FORBIDDEN HEART

Hearts of the Highlands
Book Six

Paula Quinn

© Copyright 2020 by Paula Quinn
Text by Paula Quinn
Cover by Wicked Smart Designs

Dragonblade Publishing, Inc. is an imprint of Kathryn Le Veque Novels, Inc.
P.O. Box 7968
La Verne CA 91750
ceo@dragonbladepublishing.com

Produced in the United States of America

First Edition November 2020
Print Edition

Reproduction of any kind except where it pertains to short quotes in relation to advertising or promotion is strictly prohibited.

All Rights Reserved.

The characters and events portrayed in this book are fictitious. Any similarity to real persons, living or dead, is purely coincidental and not intended by the author.

ARE YOU SIGNED UP FOR DRAGONBLADE'S BLOG?

You'll get the latest news and information on exclusive giveaways, exclusive excerpts, coming releases, sales, free books, cover reveals and more.

Check out our complete list of authors, too!

No spam, no junk. That's a promise!

Sign Up Here

www.dragonbladepublishing.com

Dearest Reader;

Thank you for your support of a small press. At Dragonblade Publishing, we strive to bring you the highest quality Historical Romance from the some of the best authors in the business. Without your support, there is no 'us', so we sincerely hope you adore these stories and find some new favorite authors along the way.

Happy Reading!

Kathryn Le Veque

CEO, Dragonblade Publishing

Additional Dragonblade books by Author Paula Quinn

Rulers of the Sky Series
Scorched
Ember
White Hot

Hearts of the Highlands Series
Heart of Ashes
Heart of Shadows
Heart of Stone
Lion Heart
Tempest Heart
Heart of Thanks
Forbidden Heart

CHAPTER ONE

Along the Scottish border
Late Summer 1349

"Ye have my thanks fer the extra apples."

"Oh?" the vendor's daughter lamented. "Do ye have to go so soon?"

He lifted his hand to her as he turned to walk away. "Another time, mayhap."

"Yer name, at least, Sir," she reached out to seize him.

He turned and set his dimpled smile on her. "Captain MacPherson."

She looked unsteady, so he offered her support with one hand on her elbow.

"Captain!" the voice of one of his men rang out.

"Ah, alas," he said, his smile waning. He patted her arm. "I must go."

She nodded and finally released him.

He set out toward Cormac MacInnes, his scowling second in command and best friend, who was shaking his head at him. "Can we not go anyplace where there are lasses who are *not* willin' to give up their goods to ye?"

Galeren tossed his new bag of apples over his shoulder and smiled. "Mac, ye would have me give up free food?" He tugged on the heavy belt that hung low on his hips. "These are large peaches in my pouch."

Mac furrowed his brows at him as if he'd just announced that he'd been infected by the plague. Mac's displeasure wasn't an unusual expression to find on his scarred face. He was normally a grisly, grumbling bastard who could make a man shyte his breeches with one of his dark glances. His friends knew him to be fiercely loyal and just a little off in the head. Galeren knew Mac longer than he knew the other three. They had arrived at King David's court together nine years ago and had remained friends ever since.

William of Lorn threw up his arms and laughed joining them. "Cap, yer peaches are swollen because ye have been chaste fer too long."

Galeren shoved his hand into the pouch and pulled out a large peach, then bit into it. "My six years is over in less than a month. Dinna worry," he said as they picked up Morgann Bell and Padrig the Giant on the way to the public stable. "Yer six-month vow will be over next month as well."

William laughed some more. "Too late fer the innkeeper's daughter back there."

"Who says she would have ye," Mac chimed in.

"Aye," the others agreed and ignored him when William began to protest. He might be the greatest archer ever to carry a quiver, but he was also the one always looking to keep things rowdy, usually at their expense.

"She liked me well enough," William told them with a careless smirk that sparked his amber-colored eyes. "It went no further than that."

"Why should we believe ye?" Giant Padrig gave Will a shove and sent him three steps forward. The others laughed. Mac didn't.

"I best not discover ye broke the vow," the scared-face Scot warned with menace in his voice. "Ye were late in meetin' up with us here. Who were ye with?"

Will laughed.

"Ye know how important the vow is to our captain," Morgann said somberly, as he said most things. He glanced at Galeren, who nodded in agreement.

"'Tis more than important," Padrig took another swipe at Will, who leaped out of the way. "'Tis the law of King David."

"Aye, he wants his men to follow David's example from scripture," Morgann was quick to point out.

"Dinna forget what ye heard here, Will," Mac warned. "We havena lost a limb or a life in nine years. If ye—"

"Dinna be dull-witted, Mac," Will teased. "If I had broken the vow and had my way with her, ye would have heard her cryin' oot in delight from yer lonely bed."

He took off running for the horses when Mac leaped at him.

Galeren laughed watching them then reached his horse and unloaded his bags.

"On a more serious note," Morgann said, coming close to him, "how long d'ye think 'twill be before we have delivered this…novice back to Bamburgh and can take a rest from travel fer a while?"

Galeren saw Padrig leaning in to hear the answer. Galeren understood. They were all in need of a soft body in their beds.

"We should reach Bamburgh and the priory in two days. That brings to mind somethin' I wanted to discuss with all of ye." He waited until Mac and Will reached them and then continued. "We are goin' to a priory. We will behave with dignity. The high steward trusts us to see to the safety of his niece. She is verra important to him." But for the wrong reasons, he wanted to tell them.

Galeren had heard of her for years—she who was to become a nun and procure John Stewart, High Steward of Scotland, a seat on the church's council. If King David died with no issue, John, who was the first son of Marjorie Bruce, daughter of Robert the Bruce, would be next in line to be king. With the church's support, no one would contest him. John was obsessed with becoming king, so he spoke of his niece often. The fact that he didn't know much about the lass hadn't stopped him from bringing her up in many conversations.

Galeren knew she had fiery red hair and a temper to match. But Galeren suspected that any lass of ten and four would rant and scream if she was taken from her kin and put into a priory. She was no beauty, with dots across her cheeks and nose and long limbs.

"What is wrong with how we behave?" Mac protested.

Galeren had to laugh–either that or throw up his hands and head home. They weren't right for this task. They would frighten the poor novice to death.

"Ye were just chasin' down Will," Galeren reminded him.

Mac offered him a rare smile. "I wouldna have hurt him too bad. Besides, John's niece will only be with us fer two days. I think her delicate sensibilities will survive us."

William jeered at him. "Hell, Mac, can ye not agree to be somewhat more pleasant fer two bloody days?"

"Not with ye around," Mac replied with a smack across Will's temple, which Will answered by jumping on him.

"They give not a care to our duty, Captain." Morgann said with disgust shadowing his cerulean eyes.

Galeren sighed and with nothing but a look of annoyance, signaled Padrig to end it.

"Captain?"

"Aye, Morgann?" Galeren answered and returned to securing his saddle.

"What is a novice? Is she a nun? Because if she is a nun, we are all doomed. Ye realize that, d'ye not? These bastards will incite curses upon our heads!"

Galeren tilted his head and gave him a curious look. He knew the lad was ten and eight—or nine, but who thought such things? "Nuns are not witches, Morgann. There will be no curses, aye?" He smiled at his somber friend and patted him on the shoulder as Mac, Will, and the quiet giant readied their horses to leave.

They would cross the border in England at night. Thankfully, Galeren's mother had been a border reiver. He had kin along the border. He had already written to them to let them know when and where they would be and to make arrangements for their safe passage along the east Marches. Everything had been set up and put into motion.

Galeren didn't want to go to Bamburgh or anywhere in England. He hated the English. They ever sought to rule the Scots and the Scots would ever fight to stop them. But he would not disobey John or King David in what he was told to do. He would go to Bamburgh with the men and hope the novice made it to Ayrshire without any damage to her eternal soul.

What other choice did he have? These were his most elite men, his friends. He would not have made an important journey with any other bunch of ruffians. They'd fought in various battles together and Galeren trusted no men like these, save for his kin.

They mounted their steeds and rode southeast. They would sleep outdoors as inns tended to be dangerous for men who thought to challenge them.

Galeren rode in no particular place among the men. If he took the lead, it was usually because there was danger ahead. While they rode, he thought about home and listened to the men around him talking and laughing. He didn't think of Invergarry but of Ayrshire—his home for the last nine years. Dundonald Castle, where John and his wife, Matilda, raised their three bairns. He smiled thinking of the children, whom he loved. John had only wed Matilda to please the church.

John did much to please the church. Sending for his niece was one of them. He wanted her around to prove to the church that he was a religious man.

"Are ye still goin' to wed Cecilia Birchet when we return home and the vow is over?"

"I dinna know," Galeren answered Morgann, looking as solemn now as his friend. "'Tis what John has asked of me. But I dinna love her."

"Many marry fer peace or some kind of alliance," Morgann pointed out. "If 'tis what the steward wants…"

Galeren nodded. He would do it if he must, but Cecilia was difficult to get along with.

The only child of John's closest friend, Lord Edward Birchet of Prestwick, Cecilia was used to having her way. When she didn't get what she wanted, she threw herself into fits of screaming at her father that he didn't truly love her. Galeren wouldn't blame him if he did not, in fact, love her. How could anyone? Galeren didn't care if she was considered the most beautiful lass in Scotland by most. Beauty faded soon after he got to know her. Oh, she didn't practice her tantrums on him. Yet. He could see the simmering anger in her gold/green eyes. She always held her tongue with him. He was certain that would change when they were married. He wasn't sure he could remain with her if she raved and ranted at him. He'd gone to John about it, but the high steward only laughed at his concerns and asked him to ponder how wild she would be in his bed. Galeren didn't want to ponder it. He didn't want a life with her. But John wanted their union. King David wanted it as well. He'd asked Galeren to try. Galeren had agreed.

Padrig was mostly always quiet, so his silence was expected.

"Ye will never have peace with her," remarked Mac. "She will ever be jealous of yer steadfast, sometimes foolhardy loyalty. I dinna think John should ask somethin' so personal and permanent of his captain."

"Especially," now Morgann joined in, "to a grumblin' banshee."

"Aye," Mac agreed. "What kind of friend does that? He is yer friend. Is he not?"

"It has nothin' to do with friendship," Galeren told him calmly.

"No? What has it to do with? Yer military service then?"

Galeren shook his head, but he had no defense and looked away. "I have my reasons. Just know that 'twill always be aboot duty fer me"

"Aye," Mac agreed quietly. "We know that, Cap. But she will be yer wife. Ye will be stuck with a screechin', spoiled child who will make ye miserable. I—we, dinna want that fer ye."

Galeren glanced around at the others. They were nodding their heads in agreement. He cared deeply for them. Even King David did not command his utmost admiration the way these four did. Aye, they drove him mad most of the time, but here he was with them yet again.

"I will never allow any wife of mine to behave so irrationally and with complete disregard for the sacrament of marriage."

"What will ye do?" Will put to him.

"I would decide when the time came. Mayhap lock her in our chamber, or someplace of her own."

"Punish her in her chambers?" Will asked with barely concealed amusement.

"Aye. What else do ye do with a destructive child? Look," he said, turning to all of them. "I am not a peached-faced lad—"

"Four and twenty," Mac pointed out as if it explained something of vital importance.

"Two years younger than ye," Galeren reminded him. Then he sighed through his teeth. "I will handle Cecilia. Dinna worry aboot me, aye?"

Mac, Morgann, and Padrig all agreed.

"Will," Galeren said, waiting for him to agree. "King David has been advised and he agrees that an alliance between Lord Birchet and John is a good idea. He has his reasons."

"What in the bloody hell do ye care aboot what our imprisoned king thinks?"

"William," Galeren commanded. "Ye speak treason against the king. Mind yer tongue."

"We dinna have a king, Cap!" Will threw up his hands and Galeren motioned to Padrig.

The giant moved quickly and surprisingly quietly. He took hold of Will and shook him by the collar.

"Take yer hands off me, Goliath!" Will demanded with a smirk. "Ye remember what happened to Goliath, d'ye not?"

Padrig gave him another violent shake to quiet him.

"Tie him up," Galeren ordered.

Padrig didn't move for an instant and then the other three stepped forward to help.

"Cap, what are ye doin?" Will asked, growing more serious now.

"Ye canna keep yer mouth shut, can ye?" Morgann reproved him. "Ye are as bad as our captain's betrothed."

Will gave Galeren an incredulous look. "Are ye truly goin' to keep me tied up?"

"Treason, Will," Galeren said and rode his horse past him. He loved Will but one day his mouth was going to get him killed. He also loved the king. He'd joined David's ranks at fifteen and the two became good friends until David was captured by the English six years later. His imprisonment didn't shake his captain's loyalty. Galeren was still in contact with him. He was and would always be the king's captain.

He continued onward while Will vowed to shoot arrows into their arses as soon as he was free. The others swore retribution with crass jokes and laughter.

Galeren shook his head. His men would not be tamed.

"What d'ye know of John's niece?" Morgann asked him.

"All I need to know. She is a novice and will become a nun next spring."

"Why does the church council want to meet her?"

"John sends fer her. He hopes that her place in the church will secure him a place on the council." He saw the sour looks on his men's faces. He felt the same way. He didn't like that John was using his niece as a piece in his game for power. But no one spoke of it.

"What is the novice's name?"

"Silene Sparrow," Galeren told him.

Morgann's lips parted as he breathed the name then he looked about to smile. If he had, it would have been the first time in a sennight. "'Tis pleasin' to my ears."

"Aye," Galeren agreed. It was a bonny name. What were they supposed to call her? How could he warn or prepare her for her journey with them? He felt as if he knew her because of all the time John had spent talking about her. He felt protective of her and a bit glad to finally be meeting her.

They reached the border hamlet of Southdean the next day. Galeren met his kin, the Hetheringtons and shared news with them about his mother, Braya, whom he'd last seen this past summer.

His grandparents had not been able to make the journey from the central Marches where they lived. They'd had a letter written and sent with Galien Hetherington, Galeren's uncle, telling him they missed him, but his grandfather, Rowley, hadn't been feeling well and his grandmother thought it best not to travel.

Uncle Galien had some dried food and fresh bread for him and his men and some long-sleeved tunics that his grandmother had sewn herself for Galeren for the cold nights.

"I will return to Invergarry when my duty is done, and I will tell her," Galeren said, sitting back in his chair in the hamlet's town hall after supper.

"You are a good lad," his uncle commended, pouring them some more whisky. "Tell me a bit about your brothers."

"Bors left the king's service. Most of the army dissolved after he was captured at Neville's Cross."

"But not you."

Galeren shook his head. "Not me."

"How long will you follow him?"

"As long as he is king."

His uncle nodded, showing his respect by not arguing the point. "You always have a place on the border if you ever decide to be a reiver." He lifted his cup to his nephew, and they drank together.

"Did I ever tell you about the time my eldest brother, God rest his soul, Ragenald was first discovered teaching your mother how to fight?"

"Ye never told me, Uncle," Galeren said with a smile and leaned in to listen.

But the tale was interrupted by the sound of a fist landing against a face. Galeren looked over his shoulder at Will shaking off the effects of the punch. The captain rolled his eyes heavenward, then he closed them when his uncle sprang from his seat and hurried past him.

He thought about the young novice, Silene Sparrow. Was she the fragile sort? How would she react to this kind of fighting?

He rose from his chair, dreading having a hysterical woman with him for two days.

He knew and understood that man's first instinct was to flee from something so troublesome. He'd felt the urge to flee more times than he could count, on the field and off. He felt it in Dundonald Castle and in his vow to Cecilia Birchet, and he felt it in Bamburgh and his vow to keep the novice safe.

But he never fled. He'd conquered the urge and faced whatever it was, head on.

But he had never faced a force like the one in his path.

CHAPTER TWO

SILENE WASN'T SUPPOSED to be out alone, but this was her last dawn in the priory—in Bamburgh, and in England. She didn't think she would ever return. She didn't know why. It came to her one night, this knowledge, this certainty that if she left Bamburgh, she would never return. Was she going to die? Because only death could keep her from the prioress and from her sisters. But, oh, she didn't want to think on it now. It was too glorious a morning to weep over what she could not control.

She'd read her morning prayers and finished all of her chores. She wanted to walk through the late burst of foliage covering the hills surrounding the small priory, to the cliffs overlooking the coast of Northumberland. She donned her chemise, tunic, and her cloth mantle, and left for her morning walk.

God understood why she'd gone out alone every morning. She'd talked with Him about it enough times.

She didn't make it more than several feet when she saw Sister Mary Joseph, the prioress of St. Patrice's Priory waiting for her at the short, metal gate. "Good morning to you, Sister Silene."

Silene was tempted to look around for a place to run. Ridiculous since she would never run from the prioress. "And good morning to you." She twisted her mantle in her hands, torn between wanting to go and wanting to obey. "Oh, Mother, I have to look upon the place of my heart one more time. Forgive my disobedience."

Thankfully, the prioress nodded her head. "Where are your wimple and veil, Sister?"

Silene's heart fell to her feet. Shamefully, she had no reply and lowered her head. "I…I…"

"My dear, you will have to wear it when in your uncle's care, especially in the care of his men and your full habit, too. That red hair of yours draws too much attention. We should have cut it closer to your head in front. It looks like a horse's mane the way it falls over your eyes like that." She brushed Silene's hair away. "Your beauty is not your hair."

"Aye, Mother Superior." Silene lifted her gaze and just as she had on the first day here, she marveled at the prioress' blue eyes that glittered and gleamed when she spoke. She was thirty and eight, twenty years older than Silene and still so beautiful, even with her jet-black tresses shaved off beneath her gray veil and wimple.

"I fear I shall never see you again, Mother Superior." There. She told her. She couldn't keep it in any longer.

"You have felt it, my dear?" the prioress asked, narrowing her eyes on the young woman and knowing about Silene's "feelings".

"Aye. In my very bones," Silene confessed to her and bit her bottom lip to keep from crying. She'd wanted to avoid this, not bring it up at all. But it frightened her to think of never seeing the prioress or her sisters again. She *had* to speak to someone about it.

"You have a gift, child," the prioress said, and seeing her tears, she patted Silene's shoulder. "'Tis not always a good thing, I'm sure. And you must remember that 'tis emotion, not evidence. Never be ruled by what you are feeling. Enjoy your emotions. Let them teach you, but never let them rule over you."

"Aye, Mother," Silene told her. She would try to remember. "I...I am also afraid of traveling alone with my uncle's men. What do I do if one of them...?" She couldn't finish. Was she allowed to kill someone if they were trying to rape her?

"Your uncle and I have corresponded often about this over the last several months. He knows the wrath of God will come against him on Judgment Day if one of His children were harmed. The men he is sending are five of his most loyal, most fierce. They have even taken vows of chastity."

"That eases my concern," Silene told her. "But sadly, I harbor anger toward my uncle for using me for his gain. I feel as if I am to be presented to the church council for very wrong reasons. I will be asked questions about my love and devotion to our Lord."

"Then tell them of it," Mother advised.

Silene nodded and promised she would. "Thank you for your wise counsel, Mother," she said and began to head back to the priory.

"Sister?"

Silene looked over her shoulder at the prioress.

"Go on, then. Go see to the place of your heart. But do not be too long."

Silene ran back to the prioress and threw her arms around the woman.

The prioress had comforted her when she'd arrived. She had been taken from her mother, her entire family, but the prioress had made certain to care for her and love her as her own.

She pulled open the gate and ran toward the fields. The hood of her mantle fell back as she leaped over thin streams and tree stumps, exposing her hair, glimmering in the sun in shades of russet and orange. Some gold strands shone when the sun hit it at a certain angle. It was cut short in the back and on the sides.

When she came to the field, sprinkled with long daffodils, she slowed, surprised to see a small bird stuck in the bramble. Its screeching stopped her as she grew closer. Its little wings flapped urgently.

"I know. I know." She spoke soothingly to it and moved the branches away. "All will be well, little bird." She parted the branches and looked up as the bird flew away.

She continued, humming and looking up at the sky often. Taking a deep, replenishing breath, she could smell the ocean. She could hear the roar of the surf in the distance.

She hurried toward the cliffs and relished the cool, briny wind in her face. She didn't want to leave the sea, but she was thankful to have lived so close to it for the last four years. She tried to visit every day, but she wasn't always able. She loved the power of the sea. Of course, she didn't know how to swim. None of the sisters did, but they often waded in the shallows and played in the water in the summer. She would miss her sisters.

What would Sister Edith do when she broke out in hives? She did so whenever she was anxious, which was all the time. And what about Sister Marjorie Anne? Who would help her learn the Rosary? Poor dear had trouble remembering anything. Who would pray with Sister Agnes when she awoke in the middle of the night with one of her night terrors?

Everyone else in the cavernous room, which housed seven beds and that many novices, complained that Agnes woke them from their sleep. Silene's bed was closest to Agnes'. But even if she wasn't close, she would not have let Agnes cry alone. It wasn't Agnes' fault her father was killed before her eyes, or that in trying to keep her six children alive, Agnes' mother turned to prostitution. Five years and five children later, Agnes was helping to pay to eat.

The prioress had seen Agnes trying to peddle herself and took her from her mother. She gave Agnes a new life. Agnes was twelve at the time. Her mother was offered a place at the priory but refused. Still, the prioress left the invitation open indefinitely.

Silene sighed and refused to cry. Perhaps she would return. Perhaps what she felt in her bones was incorrect. Hadn't Mother just warned her against being ruled by her emotions? Perhaps she would go to Scotland, stand before the church, and then come home and speak her vows next spring.

A small sob escaped her because she knew it wasn't true. She didn't know how she knew. She just did. The sob felt as if she'd been holding it in all this time. It drifted away on the breeze. She swiped a tear from her—

"Pardon me, Lady."

Silene turned to the man whose deep Highland voice startled her. The sight of him suddenly standing there made her run.

In her fright, she turned her feet the wrong way and lost her footing at the edge of the cliff.

Nay! Nay! Was this truly how she was to die? Falling to her death from her favored place?

A strong vise took hold of her wrist and yanked her back hard against his armored chest, straight into his arms.

"I have ye."

She felt the rumble of his voice against her chest and her knees quaked. She looked up into large, deep green eyes eclipsed by dark golden waves that had escaped the queue behind his head. His sculpted jaw was also dusted in deep gold. But his lips…oh, his lips were full and lush and carved in decadence.

"Let me go," she managed in a commanding tone and looked away from his mouth. She wished she had worn her habit and veil. His captivating gaze had settled on her hair.

He obeyed her order, but first he turned her in the proper direction so that she would not run off the cliff.

She stepped back and foolishly took another look at him before her feet carried her away.

Was he an angel? She gasped. He could be since he was all golden already.

But he wore men's clothes, dark hose, boots, a cream-colored léine beneath his great belted plaid of blue and black. He motioned his hand to someone else within the trees. Not an angel. A Highlander. More of them stepped out.

She ran.

She ran back to the priory and slammed the gate shut. She needed to alert the prioress that there were strange men—she stopped in her tracks. Men didn't usually travel through here. There was little reason to, unless…her belly flipped, and her mouth went dry…that man was one of her uncle's soldiers. Oh, she hoped not! For he was temptation come to life. He'd saved her from falling to her death. His arms were so strong, so hard. His heart had beat as thunderously as her own. He was tall and broad of shoulder and it was mesmerizing to see a Highlander in the flesh. He was startlingly handsome. She hoped he wasn't her uncle's man. But if he wasn't, then what were he and his friends doing hiding in the trees?

She quickened her pace and hurried through the vegetable garden and the kitchen. She finally found the prioress in the cloister.

"Mother! I nearly fe…" Oh, no! She couldn't tell her that she'd almost fallen off the cliff. That would frighten and upset her. "I met a man on the cliff. A Highlander!

The prioress narrowed her eyes on Silene. "Did you nearly fall from the cliffs, Silene?"

Silene dipped her thick, russet brows over her eyes and stared at the prioress a bit dumbfounded. How had she drawn such a conclusion? And since the prioress was correct, was her ability from God? If so, Silene dared not lie.

"Aye, I did almost fall but that was because the man frightened me nearly out of my skin!" Her enormous blue-green eyes grew larger still. "Do you think he could be one of Uncle John's men?"

"Hmm, you said he was a Highlander?"

"Aye, and he was not alone. He made a motion to others in the trees."

The prioress nodded her head. "John made mention of his Highland Elite."

Oh, Silene felt like weeping. She didn't want to travel with him. Was he chaste? Was what the prioress told her correct? She was surprised that a man who looked the way he did would ever have taken such a vow.

The heavy metal bell rang outside. Someone was at the gate. It was him. The beautiful man from the cliffs. It had to be him, come to take her away to Scotland.

"Go upstairs to your room and get your things," the prioress told her calmly. "Put on your habit."

"Aye, Mother." Silene obeyed and ran to the room she shared with her sisters. Some were there and were already looking out the window.

Silene went to it and peeked down with them. She saw him on his black steed. It was the same man in his great plaid. He sat straight in the saddle, his presence commanding. He was the leader of the four men around him. Had they all been watching her at the cliffs when she thought she was alone?

The leader spoke to the prioress and Silene wondered if Mother was affected by him at all. He and his men waited when the prioress disappeared inside.

The leader appeared a few moments later. He seemed annoyed and looked around and then up. All the sisters, including Silene pushed back away from the window. Some giggled. The rest turned to her and gave her pitying smiles. Aye, she would be traveling with him—and his men.

She thought about the scar-faced soldier who narrowed his flinty eyes on Mother and gave her an angry looking over.

Another had long, pale blonde hair tied into a tail that reached just above his waist and a long bow strapped to his shoulder.

One who didn't smile when someone said something that caused the rest of them to do so.

The last was a hairy giant who surveyed every inch of the grassy yard.

"Oh, Silene!" cried Sister Marjorie Anne. "They look positively primal. I will pray for you every single day."

Two sisters, including Sister Agnes, wept for her. Silene comforted them and then let Sister Agnes help her dress into her white scapular with a veil attached. She wore a white wimple that covered her head, neck, and chin. When she was done, she reached for her bag and squared her shoulders and then left her room alone. The prioress didn't want the sisters in the presence of such raw virility.

Silene's plight wasn't the prioress' fault. She didn't like Silene leaving any more than Silene did.

She would be brave and do this thing.

She prayed on the way down the stairs.

The men were inside the priory. She could smell them and hear their voices. Neither were unpleasant but rather invigorating, like woodsmoke and leather.

The only other men allowed in the priory were priests and abbots.

Sister Mary Joseph was standing with the handsome leader.

When they heard her descending the stairs, they turned.

The leader's gaze was potent. He stared at her for a moment or two until she shifted in her place and the prioress came to her rescue.

"Ah, here she is now. Sister Silene, this is Captain Galeren MacPherson and his men." She introduced them. Silene greeted the men with a polite nod and the slightest of smiles. When she was done, her gaze returned to the captain. He smiled, revealing a deep dimple in his right cheek. He didn't need it to make him sublime. His eyes soaked her in. She looked away, severing the compelling connection because it made her feel…odd.

"I understand ye have some fears, lass," he said, growing serious, which was, unfortunately for her, just as dangerously alluring.

She blinked at the prioress, who knew it, too.

I will be strong, she vowed silently.

"Let me assure ye," he continued, "we will keep ye safe and do ye no harm. Ye have my word. Prioress?" he asked. His voice was like silk against her ears. "My men and I are weary and would beg yer mercy fer a few hours of rest here before we start over again."

The prioress' alabaster skin went even whiter. "Here?"

"Aye. Just fer a few hours to rest in a bed. Mayhap eat somethin' hot fer supper."

He smiled. Poor Mother.

Some orders did not allow men while others housed men and women together. Theirs had no rules against it.

"Captain," the prioress said, then took a breath to compose herself and stand against his splendid countenance. "I'm sorry, but I do not want to put the sisters through being around you and your men. 'Tis bad enough that Sister Silene must be put through it. I will pray for her against you."

Well, Silene thought, she had recovered quickly. The problem was Silene didn't think it was a fair or kind prayer—and she didn't agree with it. As a matter of fact, she thought they should be allowed to rest. The sisters should be allowed to be tempted and tried. 'Twas part of real life.

"Verra well then," he said. His smile waned until it faded altogether by the time his gaze returned to Silene. He was insulted. She could feel it coming off him in waves.

She didn't want the captain to dislike her because of Mother's rash judgment. She softened her gaze on him for just an instant lest the prioress should see and feel betrayed.

"We will be leavin' then."

Silene looked at the prioress with pleading in her eyes. A few more hours to be here—to be home.

"Very well, Captain. Just a few more hours," the prioress relented. For Silene's sake.

Silene knew it was for her sake when she smiled, and the prioress smiled with her.

"You and your men," Mother said, turning back to him, her smile turning to distaste and distrust. "You and your men will stay in the northern quarter of the house. You will all eat in the great hall before the sisters have their supper. You will retreat until they are finished eating. You will leave after that."

One of his men muttered something about her list of orders.

The captain tilted his head an inch and glanced around him at his four men, who shifted uncomfortably in their spots.

The captain was still insulted by the prioress' words and her behavior, but he agreed to stay.

He said he was weary but the way he stared at her when she smiled at the prioress almost had Silene convinced that he was staying because he understood that she didn't want to leave her home yet.

The men were shown to the north quarter by two lay women. Silene attended prayer but she was distracted often with thoughts of Captain Galeren. She had never seen a man like him before. She'd only seen a few, of course. Messengers, guardsmen, priests. His fine frame had bewitched her. She said penance until it was time to eat.

She'd finally had some hours of peace until she saw him again.

The sisters were waiting for their time to eat. She heard some disturbing whispers traveling throughout the wide corridor. The whispers were about the prioress serving the men yesterday's food. The fresh meal would be served next.

Silene's belly knotted. She didn't want to think of the prioress' stingy behavior.

She ate very little and thought of how the captain had looked while he ate here, laughing with his friends. She was glad Mother had let them stay.

She used her time in the great hall to bid her sisters farewell. Agnes wept and clung to her. Silene was friends with all the novices and nuns, so her farewells took more time. She took the longest with the prioress, hugging her farewell and saying nothing about what Silene had heard about her.

She carried her bag to the small stable, where the men readied their horses. The captain was not there.

With the sisters following behind her, keeping a safe distance away, Silene marched onward into the midst of the four men. She looked around for someone with whom to give her bag. One of the men retrieved a horse that belonged to the nuns and handed it off to her. She secured her saddle as best she could and was almost done when the captain arrived with the prioress. He looked over her saddle from where he was standing and then made Silene freeze when he came steadily toward her. "Have ye ever tied yer saddle?"

She shook her head. "Nay, Captain."

He moved her aside and began untying all the knots on her saddle. "'Tis verra important that ye know what ye are doin' on a horse or they will throw ye."

She watched him untie it, then retie it again, showing her how to do it.

"Now ye try."

She took the leather straps from him and secured her saddle after the first try. He didn't let her mount but checked the saddle first to make sure it was safe.

She didn't ride horses. She'd never needed to. She'd always been content to be where she was. Only five of the sisters rode and, of course, the prioress knew how.

In her long scapular and habit, she could barely separate her legs enough to fit her foot into the high stirrup. She had to lift her skirts up to her knees. Some of the sisters watching gasped and covered their mouths with their hands.

Silene was torn between laughing and weeping. How was she supposed to ride a horse? She didn't need to wonder long when the captain's big hands closed around her waist from behind and lifted her off the ground, high in the air. She remembered to close her mouth, but barely, when she landed sideways in the saddle—gently, as if he were returning something fragile to its place.

"Thank you, Captain." She turned to him, but he was already leaving, returning to his horse. Should she tell him that she had no idea how to ride? And, oh, she was high up! She made the sign of the cross and picked up the reins. What now? She watched the man closest to her pick up his. Before he did anything else, he turned and looked at her. He dipped his dark cinnamon brows over eyes that were the color of the sea. He moved slowly, demonstrating what she should do with her reins next.

She imitated him, flapping her reins.

Her horse took off running, almost leaving her behind. She foolishly held on, bouncing on the hard saddle until her brains felt joggled. With both legs on one side there was nothing to hold on to. She slipped and bounced off the beast and into the dirt on her buns.

She heard someone behind her chuckle. A man's voice. When she thought of it while her insides settled, she imagined it was quite humorous. She wanted to throw her head back and laugh. But in the presence of men, such behavior was unsightly.

Still, she could barely contain a smile when the captain reached for her. He must have seen the amusement in her eyes and thought her odd, for he quirked his brow at her and almost smiled as well.

He took her hand and pulled her to her feet without any effort. His fingers were broad. His skin was rough and callused from wielding the enormous sword hanging from his belt. He looked as if he might speak but his gaze fixed on her forehead.

She lifted her hand to see what he was staring at and found a few tendrils of her hair had come loose in the fall from her horse. She tucked them back underneath her wimple.

"Come with me." Although it was a command, his voice remained low and quiet.

Did he mean for her to ride with him? She couldn't. She looked around, her eyes darting across the horrified faces of the sisters watching—and the prioress—

He went back to his horse and waited. She dared not look at the prioress as she went to him. What other choice was there? She couldn't ride alone. She'd be a bag of broken bones by the time she reached Ayrshire.

All the men were virile and handsome, even with scars and smirks, and too much hair. But, oh, the captain…he was almost too beautiful to look at for too long.

She didn't want to ride with him. She didn't want to leave her home. But this meeting with the church was the reason her uncle had convinced her parents to send her to St. Patrice's in the first place. They'd always told her how important it was for a man hoping to gain a high place in the church's council to have family in the church.

She was that connection. She didn't dare break it and cause her uncle to stop his aid to her family.

When she reached the captain, he was already in his saddle.

Without a thought, he reached down and plucked her from the ground. She was facing the crowd and felt her face go up in flames as she sailed into the air and landed in his lap with a soft thump. When she thought it couldn't get any worse, his arms came around her as he reached for the reins.

Silene looked at the prioress as they rode away and made the sign of the cross.

Chapter Three

GALEREN DID ALL he could to ignore the scent of her. It was slightly floral, herbal, a hint of a woodsy scent. It was oddly soothing and like nothing he had ever smelled before. He looked at the white veil on her head—like a bride.

He could deny himself the pleasure of gazing at her. He closed his eyes behind her. When he'd seen her this morning, he thought he had come upon some kind of ethereal, heavenly creature. He'd never seen a lass with hair as short as hers, or eyes that rivaled the summer sky and verdant fields.

He and the men had slept in the forest the night before. He'd awoken first and wandered out to the cliffs, drawn by the sound of the waves crashing below. And a soft cry.

He thought she might be ready to jump to her death when she sobbed as if in pain. He shouldn't have frightened her. He should not have pulled her against him, but any other way and she would have fallen. Her face was carved and molded by the Master's hand. Her hair was short in the back. In the front, her mop of bright, russet waves fell over her forehead, over eyes as big and vast as oceans. Eyes that were filled with dreams and paralyzed him with wonder. Freckles sprayed across the bridge of her nose. Her lips were perfect, like soft, plump coral in a colorful sea.

He knew who she was after she'd run away. John's niece, and her life was dedicated to God.

"Captain Galeren?"

He smiled behind her despite trying not to. "Aye?"

"I normally have prayers at this hour. May we stop somewhere soon so that I might say them?"

They had just started out. "Aye," he answered without hesitation. Hadn't she been praying all morning? If they stopped every hour, it would take a month to get to John. "Of course, we can stop." How could he refuse a soon-to-be nun asking to pray?

They trotted along with Galeren looking for a place to stop. The men were quiet, for which Galeren was thankful.

"So, what are we to call ye, Sister?"

Galeren smiled at Mac. But hell, he knew the silence couldn't last.

"I have not said my vows yet, so…Silene will do," she answered softly. So softly, the men didn't hear her.

He recalled Morgann's reaction to her name. Her name made her more familiar. It made her less of a novice and more human. The men didn't need to see her as anything but holy. "Sister!" Galeren called out. "Ye are to call her Sister."

He didn't look at her when she turned to give him a curious stare. Instead, he thought about his talk with the prioress before they'd left the priory.

"She has been raised here," the prioress had told him. "She knows little of the world apart from Bamburgh and St. Patrice's. Do you understand?"

"Aye," he had answered, keeping his impatience out of his tone. "But I dinna know why ye are tellin' this to me."

Her eyes sparked like lightning in stormy blue skies. "I'm telling you so that you will keep your hands off her. She does not understand the wiles of men like you—"

He'd had enough of her a thousand breaths ago. "Men like me?" he wanted to know, though he had a good suspicion. This wasn't the first time he'd been disliked, even hated, because of how he looked. It worked in the opposite way for most people. They liked him without ever knowing him. It was often more of an annoyance than helpful.

"I know your kind, Captain. You get through life on your physical beauty. You beguile and bewitch and always have your way. But I tell you, she will be set apart for God next spring. She is His. Beguile her at your peril."

Galeren wanted to smile at her. Father Timothy wouldn't agree, of course. Not about God, at least.

"I will remember yer warnin'." He gave her a slight bow and turned to leave.

"'Tis not my warning but God's."

He stopped and slowly turned to her. "In that case, He will tell it to me directly. Or do ye think yerself so pious and above reproach that He will only speak to ye?" He'd given her a moment to answer and then turned once more to leave. "She will be safe with me. That is my vow."

And he would keep it.

He would confess to Father Timothy in a letter tonight how he took pleasure in looking directly into Sister Mary Joseph's eyes when he put her novice in his lap and encircled her in his arms then rode off with her.

All his letters could be delivered home to the MacPherson stronghold by a paid messenger. His aunt, Julianna, used to be one. He didn't write as often as he should, and he never received a reply. Father Timothy didn't know where Galeren would be next.

He never wrote to Cecilia. He barely thought of her. He didn't think of her now.

He smelled the ocean and felt it in the air. They were going to pass the cliffs. It was a good place to stop for prayer. When they grew close, he felt her body stiffen against him.

"Is this a good place to stop?" he asked over her head.

"Aye," she nodded. "Tis a very good place." She turned and, before he could look away, smiled at him.

He smiled stiffly then turned to the others. "We will stop here fer prayer."

"Fer prayer?" Mac croaked, quite stunned, as if Galeren had suggested they ride into some English town and hand over their weapons.

"He doesna mean ye, ye savage simpleton," Will pointed out with a curl of his lips. "He means the nun."

"She isna yet a nun," Galeren reminded them. They all shifted their gazes to him. He ignored them, defenseless against the memory of her here this morning, with her fiery locks whipping across her forehead.

He dismounted and held his arms up to her. He kept his gaze on his men or the distant water rather than on her while she reluctantly fell into his arms. She was slender, as light as a veil. She felt small in his hands, and yet she was only several inches shorter than he.

He almost gave in and smiled when he set her down. "We will wait here," he offered.

She nodded and hurried to the edge.

His heart beat madly watching her run. Was she going to run to her death? Had he just made a terrible error in judgment?

He opened his mouth to call her back—

"Cap?"

She didn't jump but walked to the edge and knelt in the grass.

He blinked and turned to Mac. "Aye?"

"What has come over ye?"

"What d'ye mean?

"Ye seem agitated."

Galeren eyed him and the rest of them. "She distracts me." He shrugged it off with a grin.

"Who distracts ye, the novice?" Will asked, squinting his eyes at him. "Her?"

Galeren nodded and Mac opened his eyes wide. "What? Did the prioress put a curse on ye?"

"No one cursed—" Galeren tried.

Mac stopped him. "She is English."

"Aye, I know."

"And promised to God," Morgann added.

"And what aboot Cecilia?" from Will.

"Aye, what will ye do aboot that?" Mac put to him.

"I…" What was he going to do about what? "I will do nothin' because there is nothin' to do anythin' aboot." He laughed finally at how far this had gone and so quickly. Padrig joined him. "This is a ridiculous conversation."

"Captain?"

"Aye, Will?" Galeren's laughter faded and he sighed inwardly.

"What aboot her distracts ye? There isna one thing feminine aboot her."

Galeren wasn't sure if Will's sight was failing him. He took offense on her behalf and thought about glaring at his friend, but that would have piqued their interest even more, so he untied one of the sacks tied to his horse and smiled. "Who wants a peach? I think we are goin' to be here fer a while."

"Ye do know that there are seven sacred offices of worship and reading, d'ye not?" Morgann asked him with a grave stare. "She has four more left *today*. The first three are before dawn."

They all stared at Morgann in surprise. "Morgann," Galeren said slowly. "What else d'ye know aboot nuns and how did ye learn it?"

Morgann lifted one shoulder in a shrug. "I asked one of them back at the priory and she told me."

Galeren stared at him. "We agreed not to go near the sisters while we were there."

"Captain, I didna go near her. Sister Marjorie Anne came to me in the cloister. We spoke a little. They have a verra peaceful life."

Galeren nodded, understanding what Silene needed to be happy. Peace.

He turned to the edge and saw her kneeling in the grass, hands clasped beneath her chin.

She was even more delicate than he'd imaged. He looked over his shoulder at his men. How would she do with them for two days? How would she do with her uncle? He'd protect her from their ribaldry and raucous banter as best he could. Once he delivered her to John, she would no longer be his problem. He was mad for thinking of her in any other way but a holy one. Not only would God strike him down, but John would never trust him again. She was bonny. So what? Perhaps, seeing her in the breaking dawn with her hair ablaze and sadness in her gaze made him suffer foolish notions about her.

But looking at her now with everything covered but her face, her eyes closed in prayer…she was just as beautiful to him.

Dammit.

He regrettably realized, staring at her, that part of what made her so bonny was the sense of complete and utter calm and peace around her, coming from within her. Even now, when she was being taken away by dangerous-looking men to Scotland and the church.

He sat away from her in the grass and opened the pouch of water that had been tied to his waist. He took a drink and watched her. The men thankfully remained quiet—for the most part. He loved the men, but he didn't want to interrupt or distract her from her prayers. So far, all was quiet, and she continued.

He wondered what she asked God for. To be away from the savages as quickly as she could, no doubt. He smiled thinking about how much Father Timothy would like her.

He waited while she continued for a little over an hour, seemingly not distracted in the slightest when the men finally broke into their normal banter.

When she opened her eyes, she wiped them. Was she weeping? If she was, there was no sobbing or crying out. He wanted to get up and go to her, but his duty was to watch over her, which he was doing, not to be tempted to comfort her.

She turned to her right and saw him sitting there in the grass, leaning his elbows on his bent knees. His head was angled toward her.

He watched her skirts cascade down to her feet when she rose. He stood and offered her the pouch of water. She refused it.

"Why were you watching me pray? she asked shyly.

"'Tis my duty to keep my eyes on ye."

"Oh. Thank you for doing your duty, then."

They started walking together toward the others.

"Why were ye weepin'? Are ye afraid or sad aboot leavin'?"

"Aye," she told him. "I'm both afraid and sad but my tears were not caused by sorrow." She smiled slightly as if she had a secret—something he couldn't understand.

They met up with the others and she sat to eat some fruit before they left.

Twice, Galeren had to admonish Morgann and Mac for gaping at her while she ate—after another quick prayer. She didn't appear to mind their attention too much. In fact, he caught her a few times watching them, too. He saw the spark of amusement in her eyes when Padrig nearly fell off the tree trunk he was sitting on when Will politely asked her if she minded having all her hair cut off.

"Hair is an adornment."

And hers was like a summer sunset.

"Does God want plain wives?"

This earned Will a punch from Mac on the other side of him.

Galeren neither pushed nor punched him. He glared at him and ordered him to ready the horses. Will did not refuse.

"A person can be beautiful," she said after Will left, "the most beautiful in all the world, but if they are unjust or show no mercy, there is no beauty in them and one day what is on the inside will come creeping out."

Galeren wondered if she was talking about someone like him. He was called Galeren the Bonny back home. Did she consider his heart ugly because he was a Scottish soldier?

"We need to get movin'," he said. "We have already lost time."

He met her at the horses and lifted her to the saddle.

Two days. It was nothing. He'd traveled seven days one way to get to Invergarry last summer, and longer than that to France and England. He could do this. She was forbidden. Nothing else mattered but that and the reasons why. So, what was he doing? He wanted to laugh. He'd suffered a lapse in good sense for a few hours. It was nothing more serious than that.

"Forgive me for being such trouble, Captain."

He let out a great breath, expelling his thoughts. "Ye are no trouble at all."

"I must ask you to stop again for prayers."

His heart sank. "Now?"

She giggled and the tinkle of a hundred bells rose up to his ears. He wanted to hear the sound of it again.

"In one hour."

"Verra well." What else could he say?

"Thank you for being so kind to me, Captain."

He closed his eyes behind her, feeling a little guilty for thinking about being more aloof with her. "Ye dinna have to thank me fer that," he told her quietly.

"You are not at all what I imagined," she confessed.

"What did ye imagine?" He didn't know why he was asking.

She turned a little in his lap and blushed looking up at him. "I imagined someone who only cared for war. Someone more savage and mean."

"Ye thought the captain was Mac?" Will asked, hearing as he passed them and answering before Galeren did.

He moved on and Mac rode up in his place. "What did that bastard say aboot me?"

"He said you were savage and mean and only cared for war," she told Mac, surprising Galeren that she possessed a bold bone in her body. "A compliment of the highest form," she continued. "For a warrior, aye?"

Galeren watched with a smile as Mac nodded slowly, admitting no offense had been committed. He was still smiling when his friend rode away. She turned to look up at him from beneath her veil.

"No one has ever turned his heart away from fightin'," Galeren marveled.

"'Tis evident by his appearance," she told him softly. "Fighting is likely his whole life."

Galeren nodded.

"How can a man take offense to a friend's accolades?"

He laughed. Indeed, how could he? She was correct and it had worked on the most cynical of them all.

"So, all I have had to do all these years," said Galeren with the residue of laughter on his lips, "was compliment him?"

Her smile widened and made her sea-blue eyes dance. "Aye, 'twas all you had to do."

"Eventually, I would have two Wills on my hands!" he exclaimed in a horrified whisper closer to her ear.

She laughed. The most dangerous, powerful sound to his ears.

"How many years have you known them?"

"I have known Mac fer nine years, Morgann fer one, and Padrig and Will fer seven. Padrig and Will are brothers," he told her. "Padrig is the oldest. When they were seven and nine, their parents were executed before their eyes by the English king. Their mother was a chambermaid fer Lord and Lady Edmund Everhart. She was accused of stealin' a costly jewelry set. Padrig and Will were sent back to an orphanage in Scotland. I dinna know the entire tale. Best ye let them tell it."

She nodded. "Thank you, Captain. I will. What about you?"

He blinked. Did she want him to share some of himself with her? No. It was a bad idea. She was his charge. He had to keep his head on straight. There was no reason to get to know her better when he would deliver her back to Bamburgh and the priory in a fortnight and never see her again. "There is nothin' we need to know of each other on this journey, Sister."

"I see," she breathed after a moment. "I did not know we could not be friends."

"We canna." He could not look at her and kept his gaze on the road.

After an hour, they stopped in a forest so she could pray. Galeren was determined not to let her affect him. He had a duty to see to and see to it, he would. He didn't need to watch her for an hour while she remained motionless.

So he didn't.

No one saw the shadows coming up behind her.

CHAPTER FOUR

SHE WAS PRAYING. It was so peaceful, so quiet—and then there was a hand over her mouth, and she was snatched away without a sound. She tried to scream but the hand was pressed so hard to her face she could barely breathe. Who would do this? Where was Galeren? He said his duty was to watch her. Could the hand possibly belong to him? He said he didn't want to be her friend. She didn't know why. Mayhap he didn't like her. She didn't know the captain or his men. Perhaps it was one of his men.

She was shoved and her feet left the air. She landed on her side and hit her head on something hard.

She prayed. God, protect her!

She looked up and saw a man she had never seen before. He was dirty and wild-looking and he wore a smile that frightened her.

The sound of swords clanging came into focus. Men were fighting. She prayed it was Galeren and his men. She closed her eyes as her abductor leaned over her, and she prayed for Galeren's victory.

"You a virgin, Miss?" the man asked in a gravelly voice.

Oh please, Lord, don't let him rape me. Her heart felt as if it would burst! What could she do against him? Could she kill him with her bare hands? She would begin with his eyes.

She made the sign of the cross and he laughed.

"Is this moment worth your eternal damnation?" she asked of him.

"Aye. I will make certain it will be."

He tore her scapular and part of her chemise underneath.

"Nay!" She clawed at his eyes, ready to gouge them out—and then he was gone, lifted off her by an exquisite warrior angel with death in his eyes.

She watched for a moment while Galeren pulled the man to his feet. He looked surprised and then pleased at the condition of the man's eyes. And then he delivered a savage swipe of his bloody blade to the man's neck.

Silene squeezed her eyes shut. She wanted to scream. She'd never seen death before. She never wanted to see it again. She heard two things hit the floor, one much smaller than the other. She felt ill thinking about what they were. Her body shook. She was afraid to open her eyes.

Something soft like a blanket fell on her—it smelled like woodsmoke and the forest and rain. Like Galeren.

She opened her eyes to find him swooping down on her and wrapping her in his plaid. He slipped his arms beneath her and lifted her, cradling her to his chest.

"Fergive me. Fergive me." His deep voice played like a haunting melody across her ears. "Are ye hurt?"

Why did his asking for forgiveness make her tremble harder and want to weep in his arms?

She thought of the violence against her, and of what the man had planned to do to her. She thanked God for sending Galeren.

"Yer head is bleedin'!"

"It hit a rock. I think." She looked up at him, trying to hold back her tears. "Thank you."

"I should have been watchin' ye, lass," he said, sounding heavily burdened.

"Captain Galeren," A flash of her imagining what it would be like to touch him forged through her, making her feel warm and…guilty. "I forgive you. You saved me."

He lifted his gaze and smiled at her as they entered the camp. She almost smiled back and then looked around on the ground and gaped at what she saw. Nine men lay dead in the fallen leaves, bloody and in pieces. She cried out and buried her face in the captain's léine.

"We need to move oot of here now," the captain ordered, his chest rumbling beneath her ear. "Morgann take my horse. Padrig take the sister's."

Both men hurried off. Mac quickened his pace toward them. "Is she hurt?" he asked when he reached them.

"Aye," the captain let him know, motioning to her head. "We need to get her oot of here and take a look at her wound."

Mac leaned forward and had a look at the blood on her wimple and veil. "Dinna worry, Sister. We will fix ye up. Why is she covered in yer plaid?"

"Because the man I killed tore away her habit and ripped her chemise."

Mac's face transformed from his perpetual angry expression to one of raw fury. He ran both of his palms down his face and then tugged on his hair. "Captain, she is a nun! A nun!"

His shouting made her seep deeper into the captain's warmth and safety.

"Mac," she heard him say quietly. "Think of her right now, aye? The men are all dead. She needs help."

"Aye," Mac agreed, seeming to calm himself. "There is a small clearin' on the other side of those bushes."

"Lead us to it."

Mac showed them the way. The captain came to the other side and knelt on the ground. He set her on the grass and took a look at her. It was the kind of look that left Silene worried she was going to begin caring for him.

"I will mend ye, lass," he said so that only she could hear.

She wept softly at his tenderness, at all she had been through and seen in one day. He wiped a tear from her cheek with the backs of his fingers. "Ye are safe now," he whispered. "I willna let ye oot of my sight again."

She smiled and nodded.

He began to remove her headdress. She was afraid of what he would find. How serious was her head wound?

When he finally freed her from the covering, his gaze fell over her, perusing her in the way a man might if he had never seen a woman before. But this man had seen many, she was certain. She felt naked before him. She looked away at first, but his gaze went softer when their eyes met again.

He examined her, with Mac and the others watching and looking at her wound. Finally, the captain declared it not serious.

"Ye are cut but ye will live." He smiled at her and winked when he declared that bit of news. "I want to clean the area, and then we will do somethin' aboot yer habit."

"I have hose and a tunic and belt in my bag," she advised him. "Mother wanted me to wear my habit on this trip, but I had thought something a bit more rugged was better suited. If I had a chance or a reason to change, I would. Now, I have both."

Morgann was quick to give up his water so the captain could clean her wound. Will offered his as well, as did Padrig and Mac. The captain smiled at all of them and shook his head. "I will clean her with some whisky."

Their expressions dropped.

"Our whisky?"

"D'ye have someone else's whisky we could use, Will?" the captain asked dryly.

"This will burn," he told her a short while later, holding a cup of whisky over her. She nodded and closed her eyes then cried out at the stinging pain. His touch was light and careful. He finished by wrapping her head in the thin coif of her headdress. He and the others then left her alone, guarding her perimeter with their backs to her while she changed her clothes.

Riding her horse should be easier now, she thought, slipping her legs into a fresh pair of thicker hose. She had already been wearing boots, so she pulled them back on. She looked around and trusted that neither the captain nor his men would spy on her.

She changed quickly into her woolen tunic, leaving her torn chemise on underneath. The tear wasn't too bad, and there was a chill in the air.

She clasped her belt and pulled her hair from beneath her bandage, pushing the longer front strands free off the cloth. Her wimple and veil were stained with blood. She wouldn't put them back on until they were clean. How would she ever clean them? A river?

When she was done, she called out to Galeren. "You and your men may return."

He'd saved her. She would never forget it. How could she? Aye, what he'd done was brutal, but brutality was sometimes granted. The man had meant to rape her. She was thankful for Captain Galeren and his men. She smiled at him when he appeared from the other side of the trees. She liked the way he walked with purpose toward her.

She felt a pang deep in her heart. Something pulled it toward him. No! She would give her heart to no one. It wasn't hers to give.

"Ye look nice." His voice was temptation itself.

He'd saved her. She looked up and smiled then she lowered her gaze. "Thank you, Captain." She handed him his plaid, remembering how he had covered her with it.

"How do ye feel?" he asked. His potent green gaze was filled with concern for her. "Does yer head pain ye?"

She lifted her fingers to the bandage. "Nay, there is no pain. Where did you learn to mend wounds? On the battlefield?"

Reaching them, Will grinned at her with pity in his eyes. "We dinna mend anyone on the battlefield, Sis—"

The captain shot out his hand and Will disappeared from her vision. She covered her chuckle behind her fingers.

"Aye, 'tis how I learned it." The captain took the plaid and squinted his eyes on her. "Did ye not have a cloak?"

She blinked. She did have one. "It must have fallen off somewhere. 'Tis fine. I do not need it."

"I can go back and get it," Morgann offered, reaching them and hearing what they said. "I will be quick," he promised when his captain nodded.

"Go with him," Captain Galeren told Padrig. The giant left without a word.

"Morgann has been very kind to me," Silene told him. "You all have. I intend to tell my uncle how kind and respectful, and protective you all have been to me. I will also pray for all of you every day."

The three who were left smiled at her. The captain's smile lingered a moment longer than the rest—and they were already staring at him as if they could see right through him.

When the moment was over, he glared at them until they looked away.

"Are ye ready to go then?" the captain asked her, his smile returning yet again.

"Aye. I would like to try to ride my own horse," she let him know.

His smile faltered, compelling her to retract her words. "Of course. My horse canna carry both of us fer much longer."

"She can ride with me," Will offered.

The captain laughed as if the offer were too preposterous to even consider. "Come." He led her to her mount and untied some of the bags from the saddle. Now that her weight would be added to her horse, all the beasts would share the weight of these extra bags. None were too heavy as they had little food left.

He held his arms out to her and she stepped into them, more comfortable than she had a right to be, or had ever been with anyone else. When he lifted her up, she gazed down at the stray locks of gold strewn across his clear, beautiful eyes. Her heart began to race.

She reached for her saddle and practically leaped onto it.

He was temptation in the flesh. She prayed and fit her boots into the stirrups. She gave the reins a gentle flick and the horse began to trot away.

The captain stayed by her side, telling her what to do when they made a turn, or when they went over rocks or shallow water. She was doing well and taking command over her mount—but not much else. She found herself smiling or giggling often, not just because of him, but because of his men. They argued often, with Will usually at the core. They tried not to strike each other or swear. Their eyes darted guiltily to her often and made her want to laugh. Their banter didn't bother her. In fact, she found it entertaining. With their brawn, and their swords, and all their leather trappings, they were fierce. Of that, she was certain. But not to her.

They stopped for the next prayer and to eat afterward.

Morgann and Padrig had caught up soon after they had separated. Morgann returned her cloak to her and smiled when she thanked him, making the other four gape at him.

She denied knowing how she was able to get Morgann to smile when the captain asked her later.

She'd said her midday prayer and was attempting to get into her saddle again.

The captain let her do it on her own but did not stop Will from helping her into her stirrup.

"Your aid is greatly appreciated, Mr.—goodness I do not even know what to call you." She smiled at him.

"Will, Sister."

She nodded and heaved herself up. She made it over the saddle, landing hard on her belly. "Well," she said, a bit winded, "that was not so terrible."

"Aye, if ye want to ride around like a sack of grain," Will said with laughter in his voice.

He closed his fingers around her ankle and tossed her leg over the saddle until she straddled the beast.

When she was upright, she gasped a little at the horse's girth, but managed to keep her smile intact.

"Since ye are wearin hose—ridin' should be easier this way."

"You would expect."

He tossed his head back and laughed. "Poor lass. 'Tis not so easy to ride, but ye will do fine."

"Thank you, William."

Her gaze found the captain standing off with Mac, watching her. He smiled at her when their eyes met.

Will chuckled, looking at the both of them.

"You enjoy getting under their skin, do you not?" she said to him.

"Ye dinna know how tedious fightin' and killin' can be," he complained with a feigned sigh. "I must humor myself somehow."

She giggled behind her fingers. "You enjoy laughter." She added nothing else when he waited for more.

"As do ye," he finally guessed with a crook of his mouth.

"'Tis good medicine."

He agreed and made her laugh a little more before they set out again.

The five men rode around her, encircling her in their power and size.

"I must admit," she told the captain, riding closer to him, "I am a little apprehensive about sleeping outdoors tonight. I have never done the like before."

"We are goin' to stop at my grandparents' farm in Hethersgill before we cross the border. 'Tis a bit oot of the way, but I was told my grandsire was ill and I would see him before headin' off to Ayrshire."

"Of course," she said, liking that his family was important to him.

"We will spend the night there. I wouldna have ye sleep in the woods."

"What d'ye think John will say if we are late?" Will tossed at him. "We have already lost many hours with all the stoppin' we have done."

"I will receive his reprimands when and if they come," the captain assured him.

She looked at him when his gaze returned to hers. She didn't want him to receive reprimands. "Captain, I will take the blame for being tardy, as the fault is mine."

He smiled and her heart fluttered. "No, that willna be necessary. I can take care of hi—it."

She nodded, but she would not let the fault fall on him.

"What made ye want to become a nun?"

He was asking her to share a part of herself with him. As friends would. She was thankful and took a moment to think about her answer. "I did not want to at first. I was forced by my uncle. But 'tis difficult not to fall in love with the Lord when you learn of Him. 'Tis no longer a burden. I am happy."

His smile stiffened just the slightest.

"What is it, Captain?"

"Nothin'." He shook his head to give more emphasis to his response. "I'm glad to know that ye are happy."

But he was not smiling.

He didn't smile for the next two hours.

She had pulled back and let him ride away from her. Morgann began to slow his pace, but Mac cut him off and rode to her, ordering Morgann to stand his position.

"What is the trouble?" he demanded—but gently.

So much for subtleties. But then, this was *Mac the Menace*. She'd made up the name for him. He liked it.

"I feel the enormous weight of the task before you all to protect me."

He stared at her for a moment, his dark eyes trying to find the truth of her words.

"'Tis not yer doin', Sister. 'Tis the doin' of a man we all serve. Yer uncle."

"Aye. He is truly blessed to have men like you and the others to keep him safe."

His steely eyes finally dipped to his horse's head.

"I know you like to fight," she continued. "Your face is a testimony of your bravery."

She watched his *menacing* demeanor melt away with a smile. "Thank ye, Sister."

She nodded and used the moment to find out a little about him. "What were you like before you fought? What did you want?"

"What did I want?" He looked at her like she'd just grown another head.

"Was there a special girl?"

"I was five and ten, Sister."

"Were you stubborn and cynical at fifteen?" she teased.

"Aye. I already bore this scar and this one." He pointed to two of his scars on his face. "I fought at my father's side when the English rode through our village to claim it fer Edward. We killed ninety-four men and drove the rest away. Three days later, they returned in the night and set the village on fire. We tried to fight but the men were more concerned with savin' their families and their homes. As they should be." He paused when his gaze flicked to the captain. "I left the village and the fires and found the soldiers campin' in the forest. Thirteen men. I killed them all. When I returned to my village, I found everyone dead. Instead of buryin' my kin, I left and found the soldiers who lingered in the village when I had left the first time. I found the six of them. I killed them all. That is who I am."

Silene felt a chill run through her. He was so frank. "I'm sorry you lost so much in one day. But you are more than that."

He grunted something and rode away. She swiped some tears from her cheeks and prayed for her new friend.

They continued on in silence and finally stopped just outside of Hethersgill for prayer. She was aware of the captain's eyes on her the entire time. She tried not to let it distract her, but God knew she'd be lying if she said it didn't. She would speak to the captain about it tonight.

Still, she had to confess that she liked when she opened her eyes at the end of her prayers and saw him watching her. She wondered if he was feeling better. She decided to test it and smiled at him.

He smiled back and the setting sun returned one more time to shine on him.

"Who is cooking?" she asked, walking toward him. "It smells wonderful!"

"Padrig," he told her. "We will leave fer my grandparents' farm after we have supper. I dinna want to impose upon them by addin' six more mouths to their table."

"That is thoughtful of you."

He slanted his mouth into a dubious smile. "In truth, I enjoy Padrig's cookin' over anyone else's."

She smiled and wanted to exhale a little sigh. "Padrig is very quiet," she remarked instead.

The captain nodded. "He speaks in the silence. Ye just need to know how to listen."

What would Mother Superior say if she knew Silene liked this group of warriors?

"How was yer first day of ridin'?" he asked on their way back.

"Too painful to speak of. My horse awaits my next error so he can make me look foolish again."

He laughed softly. "Horses know how we feel. He will know if ye are afraid."

"Aye, so I am doing my best to let him know I'm not, while still being kind and gentle."

"Hmm, ye know well how to control people *and* animals."

Her smile faded. "Is that what you think I am doing?"

He shrugged and looked at the men readying to eat and then ride on to Galeren's grandparents' farm. "Morgann smiles. Mac laughs with ye. Will was even helpin' ye gain yer saddle. 'Tis not like any of them."

"They are good men."

"Aye, I know that but it doesna change the fact that they are behavin' differently. I wouldna see them hurt."

"Oh, good! We agree then." She smiled slightly, hoping he saw the absurdity of his concern.

He nodded, still looking a bit concerned.

"Captain." Her gaze on him softened. "I am making it clear to each of them that they are my friends. *My friends.* They are responding to kindness. 'Tis natural."

They sat around the fire with the men and after a quick prayer of thanksgiving by Silene, they ate Padrig's delicious hare stew with sweet and savory peach and herb sauce, mushrooms, and carrots.

She could understand why the captain enjoyed Padrig's cooking. They ate the last of the bread with a little bit of honey and washed it down with water.

"We will have to stop in a village tomorrow for more supplies," Mac said, swigging the last of his whisky.

They all agreed and set out for the home of the Hetheringtons' farm. The sun had gone down hours ago, at least two hours after six. She wasn't accustomed to staying awake after her last hour of prayer and nearly fell asleep on her horse.

"We are almost there, lass," the captain said softly close to her and her blood felt a little warmer coursing through her veins. He felt so close that she thought she might have fallen asleep and he pulled her onto his lap and whispered in her ear.

No one called her a lass. She liked how it sounded in his deep, gritty whisper.

"I do not mind."

"Ye are no longer afraid to sleep ootdoors, then?" he teased gently.

She shook her head. "Nay, I'm not."

"Yer faith in God is admirable."

She smiled, liking his humility. "He sent me you."

CHAPTER FIVE

GALEREN SAT ON the edge of the bed and held his grandsire's bony, weathered hand in his strong, capable one.

Rowley Hetherington was in his last days. His breath was shallow and weak. He didn't open his eyes to see his grandson or acknowledge him at all.

"He started his slow decline a month ago," Galeren's grandmother, May, had told him. "I wrote to your mother, but you know how long messengers take."

"Well, I am here now," Galeren told her. "My men and I are here to help with whatever ye need."

"Oh, but you have a duty to see this lovely sister to the high steward and the church," his grandmother reminded him.

"They can wait a bit," Silene was quick to tell her from where she stood at the foot of the bed. "Caring for the sick should be the first priority to all members of the church, so I'm sure they will understand."

Galeren had the urge to smile at her. Where did this courage to stand up to the church if she had to come from? Did he want her to have to?

"Captain," Will appeared at the door. "Mac got himself mixed up in a bit of a scuffle with some of yer cousins. I think ye are needed before my brother gets involved."

Galeren grinded his teeth together then let go of his grandsire's hand and left his chair. He was angry when he walked out. These could be the last moments with his grandsire and he had to take charge over selfish men—his best friend among them. He realized as he left the house, that he left Silene in there, alone with his grandmother.

"Ye can barely lift the fat of yer belly off the table," Mac shouted. "I would like to see ye lift a sword and face me, ye cowardly son of a–"

"Commander!" Galeren shouted, cutting him off. "Wait fer me…" He looked around, remembering coming here as a young lad after his grandparents left Carlisle. "Wait fer me ootside the hen house."

"Where the hell is the hen house?"

Galeren pointed then glared at Will when he snickered. "Go with him." He raked his gaze over Padrig and Morgann, the latter of whom, he knew did not find this humorous.

They both lowered their gazes.

"Jonathan of Brampton, son of my mother's cousin, what is the meanin' of this?"

His second cousin balked at him. "You take the side of a man of war over your own blood?"

"Aye, I do," Galeren told him. "When I trust that man with my life—and besides, I barely know ye. Now, why dinna ye tell me what this fight is all aboot?"

It seemed Mac had threatened to rid Galeren's kin of their teeth—without help from anyone else. Jonathan laughed while he told him, but Galeren didn't doubt Mac could do what he'd said. There were seven men here. Reivers. Some were old and some were young. It didn't matter. Mac was a ruthless madman when he fought.

"I once watched Mac walk through a sword swingin' at his face so he could get to his enemy's throat with his dagger. He doesna care what he has to go through to get to ye. Dinna put yerself in his way, Cousin. He will remove ye."

He went to Mac after his cousins promised to stay out of Mac's way. When he found his friend, Galeren expressed his disappointment in him. His old friend apologized and sent him back to his grandsire, vowing profusely to keep himself and the others in check.

When Galeren reached the room, he stood in the doorway while John's niece sat in his chair, praying over his grandsire.

She didn't cease when he came inside, proving to be comfortable in his presence while she prayed.

She remained at his grandsire's side, praying and speaking softly.

"What a wonderful gel," his grandmother commented to him a little later when she asked him for some help in the kitchen. "I do not need any help," she confessed, winking up at him. "I wanted to speak to you alone for a few moments."

He put his arm around her. "Of course, Grandmother. What is it ye wish to speak to me aboot?"

She stared at him with deep blue eyes. "I would like to…to see my daughter, Braya, one more time before I die. Rowley cannot make the trip. But after…I wish to go to the Highlands and see my daughter."

Of course, he would take her. How could he refuse such a request? "Aye. I will take ye. I know my mother misses ye. She speaks of ye whenever I visit. Uncle Galien should come as well. 'Twill be colder by the time I am free to take ye so—"

"Pardon me, Mrs. Hetherington."

They both turned when they heard Silene's voice. "Your husband is awake and asking for you."

Galeren's grandmother gave her a stunned look and then smiled and made the sign of the cross and hurried off.

Alone with Silene, he looked toward the room. "What happened?"

She shrugged her delicate shoulders and followed his gaze then looked at him. "I was praying, and I heard him speak."

His eyes opened wider as he turned to her. "Who?"

"Your grandsire."

They both smiled and then went into the room when he heard his grandmother call out for him.

Rowley Hetherington was not sitting up in bed, but he was awake and speaking very softly to his wife. When his gaze found his grandson standing in the doorway, his bright gray eyes filled with tears.

"Greetin's, Grandsire." Galeren's voice sounded too loud in the stark hush that had come over the room. "'Tis good to see ye."

"Then why are you still standing way over there?"

Galeren crossed the room in three strides. When he reached the bed, he bent to his grandsire's arms and was engulfed in a firm but frail embrace.

"How are ye feelin'?"

"Not bad. Not bad. How long are you here for?"

"Now, Rowley," Galeren's grandmother stopped him. "I told you he must deliver Sister Silene to the high steward."

"We shall see, Grandsire. I dinna think one more night would hurt."

His grandsire smiled and Galeren was sorry it had been so long since he had visited his mother's side of the family. His grandsire had almost died without seeing him again.

"How is my Braya?" he asked.

Galeren smiled. "Still as quick and as deadly as ever. She has a happy life with my father."

They spoke for over an hour, until Galeren's grandsire fell back to sleep. His grandmother remained by his side in case he needed anything when he awoke again.

Galeren went in search of Silene. He found her in the village chapel deep in her prayers with Mac and Morgann guarding her at the door on the inside of the chapel.

Joining them, the three waited in silence while she prayed.

Galeren's breathing slowed while he watched her, bathed in golden candlelight. She knelt before the small altar. Behind it, a wooden cross rose in the air. Her head was tilted upward. Her eyes were closed, and her hair was pushed off her face by her bandage.

His thoughts brought him to her abduction. When he'd found her gone, his first notion had been that she had run away. But she hadn't seemed the foolish type to put herself in such danger. She'd been taken. Under his care. But the panic and fury he'd felt hadn't been because she was his responsibility and he'd failed. It was more than that. A little more that made him want to kill them all for daring to take her.

There was no reason to keep watch over her so closely in the village. Mostly everyone who lived here was kin. But if anyone touched her, being kin wouldn't matter.

He'd asked his men to guard her and none hesitated to be about the task. They liked her. He had to watch them and make certain none of them cared for her in an inappropriate way. It wasn't impossible for she was mesmerizing, an extraordinary feast for his eyes. Whenever she stepped out into the light of day, the world came alive with color.

Of course, he could control his urges. Could Mac or Morgann, Will or Padrig? In truth, he had no idea what Padrig thought of her.

Watching her, he knew to whom her heart belonged.

She finished her prayers and stood up. When she saw him…them, she smiled and went to them.

"Captain, how is your grandsire?"

"Asleep," he told her, doing his best not to smile like a fool. "Come, 'tis getting' late.'

They stayed the night and Galeren spent more time with his grandparents.

"You fancy the orange-haired lass," his grandsire remarked. He'd awakened and was even able to keep some soup down.

"No, Grandsire. The high steward wishes me to be betrothed to another." He hadn't thought of Cecilia Birchet in days. He closed his eyes and didn't see his grandsire's sharp eyes on him.

"Do you love this woman the high steward wishes you to wed?"

"No. But even if I refused him, Silene is goin' to be a nun."

"She is not one yet. There is still time."

"No," Galeren told him gently. "I am no lout to try and tempt her from the Lord."

His grandfather's smile faded. "You are very much like your father." He sighed and then smiled again. "I like the one with the red hair."

"Silene," Galeren reminded him gently, patiently.

"Aye. She has a sweet face and a kind demeanor."

Sweet face? She was glorious to behold, like seeing a flame come to life, like wanting to dive into the deep, blue-green oceans of her eyes. The delicate cut of her jaw carved by a master sculptor.

"I need to get her to John and find a priest fer confession."

His grandsire laughed. "'Tis good to see you, lad."

"I will return to see ye again when I return her to St. Patrice's."

"Why not let someone else do it?" his grandsire put to him. "I'm sure the high steward has other capable leaders."

Galeren shook his head. "I wouldna trust anyone else to guard her the way I can. She was injured once already because I wasna watchin' her."

"What happened?"

He told Rowley about the men who had tried to abduct her and how he'd killed the man who'd hurt her.

"Good," his grandsire said. His eyes were lit with fire. Galeren could almost taste the ash. Rowley Hetherington had been a formidable, fearsome man in his younger days. But when he came home from a raid, he had a wife he loved at home waiting for him.

Galeren thought he might like that, too. He'd never had thoughts like these before. He never thought he'd live long enough to have a wife and children to love. If he were to ever marry…

"Son." His grandsire covered Galeren's hand with his and pulled him closer. "You should take her back to the priory now. She is no match for schemes of devious men. She will die."

Galeren blinked his eyes. "Grandsire, how could she die? What are ye sayin'? That I should disobey my orders from the high steward?"

"What?" His grandsire gave him a blank look. Then he said, "I'm sleepy. Bring your grandmother to me."

Galeren stared at him and gave his heart a moment to slow down. His grandsire must have fallen asleep for a moment and spoke his dream. "I will bring her to ye." He leaned to kiss his grandfather's forehead and then left the room.

Why had his grandfather said Silene could die? By whose hands? The church's? Something frigid cooled his blood and dried his mouth. Was he leading her into danger? Was the warning just words slipping from an old man's mouth? Aye. It was ramblings. Nothing more.

When he found his grandmother, she told him to see to his friends. "You know the house, my dear. Put everyone where you wish."

He looked around the house. Did he remember the rooms? Were there three or four? No matter, Silene would take a separate bedroom. He and his men would sleep in the large front room.

When it came time to settle in for the night, he walked Silene to her door.

"How is he?" she asked him, passing him a quick smile.

"My grandmother says he looks stronger than he has in a month."

"God is good."

He stopped at the door and nodded. "Father Timothy's favorite words."

"I wish I could hear more about him. Is he like the priests I will go before in Ayrshire?"

Galeren knew some of the leaders of the church. Father Timothy was not like most, but he didn't want to frighten her about the stern demeanors of the church. "No. He is different." He opened the door for her and stepped aside without going in. "If ye need anythin', I will be just ootside the door."

She seemed to forget about the church. Her eyes opened wider. "Outside the door? You…you will sleep outside the door?"

"Aye. 'Tis my duty."

"Even here?"

"Everywhere."

Her smile softened on him, making his bones ache a little. "Very well, then. Good dreams, Captain."

Why did he feel the need to keep her near? Protect her from an unseen, unknown enemy? He shook his head at his grandsire's warning.

"Good dreams, lass."

He watched her close the door then he turned and slid down the cool wood. He removed his boots, but he didn't remove his belt or swords. He trusted his men and had no doubt that Silene was safe, but it was his nature to be cautious. People could try to break in from outside.

He closed his eyes, well used to sleeping on the hard ground. He heard a sound from the other side of the door. A moment later, he felt her move against the door and tried not to smile.

"Captain?"

"Aye, lass?"

"Are you very sleepy?"

He opened his eyes and looked at the door. "No, lass."

"Nor am I."

He heard the sigh she let out almost seeping through the wood and into his bones.

"Will you tell me about your Father Timothy?"

"He is more like a grandsire to us than the town priest," he told her, pressing his ear gently to the door. "He devoted himself to my uncle, Cain, after the English murdered my grandparents and separated the three brothers. The English took my uncle with them. He was seven and raised on the battlefield. Father Timothy took care of him and taught him about God amidst all the bloodshed. When my father found his brothers, the priest took them in under his wings. He has been in all my cousins' lives from their births and has often reminded us all of how God had blessed him, puttin' him in the service of the MacPherson Clan. He is a gentle man, but he has fought on the battlefield against the English."

"Aye," she said, sounding like a satisfied cat. "I imagined he was most likely a gentle man."

He laughed softly. "Oh, how did ye know?"

"Because *you* are gentle."

"Lass, I'm a warrior," he whispered through the door.

"You are gentle with me. Back at the priory, I feared that you would not be. I prayed about it often as it weighed heavily on me. But I feel safe with you. You and your men have been very kind. Thank you."

Galeren closed his eyes. They were silent for a moment and Galeren thought she may have fallen asleep.

"Is it true, Captain? Are you chaste?"

"Aye, 'tis true. I finish my six years in less than a month."

"Six years! You are a very disciplined man."

"'Tis gettin' more difficult the closer it comes to bein' over." And being near you, he wanted to tell her.

"I...I will pray for you."

"Thank ye," he said softly.

"Good dreams, Captain," he heard her faint whisper.

"Good dreams, lass."

HE WAS AWAKENED several hours later when she opened the door and he tumbled into her room, sprawled out on the floor. He opened his eyes to find her standing over him with a smile she tried to cover with her hand. She'd taken off the bandage around her head and her curls tumbled over her eyes.

"Are you hurt?" she asked, kneeling beside him.

"No," he answered.

"Then why are you still on the floor?"

"I am a bit dazed." He sat up and smiled at her.

She giggled again and he stared into her eyes. He saw too much in them. He saw parts of her heart, sadness, regret, desire, shame. It made him feel worse. Like the worst kind of lout because he was sure he was the one making her feel these things. And yet, it took his strongest resolve not to lift his fingers to her smooth skin, not to smile and pull her in for a most forbidden kiss.

He pushed himself up and onto his feet.

She followed, rising like a flame. He took a step away and then around her and stepped out into the hall. She left the room and moved past him while he slipped on his boots.

He would keep his distance from her today. He was no monster. He would have Mac—

"I wish we could stay with your grandparents a little longer, Captain," she said, pausing to let him catch up.

"Aye." He wished the same, but it wasn't wise to remain with her longer than he needed to. "But yer uncle expects ye today and ye willna be there. We will already be a day overdue."

Her smiled faded. She stepped back. "Aye. We do not want to be overdue to my uncle. You are a very disciplined soldier."

He nodded—though at the present moment, he took no pride in it. He didn't know how much longer his discipline would hold out. He wanted to share his smiles with her, touch her cheek, her hand. He wanted to seduce her, with the hope of kissing her. But she was forbidden. He tried to see her the way, it seemed, others saw her. Not as beautiful. But then he'd watched her laughing with his men or lost in worship that made her weep. When she spoke to him, he found himself wanting to make her smile.

"In this case, lass, I must be."

She straightened her shoulders and set her chin with resolve. But her fortitude didn't reach her eyes. "You are correct, Captain," she said and turned to leave.

His resolve didn't falter. He wouldn't let it.

He swallowed as she walked away to join his grandmother in the kitchen. He wanted to go the other way, out the front door. He would leave without her. Let John send someone else, or let his men take her the rest of the way.

But it was *his* duty to take her to John, to protect her. He wanted to protect her. The wilds were dangerous, especially for women. He wouldn't leave.

He entered the large front room and spread his gaze over his men, his friends. They were all on their feet. Mac was fixing his belt to his waist. It sagged from the many weapons attached to it. Padrig was adjusting the leather straps crisscrossing his back, a long claymore attached to each strap. Will pulled on his boots, a sword at his side and a bow and arrows slung across his back.

Only Morgann stood ready to go.

"Mornin', Captain," he offered first then was followed by the other three.

Galeren let a smile pass over his lips and then looked toward the kitchen. He wasn't as disciplined as she gave him credit for being. She would change her opinion of him quickly if she knew of his foolish, reckless desire to go to her even now.

"Everythin' well, Cap?"

Galeren widened his smile on Mac. "Aye. I was thinkin' aboot…ehm…"

Mac nodded. "We know. We will miss her as well."

"Your dear grandmother has done everything she could," Silene's dulcet voice fell like the sound of bells across his ears, "but she could not get the bloodstains out of my veil and wimple."

Galeren and Mac—and the other three all turned to the sound of her.

She stood in the doorway, there being nothing feminine about her silhouette in her hose and tunic, her hair cut above her ears. And yet, she was the most perfectly delicate woman Galeren had ever looked upon.

She held her veil and wimple out to them. The blood staining both was lighter, pinker, but it was still blood.

"I cannot wear it!"

Galeren offered her a sympathetic gaze but, and he was surely going to hell for this, he wasn't sorry that she couldn't wear it. He raised his eyes to her mop of fiery hair atop her head.

"Mayhap we can find another habit fer ye, Sister," Will suggested with a reassuring smile that turned a bit mischievous when Galeren set his eyes on him.

Her eyes widened with hopefulness. "Will we be stopping in any other towns?"

Galeren unclenched his teeth. "Aye."

She smiled at him, looking relieved. It pricked him in the guts. This was who she was. Almost a nun. He had to accept it and leave her alone.

He swallowed a hundred words and nearly choked on them all.

CHAPTER SIX

*F*ORGIVE ME.

Silene said ten more Hail Marys as they crossed the border. The prayers though were not for her safety, but for her soul.

She thought about getting ready for bed against a wooden door that was surprisingly warm. She imagined the captain's body, asleep on the other side, had warmed it. He haunted her dreams. He liked her. She could see it in his eyes, in his gaze that followed her. But he was well disciplined. She was glad. Wasn't she? She said another twenty Our Fathers. It sickened her to think of the betrayal of her upcoming vows.

What kind of woman was she to fall captivated with a man just because he was gloriously handsome? Of course, there was more than that or she wouldn't have given him a spare thought. She shouldn't be sparing him any now! He was thoughtful. He hadn't complained once about stopping so often. He'd even tried to find the most peaceful, beautiful spots for her. He was patient with her and with his friends and kind to his grandparents.

She shook her head at her inability to stop thinking of him.

I need Your help.

She said one last prayer and made the sign of the cross and opened her eyes.

He was there. A few feet away, his gaze ever on her. His duty. Was it more than that? And why her? She was plain and…red with all her curls cut off. Surely the captain could have his choice of many women, she thought rising off her knees and going to them.

"We will stop in the market town fer supplies after we cross the border," he let her know, finally looking away—and then returning his attention to her. "'Tis not far."

Should she smile? No. They needed to stop smiling at each other. It was tempting.

She nodded and then walked by him, talking to God instead of the captain.

You have to know he is tempting. I cannot seem to resist him. I want to smile at him all the time—even just after an hour-long prayer of repentance. Oh, I need Your help!

"Carrot soup fer our midday meal, Sister," Mac informed her when she stepped into the camp.

"'Tis all we had left," Padrig defended while fixing her a bowl.

"Well then, we are blessed to have you to prepare it."

He smiled, proving her earlier point to the captain. Padrig was a gentle giant. Beneath all his hair, he was a darker, bigger version of Will. The captain said he did not smile often. Silene didn't agree. Padrig was shy, but he had no shortage of smiles.

"The captain ought to do all the buyin' and tradin'," she heard Morgann telling the others. "We will likely get double."

"That will take all day," Mac said, shaking his head.

"Why will you get double if the captain does the business?" she asked, accepting Padrig's bowl.

"The lasses."

"Will!" The captain stopped him from saying anything more.

She turned and laughed at the glowering leader as he took his seat beside her on a log. "What about the lasses?"

"'Tis nothin'," he muttered. "Let us eat and head oot."

She looked around at the others. They all had their bowls in their hands. "None of you have eaten yet?"

"We waited fer ye," the captain said, taking his bowl.

How was she supposed to resist smiling at him? "That is very thoughtful of all of you." She offered them her best smile after she prayed over their meal. The men prayed with her.

Her heart swelled as she tasted the soup.

As she suspected, it was delicious, seasoned with an array of spices and something sweet…perhaps a dollop of honey.

When they set out a little while later, Silene noticed that she and the captain rode apart with the men between them, but they kept gravitating back to each other. Each time they did, they looked equally puzzled at how they had gotten there. He stayed close when they crossed the border. No one tried to stop or rob them.

"I think our horses are friends." She chuckled, sounding more nervous than amused.

He agreed and then glared at Will on the other side of him when Will muttered something under his breath.

Why were his men teasing him about her? She moved her horse further away from him and met Morgann's solemn stare.

"The captain is verra protective of ye," Morgann remarked, drawing his horse nearer.

"'Tis his duty," she reminded the Highlander.

"Aye," he agreed.

"Tell me about you, Morgann. How did you come to ride with the captain at so young an age?"

"The steward fell into a ragin' river and I jumped in and saved him."

She smiled and her eyes opened wider. "That is something to be proud of!"

He shrugged and looked more somber than ever, but he would say nothing more.

"You can speak to me about anything, Morgann," she assured him. "We are friends, aye?"

He smiled and nodded but said nothing more about his past.

They chitchatted for a little while longer and then came to the large market town of Hamsertown. Silene marveled at the wood and stone houses built around the market. Trees divided stone to break through the ground and spread their branches. Vendors filled the center of the market. She gaped at the sight of colorful banners whipping in the wind about their tents. Each bore a likeness of their wares. Candles, torches, handheld bags made of leather and felt, strings of different colored wool and thread, just to name a few.

They didn't stop but rode through the town. Turning left, they saw even more vendors and flags. This area was dedicated to food. They sold various fresh and salted meat and fish, fruit, herbs, grains, and beans.

Padrig broke off first and headed to a meat vendor. Will went off with Mac, and Morgann stayed with her and the captain. But before they reached the vendors, Silene saw three small, dirty children playing with rocks. She smiled at their innocence, but it faded as the obvious became apparent. They were poor. Their clothing was tattered and stained, as were their faces. They were thin and their skin was sallow. The sight of them made her eyes burn.

"Captain, may I stay here with them?" she asked.

He looked like he might refuse her. She would stay anyway if he did. His gazed flicked to the children and then to Morgann. He nodded. "Stay with her," he told his friend.

Should she not smile at him for giving in to her wish? For her or for the children's sake, it didn't matter. Of course, she should smile at him for his kindness!

He turned away without seeing it. She was about to frown and begin reciting ten Our Fathers when her gaze swung to Morgann's.

"'Tis good that ye care fer them," Morgann told her. "Likely no one else does."

She went to the horses. He followed her. He didn't protest when she took the last of their fruit out of their supplies bag. But even if he had, she merely had to turn her gaze on him for him to remain quiet. She didn't want to have to beg him for food to feed these hungry little ones, but she would.

She carried three apples, one for each child, and approached them.

"Sister!" Morgann called out to her, meaning to stop her. "They could be ill."

She turned to look over her shoulder at him with her vision blurred from tears. "They are hungry, Morgann. Today, they will eat."

He muttered something and then pulled out a few of the carrots they had left.

"We will not hurt you," she promised the children as she and Morgann came near. They looked afraid but their eyes stayed on the food. They ranged in age from three to seven. "Are you hungry?"

The two younger girls looked up at the boy, unsure if they should answer.

"We will feed you," she promised and moved closer.

Morgann stopped her from going any closer with a hand on her arm. "That is close enough, Sister."

"Any coughing? Chills?" she asked the children. "Pain, here or here?" She pointed to her underarms and groin.

They shook their heads.

"What are your names?" she asked them as she stepped closer and handed them her apples.

"I'm Adam," said the tallest, a boy with scruffy, dark hair falling around his face. "That is Katie, my sister," he said, pointing to the middle girl with long, tangled, dark hair and huge brown eyes as somber as Morgann's. "And that one is the babe, Bethany."

Silene's smile warmed on them as they bit into their apples. "I'm

Silene."

"I thought you were a man," Adam confessed and wiped his mouth.

She laughed and turned to a smiling Morgann. "This is Morgann."

Adam stared at Morgann's sword with wonder and awe.

"What is this?"

Silene, Morgann, and the three children looked up at the captain returning with a sack tossed over his shoulder.

"They were hungry," Silene told him, only slightly worried. She knew he wouldn't be angry that she'd given the children the apples and carrots.

She noted Adam staring wide-eyed at all the weapons hanging from the Highlander's belt.

"Where are yer father and mother?" he asked the boy.

"My father is at work in his shop. My mother is home."

"Where is home?" he asked.

Adam pointed to a small cottage half-hidden beneath trees and two other bigger houses.

"Go and bring yer mother here. Tell her the high steward's men are here."

"My sisters…" Adam hesitated.

Silene moved forward and put her hand on Katie's shoulder. "They will be safe with us."

They watched the boy run off then Silene turned to the captain. "What do you intend to do?"

"Feed them."

"Cap, we dinna have enough coin fer us and them," Morgann pointed out, a worried look on his face.

Silene didn't take her eyes off the captain. Would he—

"We will have enough," he said with a flicker of resolve brightening his green eyes. She sighed when he left to get more food. Ten more Hail Marys.

She smiled and then turned back to the small, dirty faces before her. "Do you have a favorite story?"

They shook their heads.

Silene told them her favorite and while she was in the middle of telling, Bethany crawled into her lap to listen. Many times in the past, she had thought about having her own children, of being a mother. But that desire faded as her love for God grew, though it wasn't gone completely.

Smoothing Bethany's dirty curls away from her cheeks, the child stirred the desire in her again.

She didn't notice the captain standing off to the side with two sacks in his hands, watching her in silence that was louder than Adam calling to them with a woman nervously in tow.

Silene set Bethany gently on the ground and stood up with a soft smile to greet the children's mother.

"I am Sister Silene of St. Patrice's Priory in Bamburgh."

Adam's mother narrowed her eyes on Silene's hair and her clothes. "You do not look like a sister."

Silene lifted her finger to her hair and looked at the captain—why him, she did not know.

He stepped forward with the bags and dropped them at Silene's feet.

With a grateful grin, she bent to take a look inside. One bag was filled with grain and one with figs and other fruit.

"The captain has graciously supplied your family with food," she told Adam's mother. She let her gaze drift to him. All this must have come with a high price. "Thank you, Captain."

"Aye. Thank you, Captain," Adam's mother agreed, her gaze transfixed to him. And why would it not be? What female with a pair of eyes in her head did not want to look at him? "I'm Katherine, wife of Simeon, the tailor," she said, finally remembering to introduce herself.

The captain nodded. "Morgann will carry these bags back to yer home. Sister Silene will accompany ye and yer children. I will return with more food."

The children's mother nodded numbly and smiled. She turned to Silene. "God bless you and these men, Sister."

"And you, as well."

But Silene didn't go to the children's home. She hurried to keep up with the captain when he strode off.

"How did you come by so much?" she asked him when she caught up. She ignored his scowl at seeing her. "Morgann said you barely had enough coin for the five of you."

He looked around at everything but her until he finally took hold of himself and lifted his gaze from the ground.

"I can get…more from female vendors by doin' the …ehm…simplest things."

"What kind of simplest things do you mean?"

He cleared his throat. "By lettin' my gaze—" he paused for a deep breath, "—or my smile linger. If I…ehm show her attention, touch her hand." He looked as if he wanted to crawl out of his skin. "Sometimes I dinna have to do anythin' at all. They like to give me things."

She stared at him, not knowing what to say. It took her a moment to realize he was serious. She fixed her gaze on his dark, golden hair falling over his temple, and then onto his mouth, and his chin. He certainly was handsome. She could understand why women wanted to get to know him better—but they gave him food without coin?

She slanted her gaze on him and then smiled and shook her head.

"What?" he asked. "Say what ye would."

"You enjoy it."

He shrugged his shoulders. "No, I dinna like bein' given food at no cost when there are children ootside the doors starvin'."

She wanted to say something, but what? "Aye," she finally said in a low voice. "I agree." There was more inside she wanted to say, but she held her tongue. She wouldn't flirt with him, no matter how wonderful she thought he was.

"The thing is..." he began slowly, in a soft, deep tone that made her bones feel a little soft, "...people dinna realize that if they find me so pleasin' on the eyes then mayhap others do as well. And the same compliments over and over again have become empty."

"Hmm." Her heart banged rapidly and she felt lightheaded. Was he telling the truth? Was he so vain that he thought everyone considered him so delightful? She knew Lucifer had been a beautiful angel before his fall. Mother taught all the novices that was why beautiful men, or even women, could not be trusted.

Silene didn't believe it. That would mean the prioress and all the sisters were not godly. Of course, she'd never seen anyone as handsome as Captain Galeren. She prayed he wasn't beguiling her.

"I know how that must have sounded," he said after she remained quiet. "But I do hear it often. Even at my childhood home I am called Galeren the Bonny."

"Truly?" she asked on the verge of another smile. She believed that all the compliments didn't please him. And that pleased her.

"Aye," he replied. "Everyone always has an instant opinion of me—whether good or bad."

"Your men know who you are."

He smiled. "Aye, but ye know what I speak is true. Surely ye hear the same."

"Me?" She laughed. "Hear what?"

"That ye are beautiful," he said and deliberately walked away.

Had she heard him right? Did he say she was beautiful? No. She would have laughed if she didn't want to cry. She remembered hearing her father say she was no beauty and no man would likely want her anyway, just before her parents gave her up to God. She knew there was a different kind of beauty, the kind that comes from within. Mother had told her she possessed that kind. Is that what the captain saw? But what had she done to cause him to say such a thing?

She lifted her hand to the russet waves on her head and thought about it while the captain reached a vendor selling oils and spices. He left Silene to go inside.

From her vantage point, she could see him speaking to a pretty maiden, who was either the vendor or the vendor's daughter. She watched the woman smile at him and touch her fingers to her hair. He offered the maiden a slow, blatantly sensual smile, exposing that dimple that somehow made him even more handsome. He laughed at something his admirer said and then leaned over the table separating them, took her hand in his, and kissed it. A few more words and well-timed smiles later, he left with a sack of goods over his shoulder.

It was the same at almost every vendor they visited. They all wanted to give him free goods. And today, he accepted.

It was all for the children's mother.

Silene knew in that moment that if she were blind and had never seen his face, she would consider him the most beautiful man she'd ever met.

They returned to the cottage and met up with Morgann. The children ran out to greet them, eager to look inside the bags. They stepped inside and into a small kitchen, lit by the sun through a wide unshuttered window and a dying fire in the hearth. The table was bare. Shelves stacked around it held vessels of clay, some now filled, thanks to the captain, with grain.

They gave Katherine the rest, placing the bags on the table. Apples rolled out of one and three little hands reached for them.

Crunching could be heard from all around. It made Silene content to see them fed.

"Come, I have a gift for you," the children's mother said, taking her hand and leading her away.

"Oh, no. I could not."

"You must, else I could not lay down my head and sleep at night. I am a dressmaker. I have the perfect gown for you! By looking at you, I believe 'twill fit."

"But I have no reason to wear a gown," Silene insisted.

"You might." She handed Silene a gown of rich purple with white lace around the shoulders.

"Oh, Katherine, 'tis the finest gown I have ever seen!"

She shouldn't keep it. She would accept no gift for doing the right thing.

"I just cannot accept it." She felt terrible saying it, giving it up. She hurried away and joined the others.

Katherine appeared a little while later without the gown. Silene offered her a soft smile.

When it was time to go, Silene kissed Katherine and the children on the cheek and promised to visit them again.

They reached their horses and the rest of the men who had returned before them and discussed what they were doing next. "We should reach Dundonald by tomorrow afternoon if we make all the stops," Mac said.

The captain mounted his horse and moved closer to hers while she did the same. "Are ye hungry? D'ye wish to stop and eat first?"

"Aye," Padrig chimed in. "I have some new spices I would like to try."

Silene wasn't hungry but she would do anything to postpone arriving in Ayrshire. Would she ever see the captain again?

"Aye. Let us eat," she told them, much to Padrig's satisfaction.

For some reason, that made her want to weep, she felt that this would be her last meal with them all together. It was the same feeling she had when she knew she wouldn't return to St. Patrice's.

A sob rose up from some deep, sad place she'd felt since the plans for her to stand before the church were made. The sound escaped her lips. She hadn't meant for it to and lifted her fingertips to her mouth.

"What is it?"

She opened her eyes to the captain then wiped them as tears spilled over her lids. "Nothing, I—"

"Mac, make camp close by. We will find ye." He turned to her. "Come."

He rode off in the opposite direction.

She hesitated for a moment, unsure if she should be alone with him. Finally, she flicked her reins and followed him.

He stopped between the trees and waited until she reached him. "Now, ye will tell me why this is the second time I have heard that wretched sound escape yer lips.

"'Tis just a feeling I get that makes me feel sad."

"What kind of feelin'?"

She drew in a deep breath. "I do not know why I feel these things!" She threw up her hands and dismounted.

He was there with her immediately, beside her, his wonderful scent covering her. "What is it, lass?"

She grew still and stared into his eyes. If he thought as her mother and father had that she was touched, either by God or the devil for having premonitions that sometimes came to pass, he might tell her uncle. The church leaders would not wish to speak to her. Her uncle would lose his tie to the church. She thought on it, trying to decide whether or not to tell him.

He waited patiently while she weighed everything.

"This will be the last time we will all eat together." Perhaps she *was* mad for caring. "I do not know why I feel it so powerfully about some things and not others." She tried to stop speaking but everything came pouring out. Why? Why tell him? "'Tis as strong as knowing I will never see St. Patrice's again. I do not know if 'tis because I will die."

She was surprised to find the captain's face pale.

"You believe me?"

He nodded. The color still hadn't returned to him. "Does this feelin' tell ye that ye are goin' to die?"

"Nay, Captain, but…Captain, are you feeling ill?"

"Aye. Aye. I am. It came upon me quickly. I must be hungry."

Hunger. Aye. She nodded. "We should get back to the others."

She turned to gain her saddle but his fingers on her wrist stopped her.

"I willna let ye die."

She smiled at him. She wanted to tell him she believed him, but he was dangerous to be around. He made her question things—like if she was fit to be a nun.

"I will keep ye safe, Silene, and then I will take ye home."

Her smile could do nothing but remain at his vow. "Thank you, Captain."

"Ye are free to call me Galeren," he told her, his green eyes steady on hers. His mouth was slow to smile but, finally, he did. "I would give up my life to keep ye alive."

Her throat burned with emotion—this time, mostly for him. "I pray that you will never have to face such a decision."

"Trust me, Silene."

Why? Why should she? She barely knew him. Still, there was truth in his eyes. "I will try."

Something made his eyes go smoky and deep. For a moment, she felt something—like when lightning strikes close by and she felt it in her blood.

It made her look away, guilty at the foot of her vows.

"Let us get back."

Emptiness engulfed her when he rode away, a cold void that assaulted her and made her look toward him once again.

He made her weak and guilty.

When she reached the captain, she slowed her horse and then came to a complete stop.

He wasn't alone. Three mounted men blocked their path. One of them eyed her curiously, trying to tell it she was a lass or lad. Finally, he grinned with naked male intent, coming to whatever conclusion he'd made.

"Take yer eyes off her or I will do it fer ye."

Silene's blood went cold in her veins at the captain's threat. The foolish man laughed. He moved his mount forward. "I'm going to f—"

The captain's blade slid from his sheath before the other two had time to release theirs.

Silene wanted to hide behind her hands. Three against one was terrible odds. She wished she could help. *Do not let him die because of me.*

His blade flashed against the low-hanging sun as it descended on the would-be thief. She watched as the captain's blade smacked against the other and knocked it from the man's hand.

With one fluid movement, he shifted his wrist and smashed the hilt into his opponent's head. In the time it took to breathe another breath, he swung his sword at the next man. His movements were savage yet graceful and merciful. He could have killed the three attackers at any time, but he beat them all with his hands and knees.

Silene wasn't sure how many of the three had any teeth left. But she was safe and unharmed once again.

They left the men where they'd fallen and rode away. She had never seen such violence as she'd seen in two days on the road. How did anyone who wasn't skilled in battle get from place to place without getting robbed or killed?

"There is ugliness in all the beauty around us," he said setting his gaze over the surrounding landscape.

She nodded. "I was thinking the same thing. But there is beauty also."

He cut her a side glance and slanted his shapely lips.

What amused him? He didn't say. Was it because they shared a thought or two? She did like him. Was she supposed to dislike the man who fought to keep her safe? How? Was he sent to test her? No! She was afraid she would fail.

"Silene."

She closed her eyes. She liked how her name rolled off his tongue on his lyrical burr.

"I'm sorry ye are seein' so much so soon. 'Tis a harsh world. 'Tis why yer uncle chose me to escort ye. He cares fer ye."

"Does he?" she asked solemnly.

"Of course," he told her, not truly believing it.

"He cares that the church thinks he has ties to the church through me. He cares for me because I am to be a nun."

It was the first time she had confessed it. It tasted bitter in her mouth.

He was silent for a little while and rode his horse closer to hers and gazed at her.

She suddenly wanted to tell him everything, things she'd only told God. "I was given up by my parents to help my uncle. The first time he came to St. Patrice's, I thought he was coming to take me home, to take me away. I thought they had changed their minds and wanted me back. But I wrong. He left without me, ignoring my cries. I have always felt abandoned." Why was she confessing this all to him? Why were these emotions she thought she'd put away coming back to the surface? And not to a priest but to a man of war. A man who moved closer—close enough to dip his head beside her and press his lips to hers.

She should have moved away, denied him—but she didn't.

She began her litany of Hail Marys, but everything faded from her lips but him.

CHAPTER SEVEN

HER LIPS TASTED faintly like honey and made Galeren hungry for more of her. Nothing that would strip her of her dignity. He was not raised to be an animal. He wanted to touch her, take her in…

He lifted his hand and slipped his fingers under her chin, along her jaw. His full, lush lips played with hers, swept against her teeth. His legs felt soft, weak. He'd fought dozens of battles, faced great, terrifying opponents on the field, and his legs had never gone weak. He was surprised at the acceleration of his heartbeat, the clarity of his thoughts. He had to let her go. He wanted to go on kissing her for days—years. He wanted to hold her in his arms. But he couldn't. She wasn't his. She was God's.

Galeren was grateful he hadn't been struck down.

"Fergive me." Who was he asking?

"Of course," Silene answered on a quiet, quavering voice and took a step back.

"I didna mean to…"

She looked up at him waiting for more. Her fingers trembled as they reached her lips.

What should he say? The truth was best. "I meant to kiss ye…"

Saying it made his gaze dip to her lips, bringing back to mind how soft and yielding they'd been against his. "I—" he looked at the trees around them. "I didna mean to overstep. I know—He—"

"Let us not speak of it," she pleaded, appearing and sounding as guilty as he.

But he'd kissed her.

Hell. That's where he was going. She didn't wish to speak of it. For now, or forever?

They met up with Mac and the others and told them what had happened. The attack, not the kiss. Galeren didn't want to tell anyone. Mayhap a priest. Mayhap Father Timothy. Until then, he had to be away from her. Being together was deadly for their souls.

They ate and the men laughed and teased serious Morgann.

Once Silene understood that Morgann wasn't hurt, she enjoyed the banter.

"'Tis easy not to grow angry with them," the young Highlander told her, leaning in. "Their insults are weak and impotent."

"Now, Morgann," Will laughed, "let us not bring up yer bedroom troubles."

"Why not, Will?" Morgann asked. "Are ye worried the malady might strike ye again if ye speak of it? Remember 'twas ye who suffered with it, not I."

Will thought about it for a moment then was quiet.

They all laughed.

Galeren did not. Soon, she wouldn't be with them. He had worried about how she would hold up to his men, but she not only wasn't bothered by their bickering, she had them all doing their best to please her.

He shook his head, trying to clear her out of it.

He wouldn't have to concern himself with her anymore. He wouldn't allow as many stops today. If they stopped so she could pray nine times a day, they would never get to their destination. He had to tell her.

"Sister."

She frowned, mirroring his expression.

"Come fer a walk with me. I wish to discuss somethin' with ye."

"A walk?" she asked, looking worried.

"I vow I willna touch ye."

She looked like she wanted to say more, but only nodded instead.

When they were alone amidst the trees, she turned to him. "What is it, Captain?"

"I'm afraid…"

Her eyes widened. Her gaze filled with concern.

This wasn't going well. He pulled himself together. "I'm afraid we canna stop so often today."

She blinked her eyes and he felt as if she'd kicked him in the guts.

"How often may I stop?"

He wanted to look away, but he knew he shouldn't. He needed to be stern. "We will stop twice."

Now her wide, sea-foam gaze grew darker—like a storm coming in quickly from the horizon. "You expect me to give up the rest of my prayers?"

He shook his head slightly. "No. Ye can pray on yer horse."

"I cannot."

His move. Her gaze on him was steady, almost unblinking. What more could he say? That he wanted to get to Dundonald as soon as possible? To be away from her? He opened his mouth to speak.

"Is that all, Captain?"

No storm, but it left glaciers in its place.

He didn't want to keep looking at her, but he couldn't look away. "That is all."

She kept quiet and waited for him to lead the way.

He felt like hell. He needed to get back to Dundonald, back to his duties that didn't include her. The less he spoke to her, the less he would miss the sound of her voice.

He hated himself for being held captive by a novice of the church. Thankfully, it wasn't too late to forget her, resist her. He barely knew her. He didn't love her. He was taken with her, drawn to her. Nothing more. There was nothing between them.

Nothing but a kiss.

A kiss like nothing Cecilia had ever made him feel. He wiped his brow. How would he tell John that he did not want to wed Miss Birchet? How would he tell the king that he would not wed her? He would go home to Invergarry.

He wanted to laugh at being so vexed over the novice. The solution was simple. Be truthful with King David, John, and with Cecilia, and then leave Dundonald for a while, mayhap longer.

He'd suggest Mac take his place. His friend would make a good captain. He could take Silene back to St. Patrice's.

They returned to the camp and helped clean up before setting out again.

As it had so many times since he met her, his gaze wandered back to her as she rode her horse. He creased his brows. What was she doing? She held her reins in her raised palms. Was she praying?

He continued watching her with her eyes closed, honeyed lips moving in silent, secret prayer. She wasn't paying mind to her horse or where it was going.

Instinctively, he moved closer, his muscles anticipating.

"Lass?"

She didn't answer him.

He didn't like this.

"Lass!" he said with more command.

She opened her eyes and, for an instant, looked completely confused about where she was. She lost her balance.

He rushed to her and caught her in his arms. He didn't pause to torture himself further but set her down in his saddle, between his thighs.

Fool! He was a fool. He should have had Mac or Morgann do this. But having her unveiled head beneath his chin, her hips wedged between his, was the punishment he deserved.

She went directly back to her prayers, unfazed by him—having no trouble at all being so close to him.

He held her with one arm coiled loosely around her waist. He held the reins in his other hand.

"I dinna think—"

"Shh! We will speak later."

He could do that. Waiting would give him time to think about what he should say when she was ready to speak.

A moment later, she lifted one of her arms in the air.

He moved his head to see the road.

He heard her sniff and looked at her over her shoulder. He was horrified to see her face wet with tears. He wanted to know what it was that had made her cry. But he kept silent—for whatever it was, she chose not to share it with him.

When she finished and opened her eyes, they rose to his. "I am well—better."

"Aye?" he asked with concern in his eyes.

She sighed. "There is a feeling of coming gloom…" she paused to consider her words. "Someplace. I do not know. 'Tis a feeling of danger."

Danger? His grandsire's words haunted him. "D'ye think 'tis the Lord tellin' ye not to go to Dundonald?"

"But I must go. This is the reason I was sent to St. Patrice's from the beginning. My uncle never made any pretense about why I was put into a priory. I must see to this or he will cease caring for my parents."

"Perhaps at the cost of yer life?"

She shrugged her shoulders. "You of all people should understand duty. Is not escorting me to my uncle your duty? A duty of which you clearly grow weary?"

He wanted to say a thousand words, to deny her charge mostly. But he would admit that he was behaving as if she were burdensome. No matter how he felt, he should not have made her feel like a burden. "Fergive me."

She looked surprised by his apology.

"I am troubled by how I feel aboot ye."

Her eyes opened wider. A wash of claret swept across her face. She swallowed. "How…how do you feel?"

He couldn't tell her that he was beginning to care for her more than he should. He couldn't stop it. She was different than the lasses at the castle, different than Cecilia. She was honest and raw. She was not under the rampant delusion that the world was here to serve her, but that she was here to serve others. He couldn't tell her about Cecilia. Not now with her here in his arms, held secure on his horse.

"I'm fond of ye, lass."

She stared at him.

Could she feel his heart beating through his plaid? She was close.

"I am fond of you, as well," she whispered and closed her eyes, shielding herself from him, from the truth of her reply.

He understood. He wanted to be away from her. If he couldn't have her, he didn't want to torture himself being with her. If they did not stop for her prayers, they would save many hours and arrive at Dundonald faster—but she would have to pray in his arms. If they stopped, they would be together longer.

He winced at the thought, as if a dagger had just gone through him at either prospect.

"I think the faster we arrive at my uncle's castle, the better."

"Aye," he nearly groaned. He agreed, so why did hearing her say it make his blood run cold? Did she care for him as well? What would happen to them for having these thoughts?

"I will do what I can to hurry us along," she promised.

He felt gutted. He didn't want to think about why.

"Thank ye," he muttered.

The rest of the day passed in much the same fashion, with them finally having to stop for the last two prayers of the day. Galeren couldn't be so close to her all day.

By the time they settled down for the night in a small clearing, he made certain for her sake that the clearing was well lit while they settled in.

"Are ye anxious aboot arrivin' at the castle tomorrow, Sister?" Morgann asked her from his pallet.

"Aye, I am anxious," she answered in the flickering light from hers. "I do not know what anything will be like."

Galeren was listening close by.

"What d'ye want to know?" Will asked. "Everyone shytes the same way."

Lying near his brother, Padrig swiped his large fist into a part of Will that made the small man grunt in pain.

"Watch yer tongue," Padrig warned.

"Are ye vexed at meetin' the high steward and his kin, or the church?" Morgann asked her.

A smile danced across her lips that none of them saw, but Galeren heard in her voice. "I have met my uncle and his family before. Four years ago. I had only stayed at Dundonald for four days, but I remember Alexander and Margaret. Is Alex still shy?" she asked.

"Aye," answered Padrig.

"He preferred to play alone," Silene recalled.

"Alex is quiet but verra much aware," Galeren finally chimed in.

He heard Silene turn on her pallet to face him rather than the stars. "Does he have a friend in you, Captain?"

"All three of the steward's bairns have a friend in me, lass."

"Three? John and Matilda have had more then."

He liked the sound of her. He wanted to hear more of her.

Damn him.

"Aye. Wee Lizzie is three summers."

"Captain?" she asked in a hushed voice after a few moments of silence.

"Aye?"

"Is there nothing you can tell me about my cousins that will help me make them like me more?"

"Bein' yerself is part of what makes ye so—" he stopped and choked on his breath. "What I mean is…dinna try to be someone ye are not."

What would he have said? Irresistible? Charming? He had to keep watch over his mouth. "I'm certain the children will love ye, lass."

"I hope you are correct, Captain. I admit I have grown spoiled by you and the men at my back whenever I faced something new and alarming. I think about what I shall say to the church when I have to stand before them. I cannot sleep!"

He wanted to ease her fears and he thought hearing news of the steward's bairns would help. "Ye remember Margaret, aye? She was three when ye were at the castle."

"Aye. I remember her and her glossy chestnut curls, and how inquisitive she was."

"She is the jealous one."

"Oh?" It worked! She giggled softly, like music to his ears. "Who is she jealous of?"

"Me."

"That is sweet."

"No. 'Tis not," he corrected. "She will rant and rave and then not speak to anyone for days."

"Captain," she said, sounding more serious. "She needs to be spoken to. It needs to be explained—"

"We have tried. Nothin' has worked."

"I see. But, Captain?"

"Aye?"

"Why would she be jealous of me?"

He closed his eyes. No! He couldn't have been so damned dull-witted! "She would be jealous of any lass with me."

"With you?"

He stopped talking for a moment. He wished he could stop for good. "Good dreams, Silene."

"Captain?"

"Aye, lass?"

"I will miss you."

His heart took on a whole new rhythm and made his tongue betray him. "I willna be leavin' yer side, lass."

Chapter Eight

S ILENE RODE HER horse against the defensive barbican and gatehouse into the great outer court and stared, gaping at the huge castle before her. When she was here the first time, it was under the darkness of night and she had been in the back of a vegetable cart. She hadn't stayed long, four days, just long enough to meet her uncle and his family, and Mother Superior.

Now, she followed the captain and his men over the long pathway to the inner courtyard.

On the way, they passed the stable, a large gatehouse, a chapel, and a moat surrounding the inner wall and court.

Passing through the gatehouse, they dismounted, and their horses were taken.

Silene would have been relieved to be here, if not for the heaviness on her shoulders.

Riding in the captain's lap all day was pure torture. At first, she had been angry while she prayed. That changed as she became aware of one of his arms around her waist and the other hand holding the reins. Looking down at his long, tanned fingers and scarred hands distracted her. Moving around on his hard, well-muscled thighs with nothing to hold on to but his forearms had begun to make her perspire.

She was glad to be between her noon and late afternoon prayers. She wondered if the captain had planned for them to arrive at the castle at this time, giving her some time to settle in.

Her heart warmed thinking about how he'd done everything in his power to make her trip as pleasant as it could be.

"How are ye feelin'?" he asked, slowing his pace and waiting for her.

"I do not know," she answered honestly with a quirk of her mouth.

She couldn't tell him the truth about her indecision. She couldn't wait to be out of his arms and away from him, and yet she missed him already and he was still here! She wished she was in his arms again. She should laugh. She was mad.

"Ye are smilin'. That is a promisin' sign," he said with humor flashing across his eyes.

"I smile," she told him, "because I think I have gone mad.

He glanced down at her. "I dinna think one knows they are goin' mad if they truly are." His voice, along with his gaze, deepened.

She couldn't tell him that he made her melt all over and think of things she should not be thinking of. He made her smile, and laugh, and more miserable than she'd ever felt in her life.

Her prayers were more frantic and unfocused.

"Do you think I can have confession? Is there a priest in the chapel?"

"Of course," he promised. "I will bring him to ye after—"

"Now."

He looked around at the men, then sent Morgann to alert the high steward that his niece had arrived safe and sound and wished to stop in the chapel before being presented.

"Aye." Morgann frowned, obviously not wanting to leave her. But he obeyed his orders and took off through the inner gate.

"Come, we will find ye a priest." The captain forced himself to smile and then led the way to the chapel.

This was what she needed, to tell someone who would not tell anyone else. Someone who could absolve her, perhaps advise her what to do.

He'd told her he wouldn't leave her. But she didn't want to see him everywhere she looked. How would she ever resist him? How would she make him stop haunting her?

She quickened her pace and entered the chapel first, pushing open the doors.

There was a priest standing off to the right of the altar. He looked up, his stern, weathered face set toward her. "Who is there? Who comes barging into the House of the Lord?"

Silene slowed her pace. She touched her hooded head and wished she'd worn her bloodstained wimple and veil.

"Who is there?" the priest demanded again.

"Sis…Sister Silene Sparrow, niece to John the Steward, here at his command."

His frown made the creases in his face even more defined. "Remove your hood! Where is your habit?"

"'Tis in my bag. 'Tis covered in bloodstains."

"Put it on, child!" the priest barked. "You are in the Lord's house!"

She leaned down and opened her bag. She felt a hand to her shoulder. Her gaze flicked involuntarily to the priest.

"She will *not* put it on," the captain growled behind her.

"Captain, you will not—" the priest stammered.

"Who are you?" Silene asked more boldly than usual. She did it for the captain. She didn't want him getting into trouble over her.

"I'm Father Alphonsus," the priest answered. He seemed to be relieved to stop speaking to the captain.

"Have you served my uncle's family long, Father?"

"Three and twenty years," he told her, ending his declaration with a proud stare at the captain.

Silene raised her brows and asked in a more curious voice, "Do all your loyalties lie with him?"

"Aye," he replied curtly and looking insulted. "Of course!"

She sighed inwardly. She didn't want confession with him.

"What are you doing here in the chapel when you should be standing before the steward? You were due yesterday," he said. His voice was calmer but stinging, nonetheless.

"We ran into…I was…"

"Father," the captain's voice came down like a hammer. "Watch yer tongue when ye speak to her," he warned, stepping around her. "We were delayed by strict rules aboot when to speak to God and attacks by men who were drawn to her because of her veil. Her life was in danger durin' the entire journey because she was summoned here by yer brothers. I have remained silent on this. But now, I'm tellin' ye not to question her again or I will see that ye are sent away. D'ye understand?"

Silene frowned. This was not good. Threatening a priest's well-being would surely get them all killed.

"Aye," the priest answered.

What was this? Father Alphonsus gave in so easily. What kind of power did the captain have here?

"Good," he continued, unfazed by the priest's humiliation. He turned to her and without a word, set his palm on the small of her back and led her out.

"One more thing, Father." He stopped and turned to the priest. "Find Father Nathaniel and send him to the castle at once."

"He is away until tonight," Father Alphonsus let him know before he disappeared into a back room.

Alone, Silene looked into the captain's eyes. She saw a man of power and cool detachment. She didn't know what to say. Admonish him for defending her to a mean-spirited man? No. She wouldn't. She wouldn't have said anything. She was glad the captain had. But threatening him...could the captain carry out his promises? Would the steward let him? How much power did he have that made him so confident? She didn't have to wait long to find out.

The moment they stepped out of the chapel, John the Steward, with two of his children at his sides, hurried toward them.

Silene's uncle didn't question their tardiness. He all but ignored her and hooked his arm around the captain's shoulders and smiled. "Good to have ye back, Galeren." He turned to his children and called out happily, "Captain MacPherson has returned!"

His family greeted the captain and his men with much affection, boldly embracing the captain, and asking him dozens of questions.

In the midst of the merriment, the high steward looked at her and offered her a friendly smile. "A new soldier, Captain?" He looked around and frowned. "Where is my niece the novice?"

"Here, my lord." The captain angled his head to her and gave her a tender smile. "Sister Silene Sparrow, yer niece."

The steward stared at her. He appeared unconvinced. "Where is yer habit?"

"'Twas torn from me in an attack." She stared back at him.

He was a portly man with thick, dark hair worn beneath a meticulously wound *chaperon* on his head.

"We were unable to find such items in the villages. But, as your clever captain has pointed out to me, there is more desire for a woman in a habit than for what they believe to be a man."

Her uncle smiled, but not at her. "My apologies fer yer strenuous journey, Captain."

He finally turned his attention back to her. "Ye see, I sent my best man to escort ye. Do ye not agree?"

"Thank you, my lord. Aye, I do. Your men were exemplary in every task they undertook to protect me from the jackals that hide in the darkness. They were brave, curious, and compassionate."

Her uncle's smile grew—on her this time. "Captain MacPherson and his men never disappoint. And ye…" He spread his sable-colored eyes over her. "Ye look well, Niece. I should have recognized that fiery hair. Fergive me fer makin' ye wait."

"Of course, my lord."

"Come! Come inside all of ye. My Matilda awaits!"

As they headed toward the inner gate, the captain turned and let his lips curl at the corners. Everything was going to be all right.

She followed them through the gate and looked up at the two high towers on either side. They headed for a large, stone stairway along the eastern wall. Its door, when they reached it, was made of heavy wood and wrought iron hinges. Her cousin opened it.

Silene would have felt uncomfortable, even afraid entering a crowded great hall on her own. But she wasn't alone. The captain and his men surrounded her.

The captain walked inside after John and his children as if he were the master of the castle, home from a journey.

When they saw him and the men behind him, those in the great hall lifted their drinks and leaped to their feet, quick in greeting.

"Captain, 'tis good to have ye home," most declared while others shoved drinks into their hands.

The captain took a cup that was offered. Mac and the others followed suit, including Silene.

"Who is the red-haired lad?" a man called out.

The captain took a swig of his drink, which turned out to be ale when Silene took a sip. The captain swiped his mouth with the back of his hand, fully refreshed. Silene cringed, shivered and shook her head at the rest.

She felt his gaze on her. When she looked and saw that she was correct, her heart grew warm and she blushed with the heat of it.

She nodded, reassuring him that she was well.

He smiled as if he couldn't help himself, for he coughed a little and tore his gaze away.

But those watching him saw it and grew quiet.

"She is Sister Silene," he called out a moment later.

"Aye, my niece," the steward let them know. But if he was worried about his men making advances, she could have told him that every eye in this place did not doubt that she was highly valued by the captain.

Once again, he provided her safety.

"Welcome, Sister," most called out, studying her more closely for curves in her tunic and hose.

"My veil and wimple are stained in blood or I would be wearing them," she told them, tired of explaining.

The men held up their cups as soon as they heard about her clothing being bloodstained.

She smiled at them and thought it might not be so terrible here.

"My lord," the captain called out. "Where can she rest?"

Her uncle gave her a remorseful look. "Fergive me," he laughed at himself. "I am a great oaf withoot my wife at my left and my captain at my right."

His right.

"Where is yer wife, Lord?" the captain asked.

"Matilda is upstairs with our three-year-old girl, Lizzie."

"Oh?" Silene asked, her ears perked. "Is the babe unwell?"

A moment passed before the steward nodded. Why had he not answered sooner? His eyes appeared a bit glazed over by...indifference. His lips didn't curl downward, saddened to have to tell of his sick child, they were set straight and unyielding.

"May I be shown to them?" she asked.

"Why?" her uncle asked.

"To offer prayer."

"You can pray anywhere," he insisted.

Up until this moment, the captain had remained quiet. Now, he stepped up in front of the steward. "I can vouch fer her. She will do them no harm."

The steward's flinty gaze bored into him. "Ye vouch fer her with my wife and child?"

"I do." The captain wasted no more time but turned to a female servant. "Louise, take her to her mistress' chambers."

When he was done, his gaze skidded to Silene's then back to the steward. "She is as innocent as a fawn in the brush," she heard him tell the steward. "I also made an agreement with Mother Mary Joseph that I would bring her back safely. I willna shrink from my duty."

Their voices grew fainter and she and Louise left the great hall. They reached another stone stairway and ascended to the second landing, the third if there were cellars. Silene didn't know much about the castle.

"Ye have the captain's pledge," the serving girl remarked as they walked. "And his eye."

"We are friends," Silene was quick to tell her.

"He is verra handsome. Do ye not agree?"

"I'm not blind," Silene muttered. Was everyone in Dundonald jealous of the captain?

The serving girl smiled and continued leading her away.

When they reached a large, wooden door, Louise gave it a good knock. A woman called out from within.

"Come."

Louise held open the door and made a path for Silene to enter.

With her pale blonde tresses plaited and pinned up off her long neck and eyes as blue as a clear summer sky, Matilda was beautiful.

"Greetings, my lady," Silene said boldly, stepping into the room.

Matilda stood from her place at the bedside. "Who are ye?"

Before Silene had a chance to answer, Matilda gasped, recognizing her. "Silene? Silene, is it ye? Oh! 'Tis! Look at ye with all yer beautiful fiery tresses chopped off!"

Silene smiled and took a step toward her for an embrace. She was glad Matilda remembered her. She was only a few years older than Silene, and though Silene had only been here once, four years ago, and for only four days, Matilda had been kind to her, and they became friends.

"We expected ye yesterday," Matilda said, coming out of their embrace.

Silene nodded. "We were attacked. We also paid a visit to the captain's ailing grandsire in Hethersgill, and my prayers—"

"Yer group was attacked?" Matilda gasped. "Was anyone hurt?"

Silene told her what happened. Her uncle's wife seemed especially relieved to hear that the captain was unharmed.

"Ye traveled all the way to the central Marches, and then what? Ye slept in their home with Captain MacPherson?"

"And the other men, aye," Silene told her, narrowing her eyes on Matilda. Was she jealous? Silene would never tell her that he'd slept against her door.

"Good. Ye should always have witnesses when ye are alone with him," Matilda continued, looking around conspiratorially. "The captain is known to be extremely comely, and it would be difficult to convince the church that ye could resist such a man. That nothin' happened between ye."

Was Matilda trying to frighten her, Silene wondered, staring at her? She didn't look away and prove her guilt. "If the church would think so little of me that I would give up my body to a man because he is handsome, then why would my opinion of my uncle hold such weight?"

Matilda's jaw stiffened for only an instant and then her defenses faded into a smile. "I only wish to keep all suspicion off ye. Ye know how men are."

"Nay, I do not," Silene said with a smile of her own.

"They are the same, whether religious or not. They think we are all harlots. Deep down, they all believe it."

Silene hoped that wasn't true. She was sure the captain didn't think she was a harlot. Either way, she didn't want to fight with her aunt. "Tell me about the babe." She turned around and looked down at the child lying in her mother's bed.

"Aye, my Lizzie. She suffers a fever."

Silene stepped back involuntarily. "Are you certain 'tis not the Black Death?"

"I am certain."

Silene wasn't worried about catching something, even the Black Death. In the past, she had gone to a few villages with the other novices and nuns to nurse the sick. She'd been around terrible disease and had never become sick. If she did now, so be it.

She hurried around Matilda and leaned over the bed to examine little girl. Her fever was low, her breathing a bit labored.

According to her mother, physicians had done all they could. The child was not in dire distress. But they could not defeat the fever that plagued her.

Silene knelt beside the bed and looked up at Lizzie's mother. "May I pray for her?"

"Of course," Matilda whispered with a softer, kinder smile.

"WHAT IS IT?" Galeren asked after the steward told him all about the sickness tormenting his daughter.

"'Tis not the plague," John assured.

"How d'ye know?"

"No one has died. Still, the illness is difficult to go through. No one wants to get it."

"Understandable," Galeren muttered and threw himself into the nearest chair in John's private solar.

"The novice will likely fall ill," the steward proclaimed and fixed them a drink.

Galeren felt the alarming need to go get her, take her away from the sick child. But he knew she wouldn't leave.

It was his fault. He overrode John's order that she not go near his wife and child. "Ye didna tell me that the babe was a danger to her."

John handed Galeren his drink and sipped some wine from his own cup. "She willna die. And I did tell her not to go."

Galeren relented and nodded. God would care for her.

John took a seat in a dark wood chair with a hand-sewn cushion and cast Galeren a hard look. "Tell me, Galeren. It seems that ye and my niece grew close on yer short journey here. Is she fond of ye?"

"Most likely," Galeren told him honestly. "I saved her from almost bein' defiled."

The steward's eyes went dark. "Did ye kill him?"

"I did," Galeren told him with satisfaction, causing him to smile.

"Good," John said. "What else?"

"What are ye askin' me?" Galeren sat up and put down his drink. He loved Scotland. He'd grown to care for John and his family, but that fondness was growing thin from years of watching John involve himself in shady dealings that always ended up with someone innocent dying. Galeren stayed for the king's sake…and for the children.

He was loyal, putting personal feelings aside. But they hadn't gone away. He cared for John's family. He loved that the castle and village were under his control alongside the steward. Though Galeren was given authority, overall the steward had the final say in everything.

John didn't care if Silene grew ill.

"I'm asking ye what else happened between ye while ye and my niece were travelin'."

Was he jesting? Galeren wondered. He stared at the steward and let the storm go free just a little. "I will tell ye what we did, John. We stopped five, sometimes six times a day so she could pray alone—with me watchin' her. We all slept and then did it all over again. Other intervals included her bein' abducted by a group of ten men. We killed them all and got her back. We visited my kin along the border and her prayers strengthened my grandsire on his sickbed," Galeren finished. He gave John a dark look. "Anythin' else ye wish to know?"

The steward narrowed his gaze on his captain. "Dinna get so offended, Galeren. I must be certain Silene is pure and that nothin' gets in the way of her good standin' with the church."

She was a pawn. A piece of a game John needed to win. Silene had been correct. Her uncle cared little for her.

Galeren stood up from his chair. "If ye will excuse me, John. I have many things to see to upon my return."

He didn't wait for the steward's permission. Galeren did what he wanted at Dundonald. Everything but refuse to marry Cecilia Birchet. He was indebted to John for many things. The greatest thing being that John had saved his life on the battlefield three years ago when a man brought down his sword behind Galeren. Galeren would have lost his head and mayhap more if not for John's blade getting in between them. John kept him on as David's captain and his own after the king was arrested. John hadn't minded when the people of Dundonald began their worshipful admiration of his captain. People followed Galeren and Galeren was loyal to John—therefore the people followed John.

What if the people discovered that their darling captain had kissed the fresh-faced novice?

He left the solar angry and ashamed. He stood outside the door for a moment and closed his eyes while he thought about what had just happened. Did John suspect something between him and Silene? Why wouldn't he? Galeren believed what he felt for her was palpable, alive and charging the air. He believed Silene felt it, too. Could others see their attraction? Could his men? And they chose to say nothing?

He opened his eyes and marched toward Lady Matilda's quarters. Silene had been taken there. He wanted to see her. He wanted to see Lizzie and her mother. He didn't care about any damned fever.

When he reached the door, he knocked then entered when he was bid.

He should have warned Silene that wee Margaret wasn't the only one who was possessive and protective of him *and* her husband.

His eyes searched and settled on Silene first, and then on Matilda.

"Captain!" Matilda shouted then rose up to be swept up in his embrace. "'Tis good to look upon yer face again.

He smiled, giving her a place among his dearest friends. "What is this I hear aboot a sickness?"

She nodded and pointed to the three-year-old child lying in her large bed. "Lizzie was stricken first. Now, seven more have come down with it."

He walked to the bed and smiled at Silene when he saw that she was praying at the bedside. "Has she become better? Worse?"

"The same," the lass' mother told him.

He looked at the child, a smaller version of her golden-haired mother. The last time he'd seen her—a sennight ago. She'd hurried to him and pressed her cheek to his when he lifted her in his arms. "I will miss ye, Galeren," she had told him.

He bent to her and whispered above her face. "I am home, lass."

His gaze drifted to Silene kneeling on the other side of the bed.

"Captain?"

He looked down on the bed. Lizzie was awake. His smiled deepened. "Greetin's, lass. What d'ye mean by fallin' ill when I wasna here to protect ye?"

She smiled back. "Ye are here now."

They spoke a little longer and when she fell back to sleep, he prayed with Silene.

CHAPTER NINE

"SHE SEEMS BETTER," Matilda said about her daughter an hour later.

Silene couldn't help but smile at the captain where he was standing by the window in Matilda's room.

"She seems quite fond of you, Captain," she pointed out.

"Everyone is fond of the captain," Matilda told her.

Aye, it certainly seemed that way, Silene thought, remembering how the people had gathered around him, eager to share a word or a smile with him. He was not just the captain of the steward's guard, he was their friend, perhaps even the one they considered their leader.

So, it wasn't just her who thought he was an exceptional man. She felt better knowing it. She'd fallen under his spell just as the rest of them had.

"Captain, I asked Sister Silene how long she was stayin'. She doesna know. Do ye?"

His verdant gaze fell on her. "Ye werena told?"

"Nay," Silene answered.

He bit down hard enough to make the muscles in his jaw tighten. "Ye are to stay fer a fortnight. I thought ye knew."

Her eyes widened a little. She thought she was staying for a few days. Whether or not she believed she'd ever go back, a fortnight was a long time. She was surprised Mother Mary Joseph hadn't told her.

She blinked her gaze to Matilda. "You may put me to work where you need me. I will not be a burden to you for a fortnight."

"Dinna think of it," her uncle's wife told her. "Ye are kin, also our guest."

A fortnight. Silene's eyes drifted to him again. She was going to live here for fourteen days, seeing him. She felt like weeping. How could she resist him?

"I...I think I should freshen up." She needed to be away from him. To pray. To think.

"Of course, Silene." Matilda took her hand when she came near. "Thank ye fer comin' here first. Louise brought yer things to yer room." She turned to look around, likely for Louise, but she hadn't told the servant to return. "Oh, dear. Ye dinna know where 'tis, do ye?"

"I could escort her," the captain offered.

No.

"Nay, Captain," Matilda refused. "While ye traveled, she had no escort, which I intend to speak to Mother Mary Joseph aboot. Now, she is in my home and will have an escort."

"My lady, ye insult me." He truly sounded offended, Silene thought. "I am her escort. I wouldna—"

"Her reputation—"

"Will remain intact. Anyone who suspects otherwise can speak directly to me. Now," he turned to Silene as he leashed his control. "Would ye please come with me?"

"Truly, Captain. I can find the room myself. I would not be a burden. Please remain here." Her reasoning for not wanting to be alone with him was different from Matilda's. Silene was terrified. Why? She'd been alone with him before. What had changed—or was changing?

Her feelings toward him. They were growing stronger, side by side with her guilt. She had to pray. Ten Hail Marys was obviously not enough.

"My dear Silene," Matilda's smile softened on her. "I was wrong to worry aboot yer reputation with the captain." Her blue eyes deepened on him. "He has supreme control over his body and remains chaste. Is that not so, Captain?"

Silene looked at him. Was she bold enough to ask him why he and his men had made their vows? Not now. The less interest she showed in him, the better where Matilda was concerned.

"'Tis so, my lady," he answered.

"Ye see?" Matilda laughed. "There is nothing to worry aboot with him."

Silene's gaze remained on his. Matilda was wrong—but Silene wasn't worried.

She crooked her arm in the elbow he offered. Could he feel her trembling?

"Which is her room, my lady?"

"Down the right hall. Third door on the left," she told them.

"Nay," Silene paused, digging in her heels when he would lead her. "I can find the room on my own."

"What is it?" Matilda asked, narrowing her eyes on Silene. "Why are ye so determined to be out of the captain's care?"

"What?" Silene blinked at her and uncurled her arm from his. "Nay. I have imposed too much."

"Do ye love him, Silene?"

Silene almost reached for the bedpost to hold on to. Something. Anything. Why had she let him go? She was slipping off the precipice. What kind of question was this?

"My lady!" the captain objected, moving closer. He held up his palm to Matilda. "That is enough!"

Silene knew she had to say something. Denying it was pointless. Matilda would see right through her. She would not lie. She knew that no matter what she said, Matilda would not understand.

"My lady, I love everyone the Lord puts in my path. I love Mac and Morgann. I love them all. They are good, compassionate men who treated me with dignity and honor, especially this man." She looked up at him then quickly looked away, lest the lady see more.

"And even if she did love me," the captain told Matilda, silencing her with his angry stare, "'tis not wise to blurt it oot—fer someone comin' in or listenin' to hear. It could cause her harm."

"Aye. Ye are correct." The steward's wife nodded and gave Silene a happier look. "Fergive my rash tongue. I didna mean—"

"Of course." Silene smiled at her.

"I know where the room is," the captain told them and motioned to Silene to follow him.

She went.

"Ye shouldna fight so passionately to stay away from me," he admonished when they were alone. "John suspects it and, now, so does his wife."

Her eyes opened wider. What kind of trouble had she gotten him in to? "Why do you believe that John suspects anything?"

"Because he asked me a dozen questions aboot what went on between us?"

"Between us?" Her heart slammed in her chest. Their kiss! Had the captain told him that they shared a passionate kiss? She wanted to ask him, but she couldn't bring herself to mention it. Besides that, she didn't believe he would tell.

"Aye. Between us," he told her. "I canna deny that there is somethin'. Can ye?"

He didn't give her time to answer but continued speaking. She was glad he was doing the talking. She wasn't sure how much she would admit to.

"We dinna realize that we are starin' at each other or sharin' intimate smiles until 'tis brought to our attention. We panic over things involvin' the other, and we dinna know it until 'tis too late."

She nodded, pale-faced and guilty. "What do we do now?"

She looked away and closed her eyes. She hated to admit that there was something between them.

"Be aware of how we react to each other."

"It frightens me, Captain," she said in a hushed, quavering voice, looking at him again. "'Tis like an uncontrolled wind."

His wide, emerald eyes grew wider. "Fergive me."

"For what?"

He didn't tell her. He picked up his steps and continued down the hall without another word.

When they reached the third door on the left, he pushed it open. A woman inside screamed and then greeted the captain when she saw it was him. He apologized profusely and then did the same after opening two more doors that were someone else's room.

He was mortified and frustrated, but he never cursed Matilda for giving him the incorrect directions. They ended up laughing together when he finally opened the correct door—after knocking at least ten times.

"I will see ye la—" He stopped, likely realizing as was she, that they would probably not see each other much. "Farewell, Silene." He bowed before her and looked into her eyes when he straightened. "If ye need me, lass, I will come."

"I need you, Captain." She said it but she shook her head at the same time. She knew she should have remained silent. "Nay. I am wrong." She backed up and shut the door.

Alone, she leaned her back against the door between them.

"Forgive me," she prayed. "Oh, forgive me."

Outside her door, Galeren heard her cry and muttered a soft, miserable oath.

When he stepped into the main hall, he was stopped by two soldiers from the garrison.

"Greetin's, Captain. 'Tis good to have ye back," said one of the men. Alistair Desmond was his name. He hailed from Perth and arrived at the garrison in Dundonald six months ago. "How was yer journey?"

Galeren smiled at them. "Uneventful."

"Uneventful," the other man, Jack MacKinny, repeated with a doubtful arch of his dark brow. He was dressed like Desmond in boots and a plaid with a léine underneath. At his waist, he wore a leather belt that was heavy with various weapons. "Save that ye and the lads killed a large group of men after they attacked the nun."

"Novice," Galeren corrected.

Alistair tossed back his bald head and laughed. "That isna uneventful, Captain."

"To him 'tis." Will laughed, joining them. With him was Father Alphonsus.

Upon seeing the priest, Alistair and Jack disappeared.

"Truly?" Father Alphonsus asked, stepping closer. "It is uneventful for you to kill ten men?"

"*Those* ten men. Aye, Father," Galeren told him and moved away. He stopped after a few steps. "Have ye sent Father Nathaniel to Sister Silene?"

"I have not seen him," Father Alphonsus sneered.

Galeren gave him a black stare. He'd never be forgiven for striking a man of God. But the priest didn't know that Galeren cared about such a thing. "May I suggest ye find him?" he uttered as more of a command than a question.

Will laughed and pushed Galeren away. "I'm sure the good Father Alphonsus will find him."

"What are ye doin' with him?" Galeren demanded quietly as they left the hall.

"Findin' oot when our dear *novice* is to face the church and how many of us can be there to pledge ourselves to her safety."

Since when had she become *their* novice? And why did Will emphasize the word?

"And?" he couldn't help but ask. In truth, he liked that his men wanted to continue to protect her.

"In eight days and she can have no guard with her."

Galeren stopped to turn to him. "She will have a guard. Me."

His friend gave him an amazed look. "Ye intend to defy the church?"

Galeren squared his shoulders. "If I must."

Will smiled and patted him on the back before he broke away to head to another room. "Be careful, Cap."

Galeren nodded and continue on. He couldn't say it was good to be back. He'd told Alistair the trip was uneventful but, in truth, it had changed everything in his life.

He had to break things off with Cecilia. He didn't love her. He never would. He had to come to the truth that he might be falling in love with one of God's betrothed.

Ye have many, Lord, he beseeched in his mind. *I only want one.*

He kept walking, turning the corner toward the exit. He hurried and nearly walked into the arms of a lass crossing his path.

"Cecilia!"

"Galeren!" she answered, sounding just as stunned to see him almost running into her arms.

No! Not her. Not now.

"I heard you had returned. Why did you not come directly to me?" She pouted her pink lips and let her gaze go hot. She stomped her slippered foot just like a spoiled child. If she had one of her temper tantrums now, he didn't know what he might say to her. He wanted to go outside. Take a walk. Be alone.

"I didna know ye were here." He moved out of her embrace. "What are ye doin' here, Cecilia?"

She lifted her hand to her flowing, honey-hued hair and patted it. "Father had dealings with the steward and brought me along to Dundonald. He thought I might want to see you. He was correct. Imagine my supreme disappointment to learn you had not yet returned."

"Aye, we ran into some difficulties. It couldna be helped."

She pouted again.

"We will speak of it later. And of other things."

"But I am leaving shortly—"

He didn't wait for the rest, but continued walking, finally reaching for the door. He saw his plaid hanging on a peg near the entrance.

"Captain!"

He drew in a breath and turned again. This time, he saw Alex, the steward's son, and Margaret, the lad's seven-year-old sister, offering him their brightest smiles.

"What are ye doin'?" Alex asked.

"Are ye goin' oot?" asked his sister.

"Aye. I am goin' oot."

"We want to go oot, too!" one of them cried.

Galeren looked around. Where were their nurses or teachers? Anyone watching over them.

"Who escorts ye through the halls?" He knew the rules, for he had made them. John and Matilda's children must not be about alone. The steward had too many enemies.

"No one escorts us," Alex told him timidly. "Our teacher said he felt ill. He told us to find our nurse, Gwendolyn. But we couldna find her."

Galeren ground his jaw. So busy were they?

He felt something on his leg. He looked down and saw Margaret hugging his calf. "We want to go with ye!"

"Verra well. I have some things to think on. Will ye be silent if I agree to take ye with me?"

"Aye! Aye!" they promised.

"Fetch yer cloaks. Hurry. I willna wait long."

Galeren waited while they hurried to their room, which was the first door at the top of the stairs. He watched them from where he stood. He tapped his foot, greeting others as they passed.

"Nice to have ye back, Captain."

"Good to see ye unscathed from yer journey, Captain MacPherson!"

The children returned and Galeren finally stepped out of Dundonald and into the cool, crisp air. The children ran ahead, laughing and enjoying their freedom. Galeren kept his eyes on them but, soon, while he walked, his thoughts drifted to Silene and what the next fortnight was going to be like. He wished Father Timothy was here. He would tell Galeren what to do.

He watched the children returning to him. Their cheeks were red from running. Their happiness made him forget what was happening to his heart.

"Captain, may we go to the orchard?" Margaret reached him and asked.

He looked toward the castle's orchard behind them and nodded. "We must hurry, though. It occurs to me that we didna tell anyone that I was takin' ye."

The children looked at each other and then at him. He saw the worry in their eyes, and it pricked his heart. They were too young for such fears.

He smiled. A wee bit of worry never hurt anyone. In fact, it might make them more vigilant in their duties.

"Come." He turned around and marched to the orchard. He let them pick some apples and was proud of them when they picked extra for their sibling. Margaret even gave him hers.

"Ye are both learnin' yer lessons well," he told them while they sat beneath a tree. "I'm proud of ye."

"Let us also pick some flowers fer Lizzie," Alex suggested.

"Good thinkin', my lord," Galeren praised him. "'Twill brighten up the room."

It amazed him how the children could be more thoughtful than adults. He scowled thinking how John the Steward had not been to see his daughter the entire time Galeren had been there.

He didn't admonish them for not picking apples for their father. The steward liked making children. After that, he left the rearing to his wife and nurses.

"I asked Mother if I could have a kitten," Margaret confided.

From where he rested against the tree, Galeren opened one eye and looked at her. "Is this the hundredth time ye have asked her?"

"Aye." Margaret stared at him with huge dark eyes. "One of these times she will agree."

He smiled. Clever lass.

"Will ye ask her, Captain? Mother will agree if ye ask her."

Galeren shook his head. "She has said no alr—"

"But Annabelle Henry's kittens are almost all gone. I would like one. Please, Captain." Her eyes grew even wider. "Please help me."

Galeren stared at her for a moment or two. Had she learned how to manipulate at such a young age? No. She was sincere. She truly wanted a kitten. She'd been asking for a month and a half now. Galeren had not involved himself and Margaret had never asked for his help until now.

"I will have a word with her," he gave in. He tried to scowl but his heart felt too soft. When she bolted from her spot and flung her arms around his neck, he smiled.

"Oh! Thank ye, Captain! Thank ye!" she cried, pressing her cheek to his.

"Now, my lady—"

"Ye see, Alex? I told ye he would help us."

Galeren quirked his brow at the lad. "Ye doubted me?"

"No, I just know ye have enough to do already. Ye dinna have to add helpin' a lass get a kitten to yer list."

Galeren's expression turned serious. "How many summers are ye now, my lord?""

"Nine, Sir,"

"Nine," Galeren repeated, studying his wee friend and his haunting different colored eyes.

"What d'ye know of how much I do?"

The lad shrugged his scrawny shoulders. "I see ye doin' everythin'. Ye train the garrison and earned the respect of the men. Ye hold council and listen to every grievance, doin' whatever needs to be done to offer help. Ye are always first when Scotland needs her sons to fight."

"Nine?" Galeren asked, and then smiled. "Yer ability to understand such matters is impressive. But ye mustna worry yerself over these things."

"It doesna matter whether I worry or not. 'Twill still be ye doin' it all even when we are all old."

They were still. Even Margaret, who now leaned her elbow on Galeren's shoulder, did not speak or move.

Galeren didn't want to be here that long. He missed his kin. His nephews and nieces knew him less than the steward's children. But he would not mention home to Alex or Margaret. He knew the steward's wife and bairns loved him. His garrison and Dundonald's tenants loved him. They would not want to see him go.

"Even then, my lord," Galeren told him, "'twould not be any concern of yers."

"Ye are my friend," the boy insisted.

Galeren stood up and put his hand on the lad's shoulders. "Ye are loyal. Ye would be welcome among my soldiers."

"I would rather serve ye than any man I know."

Galeren's heart swelled and his eyes burned. Here was a lad of nine summers earnestly pledging his life to him.

"I am honored, my lord."

"And I want to come to Invergarry one day and meet yer father."

Galeren's smile widened and he bowed.

John and Matilda's bairns were intelligent and easy to mold with encouraging words. He would have been proud to call any one of them his own.

Alex was an exceptional child. He could often be found alone, playing or thinking—or obviously noticing the captain of the garrison's workload.

"Aye," Galeren told him. "Ye will meet him but, fer today, ye will play."

"I miss the kittens," Margaret said before long.

"Do ye wish to go see them?" Galeren asked.

"Aye!" both children squealed and jumped up and down.

Annabelle didn't live too far away and, soon, Galeren found himself watching the children play with the kittens.

"D'ye know which one ye want?" he whispered to Margaret.

She nodded and picked out a little orange kitten with large, blue-green eyes.

Galeren was disgusted with himself that a kitten reminded him of Silene.

When it came time to leave, "Daffodil" came with them.

"She will live with me until I can think of what to tell yer mother."

The children didn't care what rules he put into place. They would abide by them. They would feed the kitten and clean up after it when they took it home. They would play with it and keep it with them when he asked.

When they stepped into the great hall, Galeren was not surprised that no one raised an eyebrow when they saw the children with him. They walked through the hall without a nurse or teacher calling after them. No one would expect the steward's bairns to be left alone. He found Louise, the steward's servant. "Take them to their mother. I will send fer them shortly."

"Aye, Captain, but where is Gwen, their nurse, or Mr. Darby, their teacher?"

"I am aboot to find oot."

With Daffodil cupped in the palm of his hand, he left them and made his way to their teacher's room. When he reached the door, he knocked with the other hand.

"Captain," the teacher said, opening the door. He was not dead. Pity for him because that would have been the only acceptable reason to leave the children alone for the day.

Galeren heard a sound in the hall and turned to see Silene leaving her room. She had to pass him to get to the great hall, if that was where she was going.

"What can I do fer ye, Captain?" Mr. Darby asked politely.

"Greetin's, Mr. Darby. Are Alex and Margaret with ye?"

Darby's eyes widened a bit. "Ehm…nay…I just sent them to Gwen fer—"

"Did ye say ye just sent them?" he verified. When the teacher nodded, his jaw muscles danced at the anger brimming upward. "Then how d'ye explain that they were with me fer the last pair of hours?"

Silene grew nearer, walking slowly forward. Galeren wondered briefly if it was his tone that drew her or his angry, unblinking gaze at the teacher.

Darby's mouth closed—for just a moment. Then he astonishingly tried to defend himself. "I just woke with a fever."

Galeren took a step closer to him and reached his free hand to the teacher's face. Darby cringed, obviously thinking Galeren was going to strike him. "Ye have no fever. It didna just break since ye are not clammy."

"I—"

Galeren stepped back and held up his palm to stop him. "Pack yer things and leave Dundonald. Ye failed yer most important duty to the steward's bairns."

He turned away, unfazed by Mr. Darby's cries. He loved the children and Darby had put them in danger by neglecting his duty. If he showed mercy, others would not respect the highest duty there was. What was more precious than the lives of the young? Nothing.

"'Tis a good thing they were with me and not with one of the steward's enemies," he said with disgust. "Ye are relieved of all further duty, Mr. Darby."

He settled his gaze on Silene as he passed her. She was just as important. He moved toward her, unable to help himself.

"Leave here. Come away with me."

CHAPTER TEN

"GO WAIT OOTSIDE of Darby's door," the captain ordered one of his men who was passing by. "Make certain he leaves Dundonald."

The man nodded and left to take up his station at the door.

Silene saw and heard his power. He didn't need the steward's approval with big decisions. He was trusted. It was good to know.

"Is that a kitten?" she asked when they were out of range.

He scowled at first and then smiled. "'Tis Daffodil," he said, grabbing the kitten an instant before she leaped from his hands.

"I must take her to my room and put her down. She needs food and likely needs to find a spot."

"Where did she come from?"

"From Annabelle's," he told her. "Margaret has wanted a kitten fer a while now. Her mother has refused. Annabelle said the kittens were goin' fast and I didna want Margaret to lose the one she wanted."

What kind of soul was this that cared for the wants of a child who was not his own? He warmed her heart and made her feel the need to pray. "What will you tell their mother?"

"Nothin'," he answered. "Not fer a while anyway. I will keep Daffodil with me until Lady Matilda gives in."

He smiled a bit mischievously, charming her senseless.

She giggled.

"May I hold her?" What was she doing? She should be walking the other way. Hadn't she decided to stay out of his path? Instead, she *giggled*.

"You said the children were with you. You mentioned it to that gentleman, who I assumed is their teacher."

"He is that no longer."

Silene shivered at the finality of his voice. "I did not know you could be so void of compassion."

"My compassion is fer Alex and Margaret and their parents who trusted someone to watch over their bairns."

"Is Dundonald so dangerous?" she asked him.

"Anywhere can be dangerous when ye have as many enemies as the High Steward of Scotland. And not just enemies but accidents can kill also."

She liked that he worried about the children, that he'd kept them with him for a pair of hours. He would make a good father. Her face flushed at the thought of it, but she couldn't stop it.

"Katherine from Hamsertown gave me a gown. I refused it, as I have no place to wear it, but she smuggled it into my bag. Do you think I should give it to Matilda?"

"No. I think ye should keep it."

She looked up at him and wondered why he thought she should. She wanted to ask him, but she wasn't that bold.

"My chambers are lovely," she told him next, unable to keep her mouth shut. "I am unused to such extravagance."

He smiled, tempting her to do the same.

"I share my room at the priory with many other girls. My friends, whom I miss very much." Her eyes misted and she sniffled. "I even dream of them."

"Ye will tell me aboot them."

She nodded. "I often think of dear Agnes the most at night. She has night terrors and the other girls do not care to help."

"Ye are kind-hearted," he remarked.

They smiled at each other and continued down and around the hall.

Why was she accompanying him? Didn't he say he was taking the kitten to his room?

"Well, here you go," she said quickly, not knowing where his room was. She handed him Daffodil and turned her body to go. Her face did not wish to follow—or her eyes, which she could not pry from his.

"Captain McPherson?"

They both turned at the sound of Alex's voice.

Silene smiled at him. She doubted he remembered her. He'd been almost five when she saw him last. Quiet, pensive Alex. He'd been courteous and shy.

"Aye, my lord?" the captain answered him with Daffodil climbing up his chest.

"We are here."

"I see that," the captain said. "Did Louise not take ye to yer mother?"

"Aye," replied Margaret. "But Mother brought us back oot. She said we were disturbin' Lizzie. She gave us to Gwen, but we saw ye and told our nurse we were meetin' ye here. Ye *were* comin' to get us, were ye not, Captain?"

He nodded and grinned at Silene. "I have enlisted my lord and lady to help me care fer the cat." He opened the door to his chambers and put Daffodil down inside. The children hurried in after her.

"A fine decision," she told him. "There is much to be taught in caring for a pet."

He angled his head as if to see her from another perspective. "They are quick learners."

The light shining in his eyes did not go unnoticed by her. He cared for the children. Another man's children.

"They will be compassionate leaders," she pointed out.

His gaze on her warmed, going a deeper, richer shade of green. "Would ye care to wait ootside the door with me?"

She shouldn't. She mustn't. "I...I cannot..." she stopped. She couldn't finish. She opened her mouth to say a quick Hail Mary. It wasn't what came out. "Of course, Captain. I would enjoy waiting with you."

His smile widened. He bowed slightly, making her feel as if she were the princess on some far-off land in a more ancient time.

"Thank ye," he said in a low, quiet voice as he straightened and then leaned against the door frame.

"Tell me more about yourself, Captain," she said to keep herself from thinking of melting against him. "Tell me more please about your vow of chastity."

He crooked his mouth to one side. "I took my vows at St. Michael's in Edinburgh six years ago."

Fascinating. She wondered what kind of man made such promises. "May I ask you why you did it?"

He paused, looking as if he were thinking of his answer. "Israel's King David vowed chastity before every battle. We all agreed 'twas a good practice. I needed the most discipline."

"You?" she asked, chuckling with disbelief. "Not Will?"

He feigned insult. "Ye think Will more handsome than me?"

"Nay," she vowed with a shake of her head. "He seems more confident with women."

"Ah."

"I like that you are not like that," she told him. "I think if you let your charm fall full force on others, you would have crowds of women after you. You hold back."

His smile widened, deepening his dimple, making his lavishly green eyes dance. He wasn't holding back now.

They heard the children running through his chambers and something crashing to the ground. He hunched his shoulders and shook his head.

"Why did you not take the kitten to the barn? There is a barn in Dundonald," she said. "I remember it."

"I dinna think a baby cat would be safe withoot its mother in the barn."

"Nay," she agreed, "you are correct. But will you leave your duties to be here to let the children in and out. Daffodil should be let out three times a day at least. She needs food at all times and, mostly, she need attention."

"What d'ye suggest, lass?"

"I could help."

"Aye—"

"Sister Silene!" a women's voice called from down the hall. It was Lady Matilda. "What are ye doin' here alone at the captain's door?"

"Lady Matilda—" the captain tried.

"It looks indecent, Captain. Are ye tryin' to ruin John's position?"

"Of course not," he said, insulted.

"Ye will give account of this to my husband this evenin'." Matilda didn't give him time to answer. Nor did she look inside his room to find her children inside. "Come away," she said, tugging on Silene's arm.

"Ye must be cautious of Captain MacPherson," she said when they were out of earshot. "Dinna let him beguile ye—"

"What are you talking about?" Silene dug her heals into the wood floors and stopped Matilda from dragging her around. "Is he some kind of terrible monster that I do not know about? Will he try to force himself on me?"

"Nay!" Matilda gasped. "Captain MacPherson would never—"

"Then what is it?"

"People will whisper. Yer good name could suffer."

And her husband's name, of course.

"The captain has been kind to me, my lady. He is my friend. Should I just forget him and everything he has done for me because of a few wagging tongues?"

"Aye. Forget it all," Matilda warned. "Captain MacPherson is…mesmerizin'. 'Tis understandable that ye could be taken with him. As I told ye, everyone is."

Silene's eyes widened. "I do not know what to say."

"His vow of celibacy is almost over," Matilda went on as if she hadn't heard her. "Ye must—"

Silene held up her hand to stop her. She didn't want to hear another word. "Your words insult me, my lady."

Matilda's eyes opened wide. "I am tryin' to save ye from further insult."

Silene nodded. Her uncle's wife was correct. But staying away from the captain was already impossible.

"How is Lizzie feeling?" she asked, cutting off the bickering. And she was genuinely concerned for the child.

"She seems better, Silene." Matilda's smile softened on her. "She was up and playin' fer a bit this mornin'. Will ye not come and pray fer her again?"

"Of course."

Matilda showed her to her chambers.

Silene's first afternoon at Dundonald passed with her thoughts and prayers on three-year-old Lizzie and no one else.

Matilda invited her to sit with her and the steward at supper and Silene accepted.

The captain would be there to obey Matilda's demand that he give account of why they were alone outside his door. Would they eat together? Would the other men be there? Was her premonition incorrect? She hoped so.

"I purchased a new habit and all this—" she circled her fingers in front of her face, "that ye wear. 'Tis waitin' fer ye in yer bedchamber."

"You found one so quickly," Silene remarked.

"Aye. Well, ye are John's tie to the church. We want ye to look perfect. Now, I couldna find a white gown, only gray. But there is a white overcoat so ye should feel fine in it."

Silene thanked her, though she was only supposed to wear white, and finally retired to her chambers to change for supper.

She eyed the folded purple gown from Katherine, Adam's mother. She was tempted to run her hand down the soft silk. She'd never possessed anything so fine.

Why had the captain told her to keep it?

Louise arrived a short while later to help her into her clothes. Silene didn't like the serving girl serving her. If Silene wasn't a novice, she would have a lower duty than Louise had.

"I should be serving you," she remarked while Louise fit Silene's wimple and veil into place and tucked all her hair underneath.

Louise laughed and promised to let Silene braid her hair later.

"Tell me, what do ye think of Captain MacPherson?"

The question surprised Silene and she wasn't sure how to answer—though she was getting sick and tired of answering it.

"I think he is well liked by everyone."

"Even ye?" Louise asked.

"He is my friend, Louise."

The servant eyed her. "No one wants the captain as a friend, Sister. I only ask because there are whispers goin' aboot that the captain cares for ye and he is…betrothed, after all."

What? Betrothed? No! He would have told her! Silene did everything she could to keep quiet. She wanted to weep but she had no right.

"'Tis surprisin' and dishearntenin' to many of us."

"Why is that, Louise? He is betrothed. What should you or anyone else care about what he does?"

"He doesna love Cecilia!" Louise nearly yelped.

"Who is this Cecilia?" Did she truly want to know? "Is she here?"

Louise stared at her, looking hopeless. "He didna tell ye of her," she spoke Silene's fear out loud. "She is Lady Cecilia Birchet and she isna well liked. Well, not by the other ladies. The men like her well enough. She is, after all, considered to be the most beautiful lady in the three kingdoms."

Silene didn't think it could get any worse. She was wrong. He was betrothed to the most beautiful woman in the three kingdoms? How could she be such a fool to think he would care for her? She was plain. Oh, she wanted to crawl in a crevice somewhere.

"She was here earlier," Louise continued, clearly up on the latest gossip. "She left with her father. I heard she saw the captain and he hardly spared her a glance. I wonder if ye are the reason." Louise gave her a good looking over and shook her head with distaste. "But why should he love ye? Ye are not shapely and yer hair has been shaved off. Ye are not what any of us would have expected him to care fer."

Silene bristled in her spot. They behaved as if he belonged to them, as if they knew everything about him. She was certain they did not. She knew even less apparently. He was betrothed. She wanted to ask when this marriage was to take place. But she didn't dare stir up suspicions by asking questions.

"Louise, if the captain were available, which he is not, and if I were available, which I am not, he still would not care for me. He is merely protective of me, as he would be to a little sister."

"He has no sisters," Louise informed her.

"There, you see?" Silene insisted, trying to calm herself. He was going to marry someone else. What else hadn't he told her? "He thinks of me as the sister he never had."

Louise looked her over in her religious garb. "I guess I believe ye.

But if he does care fer ye, ye would be mad to let him pass through yer fingers. He is a verra powerful man."

Silene didn't care about his power. She cared about the man he was with or without it. But she did wonder what his position here was.

"What does he do here?" she asked Louise.

"He is in charge of everythin' and everyone, jointly with the steward. As I understand it," the servant told her, "they have been friends fer a long time. The captain takes care of everythin' while the steward takes care of verra little."

"Foolish of my uncle to do such a thing," Silene muttered, and slipped her prayer beads around her neck. "He will lose the trust of his people. He will lose them to the charismatic captain."

Louise cut her glance to her and nodded. "Mayhap," she said in a low voice. "Mayhap there truly is nothin' between ye."

Silene turned to her, her patience at an end, her voice laced with ice. "Louise, let me assure you for the last time. There is nothing between me and the captain. I am to be a nun. Do you understand that if you soil my good name, you hurt the steward and make him your enemy?" She paused and let her words sink in. "You are to cease your gossip, or I will be forced to tell Lady Matilda and the captain. Do you understand?"

Louise stared at her for a moment and then bowed her head. "Aye, Sister. Fergive me."

With her head still hung, she led Silene to the supper table in the center of the great hall. It was where the steward and his family sat every night with the captain.

She sat. The captain was not there. His men sat at nearby tables, smiling at her when they caught her eye.

Silene's heart thumped hard and fast. She reached for her cup and hoped it contained something mild.

It didn't.

Her nostrils burned just smelling it.

"Sister," her uncle began as he set his attention on her. "Tell me, how is it at St. Patrice's? How is Mother Superior?"

"She is well." Silene was glad he asked for her as Mother Superior spoke of him often.

While they waited for the food to be served, they spoke of the priory and of Silene's dedication to her vows in the spring.

"Captain MacPherson is tardy," the steward said to his wife and to her. "We willna wait fer him."

Silene listened and then she prayed. Perhaps he wasn't coming. Perhaps it was better if he didn't.

But finally, he arrived.

She remembered the exact moment he entered the great hall. It was during her third bite of food. It was as if someone threw open the shutters and sunshine came bursting in. He stepped through the doorway and made his way to her table. She watched as he was stopped a dozen times by men seeking his advice, women wanting to talk, and servants wanting to serve him.

She wanted to ask him about his beautiful betrothed.

He wore a white léine beneath a short coat of embroidered black. His long, strong legs were encased in black hose and leather boots. The coat only reached his hips. His hose were not overly tight but the bulge peeking out from beneath the hem made Silene's blood sizzle.

Streaks of gold eclipsed his eyes that had already found her.

Her uncle was patient while the captain stopped at Mac's table and laughed with Padrig. Silene missed sitting with the men, laughing with them. She may have sighed. She straightened her shoulders and turned her attention to her uncle and his wife with dreadful anticipation.

Their gazes were steady on her while they waited.

Silene's belly balled into a knot. They knew! They knew she cared for him. Surely, they could see it in her eyes, her darting glances. They could likely hear her heart beating, pounding like a drum.

She took a sip from her cup. Whatever was in it was starting to taste more like wine. Rather pleasant wine. She forgot the people she was sitting with and watched the captain share a furtive glance with Alex and Margaret.

He set his gaze on her table. On her.

Was he about to smile or scowl?

"Captain," her uncle called out and startled her. "We tried to wait. Ye are tardy."

Silene looked into her bowl. She didn't dare look at him taking his seat at the steward's right, on the other side of the table.

"Aye," she heard him say. "Fergive me. Many sought to speak to me on my way to supper."

"Aye. We bore witness," the steward said dramatically. "Did we not...Sister?"

Silene's face burned. He'd been watching her watching the captain. It was as if she could not control herself. She was mortified and finished with her supper.

"Sister?" His husky voice drew her gaze to him and set her spine on fire. "Fergive me fer makin' ye wait here with this pompous fool."

He eased her with amusement, and then he smiled at John, as if it were said in fun.

"Captain," Matilda said, ignoring how he had just mocked her husband. "Is it true ye had to look after two of my little ones today?"

The captain's spoon paused at his parted lips. His gaze flicked to the children's table. "'Twas no trouble, my lady. They are well-behaved and rather fun."

"I am pleased ye think so highly of them," their mother offered. "Ye can keep them with ye since ye threw their teacher oot of Dundonald."

The captain lowered his spoon and his voice. "I dismissed their teacher because he left yer children to their own defenses today. If ye wish me to look after them, I will."

"Nonsense!" the steward slammed down his cup, drawing much

attention to himself. "The captain isna here to watch over my bairns. I willna—"

"I will do it, my lord," the captain told him. "I dinna mind. If I have things to see to that are dangerous, I will lock them in my chambers. They will be safe with me."

Silene listened, looking up at him now and then while he spoke. This is what he did. He kept others safe. Her, the children. Heaven knew how many others. She was quite sure he did all this for Daffodil and the children. This would give them time to play together.

"In the meantime, my lady," the captain said as he fixed his steady gaze on Matilda. "'Twill give ye time to find a more responsible teacher fer yer bairns."

"Aye, Captain," Matilda promised, granting him absolution for releasing the teacher. He was, after all, looking out for her children's safety.

"What happened today that ye wanted me to know?" the steward asked him and then looked at his wife.

Silene flashed Matilda a glare.

"There is nothin'," the captain assured him. He obviously didn't feel the need to explain why Silene was alone with him in front of his open door.

Across from him, Silene smiled subtly.

"Captain." Matilda kept her voice low and as dispassionate as she could. "I only bring it up because I dinna want tongues flappin' and my husband's reputation bein' soiled."

Ah, the truth. Finally. It was, of course, her husband's reputation that concerned her. Not Silene's.

"Well? What happened?" the steward demanded now.

"Nothin' happened," the captain told him, sounding irritated now. "One of the men's cats gave birth to kittens and I accepted one from him."

"Captain, a cat? Why would ye?" Matilda complained.

"I ran into Sister Silene in the hall," the captain continued as if she hadn't spoken. "I asked her to say a prayer over the small kitten. Yer wife came along and thought…well, I dinna know what she thought."

The steward looked annoyed with his wife. "Was the novice in yer chambers alone with ye at any time?"

Silene was offended that her uncle hadn't asked her the question. Did he not think he would get the truth from her?

"No, John," the captain answered. "Yer bairns were in my room feedin' the kitten."

John tossed his wife another angry scowl. "Mayhap ye should quit concernin' yerself with the captain's doin's."

Matilda wasn't finished. "Of course. Fergive me, but there is one more thing, Captain. Why would ye get a kitten when ye know 'tis what Margaret wants most?"

The captain exhaled and quirked his mouth just a little. "I think that is the verra reason I accepted it."

Her husband laughed, but not to mock her. "Ye are clever, Galeren. One way or another, ye procured the pet fer my daughter withoot even needin' my wife's permission."

The captain tried not to smile but Silene could see a hint of humor around his mouth.

"Ye are much like yer father," the steward added. "A sly fox."

Galeren laughed softly but shook his head and looked at Matilda, as if to say none of it was true. He hadn't tried to fool her. Matilda didn't seem to mind for too long and, once again, forgave him.

He didn't use his innate charm for any malevolent purpose. He had done her no great harm.

Silene was glad that she forgave him so quickly and they could finish their meal.

Matilda turned to her. "Silene, ye imp. Why did ye not tell me of this animal the captain and my children adopted?"

Silene took another sip from her cup. "I am forbidden to speak of something someone tells me in confidence."

That seemed to mollify her uncle's wife and she finally went back to eating.

Her uncle and his wife were quite different from what she expected. She hadn't expected that Matilda would be so fond of her husband's captain. She wondered what the church would think of that.

"If you will excuse me." Silene rose from her seat and swayed a little. The captain was up in a flash. She held up her hand to stop him from perhaps leaping over the table to help her. "'Tis time for my prayers and then bed." She turned slowly toward her uncle. "Thank you for supper, my lord."

She left the table without looking at the captain. She could be easily read—it seemed—around him. She hurried to her room and disappeared inside. Oh, she drank too much!

She pressed her back to the cool wood and finally let herself breathe and sway on her feet.

Were those footsteps she heard in the hall?

Someone knocked on the door. Three raps that made her want to leap from her skin.

"Go away," she spoke out on the softest sigh.

"Silene," his husky, Highland burr stirred her blood, her soul.

She closed her eyes and prayed for strength.

His voice came through the door and tore through her. "Silene, pray fer me."

CHAPTER ELEVEN

THE NEXT SENNIGHT went by in a blur of prayers and practicing going before the church council. Silene also spent time with the captain, the children, and Daffodil. She helped them smuggle the kitten into Lizzie's room so the two could meet.

One more little soldier in the captain's army.

Silene's duty was to distract Matilda and get her out of the chambers.

She almost failed when Matilda refused to leave her daughter alone.

"But she is so much better. And I will remain with her," Silene offered. "Or do not go at all. 'Tis up to you. I will just go tell Captain MacPherson that you are unable to go to him."

"Is he hurt?" Matilda asked, concerned.

Silene felt terrible for deceiving her, but the captain promised to go find her and speak to her about last night at the table. So, she was not really lying.

"Nay. He is not hurt.

"Fine then. I will go. Where is he?"

"In the great hall."

"If my husband looks fer me, tell him where I am."

Surprised, Silene nodded and felt worse. Matilda wasn't overly fond of the captain. Perhaps she was concerned for him—as any friend would be.

She watched Matilda leave and closed her eyes to pray while she waited for the captain and the children.

"Where is Mummy?" came a small, quavering voice.

Silene spun around and smiled at Lizzie, swallowed up in the large bed.

"Greetings, Lizzie. I am Silene." She sat in the chair beside the bed. "Your mummy will return in a few moments. How do you feel?"

The three-year-old girl nodded, which Silene concluded, meant that she felt well.

The door opened and Margaret came skipping in with Daffodil in her arms. Her brother walked in with a bit more dignity. Silene smiled at the captain when he strode inside last.

"Lizzie, look! A kitten!" Margaret held up Daffodil for inspection. It meowed and Lizzie smiled and held out her arms. She laughed when Margaret set the kitten down on the bed and it hopped up to Lizzie's face and meowed again.

"Where is Matilda?" the captain asked her.

When Silene guiltily told him, he offered to leave and go find her.

"Not yet. Let Lizzie play with the kitten a little while longer. But you should not keep taking the kitten to Lizzie in secret. A babe's laughter is a soothing sound for a mother."

"Aye. Ye are correct," he admitted. "Where are ye goin?" he asked when she smiled at Lizzie and turned for the door.

"I have confession with Father Nathaniel today. I believe I will be with him a little longer now."

The captain's smile was like the dawn after a long, harrowing night. It was also contagious—more so than Lizzie's fever.

She hadn't asked him about his betrothed and he hadn't offered to tell her. She wondered when he would.

"This is the first time I have seen ye in two days. I'm thankful that ye havena sent me away."

She wanted to agree but frowned. "I cannot stay."

He nodded and drew in a deep breath. "Will ye tell Father Nate aboot me?"

Should she tell him? "I have not yet decided what to tell him. I fear things will get back to someone in the church and damage John's dream."

His gaze roved over her face, the only part of her showing in her full habit. He took her in like a lost man in a desert finding an oasis.

He said nothing. His eyes spoke for him. He wanted to kiss her, not just her lips, but her chin, her neck…lower. He wanted to ravish her.

"Captain, I—" She wanted to ask about Cecilia Birchet. But she didn't.

She was too afraid she felt the same way about him and turned away.

"I must go." She hurried out of the room—keeping Lizzie's laughter in her thoughts instead of the heat of the captain's gaze.

She found Matilda returning to the castle. When Silene told her the captain had gone to her chambers with the kitten and he waited for her there, she muttered an oath, but Silene knew she wouldn't remain angry for long.

When she thought about it, she realized the captain didn't need her help with Matilda. He had but to smile at her and she would give in. Silene wondered if she was so easily moldable in his hands.

She left the castle and made her way to the chapel. She slipped inside and looked for the priest. He'd come to her the day after she arrived but Father Alphonsus had been with him, so she didn't get to say much.

She had much to confess. She asked him if it was a sin to change her mind about saying her vows. It didn't go well. First, he warned her of her uncle's ire, and then he warned her of God's.

After her prayers and penance, Silene left the church. She wished she could talk to Agnes or Marjorie Anne. The sisters would never betray her. Would Father Nathaniel? Oh, why had she told him anything? He said God would be angry with her. She wrung her hands together and prayed as she hurried over the drawbridge and stepped through the inner gate. She didn't want to go back to the castle yet.

She spread her gaze over the sunlit yard. The villagers were out and about. Perhaps someone needed some kind of help.

She started forward and spotted the captain descending the stairs behind Alex and Margaret. She hid behind the western wall and watched him step onto the grass. Daffodil was curled up in a tiny bundle at his neck. They walked away from the crowd and went behind the bakehouse and into the gardens of Dundonald. The children ran ahead and squealed with delight when the captain set the sleepy kitten in the grass. He called something out to the children.

Silene wanted to get closer. She couldn't see the kitten from where she was but from the children's laughter and the captain's beaming smile, the little feline must have been doing something to please them.

She stepped out from her hiding place. He saw her immediately though he made no move to go to her. She could feel his eyes on her, facets of emerald, hooded, curious eyes. Her cheeks burned when he smiled and then turned to look over his shoulder to make certain they were alone.

"Did you speak to Lady Matilda?"

"Aye. She agreed that Daffodil was a bonny cat. But she still refuses to let the children keep her."

Silene frowned but, as she suspected, Matilda wasn't angry with him. He hadn't needed Silene today. He wanted her there. He liked her being here now. He hadn't stopped smiling.

"Did ye speak with Father Nate?"

"Aye."

"Good. D'ye feel better then?"

"Nay," she shook her head. "I feel worse. He told me God will be very angry with me if I changed my mind about my vows. That is not what I wish."

He swallowed hearing how she thought about not saying her vows. Then he nodded—and then shook his head. "Why would He not tell ye what to do? If ye are aboot to do somethin' so terrible as to fall in love with me and anger Him…why would He need a priest to tell ye not to do it?"

He said she was falling in love with him. Was she? "Because I can pretend that I do not hear."

He was quiet, searching her gaze. "I dinna believe it, Silene."

"You are temptation of every kind, Captain."

He scowled. "I dinna want to be a temptation fer ye."

She smiled, loving his guileless nature. "You must realize that you are difficult to resist."

"Then dinna resist. Let us go before Father Nate together—"

"And your betrothed? What of her?"

He barely missed a breath. "What aboot her? I never loved her. I dinna wish to marry her. I was doin' John a favor and plan on breakin' it off."

"Oh," she said, a bit taken aback by his response. Louise said he didn't love the woman. "I see." She felt better but… "Why did you not tell me?"

"I meant no—" he began but then stopped and began again. "I was afraid of speakin' to ye aboot one more obstacle."

"Aye," she understood. "I do not know what the Lord wants from me anymore." She wiped a tear from her eyes and smiled down at the kitten running through…daffodils. That was why they gave her the name.

"You truly do not mind having them with you?" she asked him.

He set his gaze on the children and shook his head. "No. They are no trouble."

Oh, it was easy to like him.

"Captain?"

"Please, call me Galeren. Everyone calls me captain."

She smiled. "Galeren. That is an interesting name."

He took a moment to exhale. "My father does his best to live like the legendary knights of Arthur Pendragon. He named me after Sir Galahad—a knight perfect in courage, gentleness, courtesy and chivalry."

Her smile widened. "I like those traits, my lord. They are good values."

He nodded. "And even more valuable is the one who recognizes them."

He was easy to like. Aye, to love. Did she love him? How would she know? She'd never been in love before.

"I have never heard of yer name before," he told her.

"'Tis the name of a flower." She smiled when his gaze went warm on her.

"You have a rare heart, Cap—Galeren," she corrected and blushed a streak of crimson against walls of pure white. "You possess every trait I value."

He moved closer, more aware of her then anything else.

"I want to close my eyes and listen to you speak," she told him, and he smiled.

"I want to smell ye on my clothes."

No. They had to stop. She marveled at how easy it was to slip right back into him and forget everything else.

"People cannot know that the man they follow fought against God for me or that I stole you from your betrothed. They will leave your side."

He shook his head but didn't look at her again. "I dinna care aboot their accolades. I am compelled to go home to Invergarry and leave everythin' behind."

She stiffened her spine. What should she say? "You should leave tonight then."

He nodded and she was tempted to clutch his arm. She didn't want him to go. He had to. One of them had to.

"I must go, Captain. I will see you again when I return home, I hope."

He didn't move.

She wished he would say something.

"My dear Captain, what is this?" A high-pitched female voice sounded close by. "You are the watcher of bratlings then?"

The woman was behind Silene and when she made herself known, the captain and the children balked.

"Is this why you did not have time for me? I was gone. Did you even notice, Captain?"

Silene turned to find a most beautiful young lady sauntering toward them. She had lovely golden hair and hazel eyes that changed beneath the sun from gold to green.

"Cecilia," the captain drawled, clearly not happy to see her. "Is yer father here? We need to speak."

Cecilia, his betrothed. Silene's belly sank. Why should it? She was also betrothed. Had she forgotten so quickly…again?

"Sister Silene, may I introduce Miss Cecilia Birchet of Prestwick."

"His betrothed," Miss Birchet supplied quickly. She eyed Silene's gray habit and veil suspiciously. "Well, are you a nun or are you not?"

"I am not," Silene told her. "But," she added when Cecilia Birchet looked about to tear out her own hair, "I will speak my vows in the spring."

She'd meant to soothe Miss Birchet's nerves. Silene was sorry for her. She imagined what it must be like to love him and not have his love in return.

But she didn't think her promise would cause the captain to scowl so fiercely.

"Go away, Miss Birchet." Margaret ran up to the captain and leaned into his leg. "Dinna touch Daffodil."

"Margaret, ye are bein' rude. What have we talked aboot?"

"But Captain—"

"Ask Miss Birchet's pardon," he demanded. "Now."

"I ask fer yer pardon, Miss Birchet," the little girl obeyed through clenched teeth.

Silene wouldn't smile at her. Not now. She would not undermine what the captain said. Not when he was correct. He was teaching the possible king's children humility.

"Granted," Cecilia allowed then shooed her away. "Now, why do you not take your brother and your cat and go play?"

Margaret's eyes filled with tears. She took Daffodil from her brother's arms and ran off.

"I will see to her," Silene offered and hurried off with Alex.

She heard the captain's hard voice as he warned Miss Birchet never to speak to the children like that again.

She didn't wait to hear anything more but rushed to Margaret. She found her sitting on a bench in her mother's orchard. She clutched Daffodil and wept into the kitten's fur.

Silene reached her but said nothing right away. Instead, she sat next to her and petted Daffodil. Finally, she spoke softly. "It takes great strength to apologize."

"I dinna care aboot strength," the little girl cried. "I just want her to leave Captain MacPherson alone!"

Silene remembered the captain mentioning the child's jealousy. But Margaret wasn't jealous of Silene at all. She wasn't jealous of Cecilia either. Margaret didn't like the captain's betrothed. It wasn't difficult to see why. Cecilia treated the children like pests, only giving them her attention if she had to. Who would want their friend to wed someone like that?

But it wasn't about Miss Birchet. This difficult lesson was for Margaret.

"I agree with you," she whispered to the girl. "I do not want him to marry her either." She drew her finger to her lips and smiled.

Margaret smiled back. Soon though, it faded, and she tilted her lips to Silene's ear. "I saw her kissin' someone else."

Silene closed her eyes and commanded herself to breathe. "Are you certain it was not the captain?"

"He was on his way to get ye," Alex told her.

They loved him. If Cecilia was betraying him, it was perfectly understandable that they didn't like her.

"Did you tell him? Or anyone?"

Margaret and her brother shook their heads. "He willna care," Alex lamented. "He is only marryin' her because my father wants him to. I have heard his conversations with my father."

"May I come near?"

They all turned to see the captain paused a few feet away. They nodded and he took a step forward. How much had he heard?

"I have decided not to wed Miss Birchet despite what yer father wants. But I will be the one to tell him, aye?"

They grinned and nodded.

He went to Margaret next. There being no room on the bench, he knelt before her. "I'm verra proud of ye, lass."

She looked at him over Daffodil's head. "I'm verra angry with ye."

"I know," he said softly, as serious and somber as she. "But I would have ye fit fer a noble court, my lady."

Margaret smiled and handed him the meowing kitten eager to get to him.

"Captain," Alex drew his attention. "We have something to tell ye."

Silene rose from where she sat and refused the captain's offer to stay. She didn't know how he felt about his betrothed. The news was private, so she left them alone.

Imagine, she thought while walking to the castle, being betrothed to Galeren MacPherson and kissing someone else! She wondered who it was. Her uncle? No. The children would have recognized their own father.

She heard her name being called and turned to see Margaret and Alex laughing and calling while they raced to reach her.

"I win!" Alex shouted.

"Sister, why did ye leave?" Margaret asked her.

She wasn't sure she—she heard his heavier footsteps approaching. She smiled seeing tiny Daffodil sitting on his shoulder and playing with the hair at his neck.

"They would run all day if they could," the captain laughed, not out of breath at all.

"They never tire," she agreed.

"Where are ye off to?" he asked.

"Prayers."

"Oh." He looked around and smiled at the children. "I was thinkin', we are goin' explorin' tomorrow and we would all enjoy it if ye would accompany us."

"What about—?" There were so many things to consider.

"We have agreed not to think aboot anyone else fer the day," the captain told her.

She smiled. She wasn't sure she could do it, but she would try.

Chapter Twelve

Galeren watched Silene chasing the children while Daffodil leaped through the grass like a ball of orange fur trying to keep up.

He smiled when she caught Margaret up in her arms and tagged a laughing Alex.

He wanted to join them when they collapsed onto the grass in a tangle of arms and legs.

Laughter filled the small, sunlit clearing and Galeren's ears. It seeped into his heart and made him long for things he'd never wanted before. A loving wife…bairns.

They had met before breaking their fast. Galeren was early, as were the children. They hadn't waited long for Silene. She was just as eager to start the day as they were.

She intelligently wore her hose and tabard instead of her novice's robes. She did wear her wimple and veil though. Galeren wished any of it helped keep his mind on what she was going to be.

They started off with Margaret riding with Silene and Alex riding with Galeren, who also carried Daffodil in a small pouch at his side.

Their first stop had been the Firth of Clyde, where they explored caves hidden along the coast. They waited a bit while Silene prayed, and then they ate their first meal together.

He'd taken them along the coast to a long stretch of rocks and reeds and vendors set up with their banners snapping in the wind.

Soon, the vendors would be gone from here, not to return until next spring…when she was—no. He promised the children…himself, not to think on the future today. They rode to a small forest close to the castle, to a sunlit glade and ate their midday meal.

With a light step, he moved quickly now, scooping up Daffodil as he went. When he reached them, he knelt in the grass with them and laughed. They played a game where he was a mouse, hoping not to become a rat. They searched out edible berries and ate them while the sun warmed their chilly bones. Daffodil finally collapsed in the grass, asleep. The children were next with Margaret sleeping on Galeren's lap under a nearby tree.

"This is not the first time you have kept the children with you," Silene said softly, sitting next to him. "All of the steward's children."

Galeren shook his head. "I help Alex learn defense and good character."

His hand lifted to the streak of scarlet burning from one of her cheeks to the other. "Ye blush." He smiled. "Why?"

"'Tis nice to see a man of good character. He is pleasing to the eye."

He raised a curious brow at her. "Is he?"

She nodded, appearing mesmerized by his full attention.

If she were someone else, he would have leaned in and kissed her. He'd stopped seeing her veil and wimple. He saw only her face. The face he was falling in love with. He couldn't fight it. He knew it was wrong. He wished she didn't wear it, but she did, and he still wanted to kiss her.

He felt the kitten's sharp little claws in him and looked at his ankle. He smiled watching sleepy Daffodil climb up his thigh, his hip and then crumple up in his léine next to Margaret's head and purr.

He should feel disgusted with himself for being so lost to a kitten and a soon-to-be nun.

But he didn't.

He returned his attention to Silene, ready to apologize for being distracted. She was wearing a dreamy smile.

For a moment, he forgot to breathe. When he remembered, he wasn't sure he wanted to.

"The hour of my prayer approaches."

He nodded. What was happening to him? He had never felt this way about a woman. Why did it have to be her who stirred his heart and compelled him to change his path and lead him on one that would likely get him thrown out of John's court and excommunicated? Not to mention what God would do to him.

He watched her rise up and brush grass from her hose. She made her way to a large tree and went to her knees.

There were women everywhere. Why was he allowing this one to claim what he'd given to none before her?

He wanted to tell her, to hold her.

Instead, he sat, watching her, praying with her that they be blessed in a union and not punished for this. Father Timothy would remind him that God was good.

He wanted to take Silene home to meet the old priest. He tried to stop himself from seeing her comfortable as his wife in Invergarry. But his mind wandered in the quiet of the forest where they played and slept the afternoon away.

When she was finished, they woke the children.

"They love you," she noted with a tender smile when they clung to him and wiped their sleepy eyes.

"And I them," he replied, rising up with two children and a kitten hanging off him.

What did she think about never having children? He wouldn't ask.

But there was something he would ask her. "Why are ye goin' to say yer vows when ye are still so young? Yer prioress was married to a baron before he died and she gave her life to God, was she not?"

She didn't answer right away and then waited while he set everyone and everything down.

When the children were out of earshot, she cleared her throat. "I have never met a man…like you before." She looked down at the grass and lowered her voice when his smile deepened on her. "I never thought I would…*want* to meet a man like you."

"And now that ye have?" he pressed gently.

She looked at him. "I…I do not know."

He didn't want to push her too much, or at all. He was falling in love with her. If she wasn't falling for him naturally, he would leave her alone.

But the way she looked at him. It was the same way he was sure he looked at her. With delight and desire, respect and passion.

"Captain, we found a spider!" Alex called out from the huddle he was in with his sister.

The arachnid must have jumped in Alex's direction because he yelped and leaped away. Margaret stood in her spot laughing at him.

"I think they had fun today," Galeren told Silene while he laughed with them.

"'Tis important to you. Why?"

He thought about it for a moment. He knew things about the King of the Scots, just thirty-three years old and a prisoner of England. Things King David had told him during their friendship. He was married, though in name only, at the age of four. He never played. He wasn't allowed any friends. He grew into a somber man, awkward around others and probably perfectly happy alone.

He saw the same thing happening to John's bairns. Friendships were important, but safety more so. Because of that, they were alone most of the time.

"They are children. They need to play."

She nodded. But he saw the shadows cross over her eyes.

"Did ye not play as a child?" he asked her, drawing a little closer.

She shook her head. "I was the oldest. My mother was often ill, so I did much of the work. And then I was sent to St. Patrice's."

Galeren wanted nothing more in his life in that moment than to teach her how to play. "Ye are verra bonny, Silene."

She had the most peculiar reaction. It was different from any he'd ever seen when he told a lass she was bonny. She covered her mouth and gave him a little laugh. He looked at her curled lips when she dropped her hand away from her face. He thought about taking her face in his hands and touching her beauty as if to convince himself she was real. Kissing her…

"Silene," he whispered, then glanced at the children. They were busy tying leaves together and putting them around the horses' necks. There would be trouble if one of them saw him and the novice kissing and told.

"Galeren," she said on a siren's breath. He forgot everything else and became captive to her alone.

She seemed to have trembled in her skin. He ached to hold her. He moved closer, dipping his head, tasting her sweet breath.

"You have me going in circles and I do not want it to stop." She rested her palms on his chest, leaned up on the tips of her toes, and pressed her lips to his stubbled cheek.

When she withdrew, he took hold of her wrist and pulled her back to him with the graceful ease of a dancer pulling his partner back into his arms. He pressed his lush, sensuous lips to her mouth and covered her, engulfed her in strength and tenderness. She felt right in his arms, as if she belonged there. Could they stay like this forever, locked in each other's arms, their mouths sealed in passion's kiss?

No. If the children saw they would have to live with a secret.

He withdrew. His legs felt unsteady. His head felt as if he'd just finished his fifth ale.

He groaned her name.

Her face grew red. Her eyes widened with…what was it? Horror? No!

"Forgive me!" she cried and turned and ran to her horse.

He opened his mouth to stop her, but the children were still playing and weaving leaves. They hadn't seen their kiss. He almost breathed with relief. He didn't want to draw their attention by calling out—demanding that she return to him. Aye, he would demand it, and she would surely ignore it. He would do anything to keep her near, but the things he wanted could be dangerous to her—possibly cost her her life.

The steward had his own army. Would he send them after Galeren and Silene if they left? Galeren couldn't fight them all and he didn't want to. Most of them were his friends.

He clenched his jaw to keep quiet as she mounted her horse.

"Come children. 'Tis time to go," he called out.

He thought he might seek out Father Nate to confess but God knew he wasn't sorry he'd kissed her.

He lowered his gaze and felt the weight of what he'd done. What he wanted to do again.

"Does somethin' trouble ye, Captain?" Alex asked, coming near him. He should have known Alex would notice something.

"I'm just sorry to see the day end," Galeren told him as Silene gained her saddle.

"We must remember it," she said as he lifted Margaret to her. "Keep it locked away in a box of treasured memories."

"I would have more of them," he disagreed, shaking his head and staring up into her eyes. "Not just a memory of one."

She said nothing but rode away with Margaret.

"Ye like her," Alex said when he, along with Daffodil, rode out of the glade.

"Aye," Galeren admitted what was obvious instead of lying and losing the boy's trust. "Dinna ye?"

"Aye. She is fun," the lad said, turning his smile on Galeren.

"Oh?" The captain arched his brow and quirked his mouth. "Am I not fun?"

Alex squealed with laughter when Galeren lifted him out of the saddle and held him suspended over the ground.

Part of Galeren never wanted to leave Dundonald and John's service. The steward would most likely be king. Mayhap Alex would take the throne or John's brother, Robert.

None of the children's teachers could teach them the things Galeren could.

If Scotland had a king who considered the good of the people and who could fight if he had to and respect the Highland way of life—well then, Galeren's kin would do well.

Aye, soon, he would be going home to Invergarry, but not too soon.

Morgann met up with him and Silene on their way back with the children.

"Captain, the steward dispatched me to find ye."

"Did he say what 'tis aboot?" Galeren asked him.

Morgann shook his head. "But he was with Lord Birchet when he sent me."

Galeren grew angry. He was also worried. This had to do with Cecilia. His belly tied into a knot. He glanced at Silene and said nothing the rest of the way.

When they reached the castle, he asked Morgann to escort Silene and the children back to Lady Matilda.

Silene said nothing and followed Morgann.

What had Cecilia told her father? Good! He was glad her father was here. Now, he could tell them his decision. He would not marry Cecilia.

He climbed the stairs to the solar where Louise told him to find the steward. He would deny anything concerning Silene.

He knocked. The steward called from the other side to enter. He did so and saw Lord Birchet and Father Alphonsus. The three men sat in high backed, upholstered chairs, two of six created for the steward's pleasure.

"Ah, Captain, have a drink and take a seat." John offered him a warm smile.

Galeren forsook the drink and pulled another chair opposite theirs. There, he waited for them to begin.

"Captain," the steward said, "I think 'tis time fer ye to wed Miss Birchet. Do ye not agree?"

"No, my lord, I dinna agree." He breathed while the men around him gasped and glared at him.

"Then what my daughter says is true," Lord Birchet's dark eyes narrowed on him.

Galeren drew his brows together. "What did she tell ye?"

"Captain MacPherson," Birchet began. "What were you doing with the nun, alone with the steward's children?"

"Sister Silene happened upon us." He hated having to explain, and even more that his old friend, John Stewart, was a part of it.

Lord Birchet opened his mouth but Galeren continued silencing him. "Yer daughter isna someone I would choose as my wife."

"Miss Birchet is renowned for her beauty," John said as if Galeren didn't know.

"Beauty fades," he replied. "And then what is one left with? A monster."

John's stare went dark. "We agreed on this, Captain. Why are ye changin' yer mind now? Tell me if it has to do with—"

"Ye know I dinna love Miss Birchet, my lord. We have had this conversation a hundred times."

"Why do you not love her?" her father joined in angrily. "Is there someone else preventing it?"

"No, my lord." Galeren told him, angry for the insinuation. They suspected something. They had no proof. All Cecilia saw was him and Silene laughing.

"I canna love a woman whose interest in herself alone comes before all else."

"Captain MacPherson," her father gaped. "You dare insult my daughter?"

Galeren regarded him soberly. "Aye, I dare. Yer daughter is spoiled, ruined fer many men. Me bein' one of them."

"What aboot my niece?" the steward asked him. "Is she ruined as well?"

What was this betrayal? Galeren stared at him. Was John willing to disregard their nine-year friendship, the years Galeren had given in Scotland's service?

"What aboot her?" Galeren asked. "She is to be married to God, and even if she werena, she doesna suit me," he thought it best to say at present. "I will say this fer the last time, my lord. The novice was under my care. We became friends. We will always be friends. But to imagine what is inside yer heads would surely insult her betrothed—and me."

Galeren paused for a moment. "Further, the steward will attest that I have taken a vow of chastity fer six years and have kept it. That is why he sent me to retrieve his niece. He knew she would be safe with me. And she was. Now, put an end to yer suspicions aboot her."

The three men balked at him then looked away. "Nevertheless," Father Alphonsus said, breaking the silence. "You will wed Cecilia Birchet."

"Why does this concern ye, Priest?" He didn't care about the answer. He wasn't marrying Cecilia. "Why is it so important to ye all that I wed her?"

"I will be king one day," John said. "Lord Birchet will have an important place at court. He is a longtime friend."

Not good enough. Galeren shook his head.

"Captain, ye will obey me," John's familiar voice raked unfamiliar words across his ear. "Ye are loyal to me and no one else. The day that ye are no longer loyal to me is the day I throw ye oot of Dundonald."

If this was how it was to be, so be it. Galeren's dark glare made the other two men back away.

"I have served ye loyally fer many years, John. Would ye dishonor me?"

"Aye. I would."

Galeren's blood boiled. "Verra well, I will leave today."

"I told you, John," Father Alphonsus said. "'Tis because of your niece."

Galeren stopped on his way out. "Father, why would ye spread an untruth that could harm her?"

"Captain," the steward said. "If ye leave, I will assume 'tis because of Sister Silene. I will keep her here fer questionin' and if I discover there is somethin' deeper than friendship between ye, Father Alphonsus will see to her punishment."

Galeren's murderous gaze flicked to the priest. So, John would have Father Alphonsus punish her. He wanted to laugh at the priest. Galeren wouldn't let anyone hurt her.

"John," he said, using the steward's familiar name and slipping his gaze to him. "If ye wanted me to stay so badly, ye just had to ask."

"Ye do what ye want," the steward pointed out. "After all these years I know what moves ye. Ye try to be what ye think would make yer father happy."

Galeren shrugged his shoulder, letting the words fall away. "If I share the values of my father, that is a good thing."

He turned to Lord Birchet. "D'ye truly not care if I will make yer daughter unhappy?"

"Some marriages are unhappy ones, Captain," her father advised.

"Cecilia can seek happiness outside of your marriage."

Aye, Galeren thought. She was already on the prowl, kissing men while he was away.

He couldn't do it. John would not have his own niece harmed.

"I canna do it, John. Farewell."

"Bring Sister Silene to me," the steward said to someone in the shadows.

Galeren remembered his grandsire's warning again and stopped. "All right," he ground out. "I will do as ye say. But not fer another month. That is when my vow is over." It wasn't the truth, but the church would never force him into marriage while he was taking a vow of chastity.

The steward threw up his hands. The priest glared at him, as did Lord Birchet.

Galeren walked away and left the solar. Let them think what they wanted. He wasn't marrying Cecilia and Silene wasn't going to be harmed by anyone.

He would make certain of it.

Even if it cost him everything.

Chapter Thirteen

Silene knew she was being punished. Why else would God be keeping the captain from her? No. She asked for this, didn't she? She prayed not to see him, not to be tempted by him. Wasn't God just answering her prayers? Three days! Three days and she had not seen him. What happened at that meeting with her uncle and Lord Birchet? Did he leave Dundonald so he would not have to wed Cecilia?

Was it for the best if he had?

She saw Father Nate on her way to the church and smiled that he was going the other way, glad that he wouldn't be at the church with her. She wanted to be alone.

"Good morn, Sister," he said, looking her over.

She bid him good day and continued on her way.

"Have you been studying the rules upon meeting the men of the church?"

"Aye. I practice every day, Father."

He smiled. "Do not falter before them."

What did he mean? Why did it make her belly tighten? Why was he helping her?

"I will try not to. Thank you, Father."

She turned to go once again. This time, his fingers closed around her wrist, stopping her.

"I have been praying for guidance about what we spoke about in confession," he whispered. "I think the Lord has led me to a different conclusion."

Silene's eyes opened wide and grew bluer. Of course, he was going to continue to chastise her. "Father—"

"Silene, you are not yet a nun. You are allowed two years to decide because people change their minds. 'Tis all right to change your mind. If the Lord sent the captain—"

Her heart accelerated. "Why do you mention him? I never said—"

"'Tis obvious if one just looks. He corrected one of his men who called you a nun as if he never wanted to hear those three letters together again."

Silene recalled him doing the same with the men when they traveled here. "That means nothing." He said their feelings were obvious to anyone who looked. What if someone from the church found out? But one of them already knew. Father Nathanial was part of the church. Was it obvious to Father Alphonsus, too? What would she say before them if they asked?

"You mistake friendly fondness for something it is not. The captain and I are friends. Good friends. Like he and Lady Matilda are. Do you understand now?" she asked softly with a gentle smile.

He nodded and backed away. "Fergive me." He buried his hands in the folds of his sleeves and left her alone. The instant he turned to go, her smile vanished, and tears burned her eyes. She hurried through the inner gate and reached the church. She opened the heavy, creaking door and looked over her shoulder to make certain no one was behind her. Her veil nearly came free and flew away when a mighty wind blew in from the north.

The north—where the captain's kin lived.

She stepped inside and looked toward the altar. Father Alphonsus wasn't there. She was happy to find the church empty.

She slipped into one of the benches and closed her eyes to speak to the Lord.

What should I do? Is what Father Nathanial says true? Would You forgive me for not going through with my vows?

She heard the church door opening and letting the wind inside. She turned to see Galeren stepping through the outer hall. Their eyes met in the light of dozens of candles. His golden hair fell around his face, his shoulders. She smiled and his expressive eyes glistened like emeralds in a summer pond.

She watched him as long as she could until he sat behind her and to the left. Where had he been these last three days? Had he been alone? Was he here to pray?

Now that he *was* here, she couldn't concentrate. She opened her eyes and stood up. Why could they not sit together? What rules were they breaking?

With that question burning in her head, she slipped in beside him on the bench. His masculine scent of woodsmoke and pine wafted through her, over her, engulfing her.

"Am I interrupting?" she asked him in a hushed voice.

He flashed his dimple and shook his head. "I wanted to speak to Father Nate but speakin' with ye is better."

She felt her face go flush. "I just saw the father. He was heading for the castle. He stopped me, wanting to speak. At first, I was not interested, but then things changed."

"What d'ye mean, lass?"

She told him what the priest had said. He appeared to be having the same reaction she'd had.

"What d'ye feel aboot it?" he whispered. His deep, honey voice covered her.

"I…I prayed for guidance."

She could feel the need in him. The need to come closer, cover her, kiss her until…

"You never told me how your meeting went with my uncle and Lord Birchet…and where have you been?"

"Just tryin' to stay away. They want me to marry Cecilia. If I dinna do it, John has threatened to punish ye."

Her face drained of blood. She felt lightheaded. She prayed to not to pass out. "You have to marry Cecilia?" She didn't want to ask, to hear him confirm it. But she had to. When he nodded, she shook her head. "Do not do it, Captain. Do not worry about me. Let him do his best. I will survive him. But do not marry that woman and be unhappy always."

"No! I willna have ye suffer." His whisper rose and echoed in the empty sanctuary. His gaze darted around, and he lowered his voice. "That is why we must leave. I already sent a missive to my home in Invergarry tellin' my kin to expect me. I want ye to come as well."

Silene opened her mouth to speak. What should she say?

"Silene, come home with me to Invergarry."

She swallowed and it felt as if her heart were going back down—or trying to. Invergarry. In the Highlands.

She had to go else they would harm her to get to him. It meant they knew he cared for her! He cared for her. She wanted to rejoice but she couldn't.

God couldn't want this since there was danger involved.

"Why do they want you to marry her so desperately?"

"They both believe John will be king. Birchet wants a connection now. But now I believe 'tis just to keep me from ye. I agreed to wed her months ago, but John knew I didna want to take her fer my wife."

"Is there any part of you that loves her?"

He shook his head. "No. There is no part."

No. He couldn't marry Cecilia. Who should he marry then?

Perhaps this was…what God wanted. Perhaps now that the captain was free, he would ask her… would she?

She closed her eyes and prayed some more. After a few moments, she opened her eyes again. "When would we leave?"

"I have a month before I am expected to wed Cecilia, but..." he paused and clenched his jaw, making the muscles dance. "Ye spoke true that this is all aboot ye goin' before the church and securin' John's place on the council. That is all he wants. But unless God takes me from this earth—"

She covered his mouth with her hand. "Nay! Do not say such a thing!"

He removed her hand from his mouth and kissed her palm. "Nothin' will keep me from ye."

Help! What should I do?

"Go before the church, Silene. 'Tis what yer uncle wants. Tell them what they wish to hear aboot yer uncle. Ye and I will leave quietly after that. I will tell them I am returnin' ye to the priory. Ye and I can—"

"Galeren," she said, stopping him. "I feel as if I am in some kind of trance. I do not know if I can trust my thoughts, for they are always about you. I need time to think clearly—to pray without you being there, as well."

He let go of her hand. His absence was painful, agonizing when he nodded and rose from the bench, and left the sanctuary.

He was giving her what she wanted. Time. Why did it feel so terrible?

Was her oldest prayer being answered? A prayer for a kind, handsome husband, to be in love and to be the mother of his children. Warmth filled her as she remembered.

She wasn't giving up God by letting Galeren MacPherson into her heart. There was room enough for them both. But could she stand before the church leaders and pretend she wasn't thinking about stepping away from her vows?

She left the church and looked around. She didn't see the captain or any sign of the children as she headed back.

On her way, a woman with a long, yellow braid hanging over her shoulder came out of surrounding trees. She wore a drab kirtle of tattered tan and brown skirts. Her cloak was moth eaten and tattered.

"Are ye the novice?" the woman asked.

"Aye."

The woman's deep blue, fathomless eyes moved over her. "Be attentive, gel. Everyone is not who they claim to be. He deceives. He deceives and the captain does not know."

"What?" Silene blinked. "Who are you? Who deceives?"

But the woman hurried away into the woods.

Silene stood in her spot long enough to draw attention. What did she mean? Who wasn't who he claimed? Why was someone hiding his true purpose?

"Sister?"

She looked up at Mac and smiled.

"What are ye doin' here? I saw ye just standin' here lookin' like ye were lost. Are ye all right?"

"Aye," she told him. "There was a woman here with me. She just ran off."

"What did she want with ye?"

Silene sealed her lips. Mac could be up to something. No. Not Mac.

"She wanted prayer," she told him just the same.

He nodded and walked her back to the castle. They spoke about Daffodil the kitten and a lass of the same name who Mac thought was pleasing to the eye. Silene missed Mac. She missed the four of them bantering all day. She loved that one or two of them even started praying with her before they came to Dundonald. Mac was one of them. Morgann was the other.

When they reached the doors, Mac bid her a good day. "Twas good seein' ye again, Sister."

Mac would never betray Galeren. He was Galeren's best friend, and a good one to her, as well. She hoped he was genuine. How would she know? What did she know of men? Friends?

She headed for her chambers but stopped when she heard her name. She turned in the hall to see her uncle, the steward.

He hurried toward her. "I was lookin' for ye."

"You found me," she said with a smile, despite his stoic expression.

"The leaders of the church are here. Over a dozen bishops and priests are here to meet ye."

What? Today! No! "Uncle, I—"

For a moment, his gaze softened on her. "I know. I wasna expectin' them either." He clenched his jaw and straightened his shoulders. "I hope ye are ready fer them. If ye are not, then go practice. They expect certain rituals to be performed. Ye are to know what they are. Vanquish *all* distractions. There will be an informal gatherin' in the town hall at dusk. Dinna fail me, Niece."

"How could I fail you?" she asked with a quirk of her brow.

"Ye will remember what ye are and forsake all others. I dinna care what ye feel. Ye will put it all aside and fulfill the purpose fer which ye were born."

"I need more time, Uncle."

His eyes opened wider then darkened on her. "More time fer what?" He didn't let her answer. "To decide if the priory is right fer ye? Let me help ye, Sister. If ye say or do anythin' other than speak yer vow next spring, I will make yer life and the life of whoever is with ye a livin' nightmare. I will destroy what ye desire."

"You threaten me?" she asked, trying not to sound as incredulous as she felt.

"I see it more like a promise." His grin looked almost misshapen with satisfaction. "Remember. Dusk."

He left, disappearing down the hall. She needed to go to confession about how she felt about her uncle. He sought prestige and little else. He didn't care about her, so there was nothing else to say.

When she turned down the corridor, she saw Will huddled in a shadowed corner laughing with a woman.

Silene smiled and ducked into her chambers before they saw her. She shut the door and locked it. She leaned against the other side for a moment and then went to her bed. What was she to do? The captain wanted her to leave Dundonald with him—perhaps leave St. Patrice's.

She wasn't returning to the priory. She'd known it before she left. Was she going to Invergarry instead? Or would her uncle make good on his threat?

Where was the captain? She wanted to go find him. She wanted to tell him that her uncle had threatened her. No. He didn't need to know. Not yet. Why rile him up and draw more attention to them? She had to go before the church whether she went with Galeren or not. She had to ease her uncle's suspicions and prove that he was favorably tied to the church—after he'd just threatened her. She couldn't do it.

Closing her eyes, she breathed and tried to remain calm. They were going to ask her about God. *That* she could do.

Would the captain be there? John had said it was informal. Did she want the captain there? Would she draw strength from him or let him sap her of it?

She made the sign of the cross and removed her veil and wimple. She felt hot. It was hard to breathe.

What was she going to do about the captain? Did going with him mean giving up her vows? Not unless she went to his bed as his wife. If she chose him over her vows was it forgivable? Father Nate confused her. She had the comforting feeling that it was.

She breathed out a little laugh. Who knew if Captain Galeren even wanted a wife? Oh, the questions were making her feel mad.

She looked around the room to the folded gown smuggled into her bag by little Adam's mother in Hamsertown. She went to it. She hadn't unfolded it and she'd barely touched it. The captain had advised her to keep it. She ran her hands over the soft purple silk. She couldn't imagine how much fabric like it cost.

She had to have gone mad, indeed, because she peeled away her habit and picked up the silken bundle. She smiled as all logic left her and she imagined herself showing up in it tonight at the town hall.

She let the folds spill from her hand and held it up to admire its shape and cut, and the delicate silver stitches along the square neckline.

With a rush of heat going through her, she pulled the gown over her head and ran her arms through the tapered sleeves. She felt the breath leave her body at the feel of the silk falling over her body. She had never owned anything so luxurious and it had been a gift! She wished she had a mirror, but she ran her palms down the dress, feeling the slightly loose fit and expert craftsmanship.

She could never wear it to meet members of the church. She smiled at her silly ravings. She would be excommunicated and perhaps her uncle would be kicked out of the church with her.

She pretended to be married to the captain, waiting for him in the bedroom while he bid good eve to their last guest. Soon, he would be here. He would ravish her, unable to resist her another instant—and no longer having to.

She closed her eyes, feeling his breath on her, his woodsy scent covering her. His sumptuous lips roved over hers and down her chin to the thrashing pulsebeat at her throat. He kissed her and held her waist in his hands.

Her eyes opened. Stop! This would do her no good if she were meeting the men of the church tonight.

She grew serious. She had to be the epitome of purity. That's what they believed. The truth was that she wasn't pure, and she didn't know her uncle. He paid for everything she needed but he had visited her only once. If they asked her what she thought of him, she would tell them that he made certain she always had what she needed. Hopefully, he did the same for her family. She would tell them nothing else until her uncle threatened her again. Then, she would tell them that.

She stepped out of the gown. She never planned on wearing it and packed it into her bag.

She donned her gray robes and sat in a chair by the window. She took out her beads and her small book of prayers and there she stayed until the sun began its lazy descent.

When it came time to leave, she put on her wimple and veil, tucking every strand of her hair beneath.

She felt more peaceful and ready to face them. She searched the halls for the captain and hated herself for it.

Before she reached the town hall, she saw the lights from dozens of candles and the hearth fire glowing from inside.

What would these men be like? She would find out soon but, first, she spotted someone waiting outside the doors. Her escort? Was her uncle so thoughtful? She didn't think so.

As she grew closer, she saw who it was. The captain. He wore a hooded mantle and dark boots. When he turned to face her, her heart melted at the masculine beauty he possessed.

"Captain." There was so much she wanted to say to him. So much waiting to roll off her tongue, held back by strength she didn't know she possessed. "What are you doing here?" He wasn't alone. Mac, Will, Padrig, and Morgann were there, smiling at her, soothing her nerves.

"How d'ye feel?" he asked, looking her over.

"Anxious, I will admit."

"Remember what I told ye," Will drawled. "They shyte like the rest of us."

Now, instead of whacking his brother with his fist, Padrig nodded.

"We just heard aboot the gatherin'," the captain said. "John planned it withoot my knowledge, which speak volumes to me. I am goin' to escort ye inside and whoever doesna like it will have to stop me himself."

"He will have to stop us all," Padrig said.

"I will stop you all right now!" she argued. "You must not come inside with me. The moment they see you they will draw conclusions." She looked at Galeren. She hadn't told him that John threatened her life. There was no time now. "Please, if you were hurt…"

"Verra well. We will do as ye ask," he comforted. "But we will remain ootside and escort ye back when this is over."

She turned to the door, opened it, and stepped inside. Into a sea of men who all turned to look at her as she entered, leaving the five warriors outside.

All went silent for an eternal moment, and then someone cleared his throat and the buzz of their voices began again.

"Well now," said a man suddenly standing behind her. "This must be Sister Silene."

"Aye, my dear niece." John hurried over and introduced her to the men.

Her heart thumped hard in her chest but remarkably, she didn't feel anxious or afraid.

"Sister Silene, 'tis a delight to meet you," said a bishop. He was a tall man with foggy, brown eyes and thin white hair that fell over his large ears. He'd been introduced as The Most Reverend Thomas Graham, Bishop of Glasgow. "May I ask, when did you take your vows?"

Her eyes opened a little wider, and then she remembered her habit and smiled. "Oh, Your Excellency, I have not spoken them yet. I am a novice. My white habit was destroyed while traveling here. The steward's kind wife found a gray habit for me to wear for now."

The bishop's smile was laced with regret. "When will you take your vows?"

"My ceremony is next spring."

He glanced at a group of leaders standing close by and listening.

"Stewart?" called Abbot Neville of Scone. "We were told she was a nun."

"She practically is one!" her uncle defended.

"Practically," said Abbot Neville for all to hear, "is not good enough."

Chapter Fourteen

Silene stepped into the brisk night and looked up into Galeren's eyes. He was the last person she wanted to see. She looked away.

"Captain," she managed to speak. She didn't know how. "You and your men may go. As you can see, I have two escorts, Father Michael and Father Benedict."

"What is it? What has happened?" Galeren asked, not paying attention to her introduction. He looked angry, frightened. He moved to touch her, but she stepped back before her two escorts took notice.

"Please, Captain," she pleaded softly. "Go. We will speak another time."

She didn't want to see him, smell him, feel him in her blood. She didn't want to talk. She needed to be alone to shiver and weep in private.

She was falling in love with the captain. Falling in love with a man.
Are You angry?

"Please excuse me, Captain." She turned on her heel and left. He didn't follow her. She was glad. She didn't want to explain.

Her time had come to an end, taken from her. The church would not offer her uncle any favor or place on their council for having a novice in the family. They were stretching things accepting a nun. They were quick to remind the steward of it.

But they were here, her uncle had pointed out. Why couldn't she speak her vows now? They agreed. There was to be a ceremony in two days.

Two days. Not next spring.

She walked, stunned and numb, back to her chambers. She didn't remember when her two escorts left her.

Two days.

She entered her chambers wishing she'd never met the captain. If she hadn't, she would have been thrilled to say her vows in two days. Now, her heart was breaking.

If he hadn't come for her, she would have spoken her vows to God and if she had met Galeren later, it would be too late for anything…

Was this feeling that it *wasn't* too late so comforting because there was still time to do something about it?

She wanted more time to pray. She had a lifetime decision to make in just two days. Speak her vows to help her uncle or run away with the captain.

If she ran away, her uncle would have no more need of her and would likely have her followed and killed for shaming him. He'd already promised to make her life, and whoever was with her, a nightmare. She didn't doubt him.

Not only would her decision change her life, it could cost her her life, as well. Or Galeren's. Or both.

She pulled off her veil and wimple, everything down to her chemise and boots, everything but her beads around her neck.

Even if God wasn't angry with her, riding to the north with an army on their backs didn't appeal.

She fell to her knees before her bed and clasped her hands together. She'd been trained since she was fourteen to give her life to God. Why would He send a man like Galeren MacPherson into her life?

Why did Galeren find her the most peaceful places to pray? Help her feed Adam and his family? Fight with savage passion for her? Adopt a kitten to please a little girl?

Someone knocked on the door. She thought it might be the captain and was tempted to open the door just as she was.

"Go away."

"Silene." It was Bishop Graham's voice. "May I have a word with you?"

Was she allowed to deny a bishop? She sighed and rose to dress. "Coming."

When she opened the door, she found the bishop's warm smile soothing.

"Come in, Your Excellency."

"Father is fine," he corrected gently and entered.

She left the door opened and walked around him to face him and smile.

"I wanted to speak to you about what will happen a pair of days from now."

She wrung her skirts and wondered if he would notice that she wasn't breathing.

"Vows are a promise to God, child."

"Aye, Father, I understand."

"If you say them," he went on anyway, "you must not go back on your word."

She nodded. What did he know? Why was he here?

"What is it that brings you such sadness and regret?"

She blinked. Did she dare lie to a bishop? She felt ill. Was she that transparent? "How…how did you know I was troubled?"

He smiled and his ears appeared even larger. "My dear, when we told you that you would be saying your vows now instead of in the spring, you looked as if we had just destroyed all your hopes and dreams."

She didn't know what to say. She couldn't tell him about the captain. Her heart drummed. She drew her fingers to her brow. She missed having someone to talk to whom she trusted. She missed Agnes and the others.

"I cannot repeat what you tell me in confession," he assured her.

"I…I am unsure."

He lifted a bushy brow. "About what?"

She closed her eyes. If he went to her uncle or any of the others, all would be lost.

"Saying my vows," she confessed to him.

"Why?" he asked softly. "Is your faith fading?"

"Oh, nay, Father. My faith is not in danger." Her life was, but she couldn't tell that much to him. He would have to do something to protect her and would have to repeat what she told him.

"'Tis my heart."

"Ah, I see."

She lifted her gaze. "You do?"

He nodded. But his smile hadn't returned.

"I hate that I feel so terrible about something that stirs my heart so wondrously."

The bishop was quiet for a while, and then he asked, "And he has made you question a life in a priory?"

"Aye, Father."

He sighed, either with frustration or acceptance. He was difficult to read.

"What should I do?"

He shrugged, stretching his dark blue robes across his chest. "I cannot tell you what to do. I can only tell you that a sister is something you should *want* to be. You can still serve the Lord either way."

She nodded and smiled. She believed it to be true.

"Seek His guidance," he told her, finally smiling back. "You will find it."

"May I ask," she began and continued when he did not refuse, "what will happen to my uncle if I do not speak them? How will he be affected?"

"Silene," he said on a whisper, "you cannot speak these vows to God for any other reason than that you wish to dedicate your entire life to Him. If you say them to appease your uncle…" he shook his head instead of continuing. "You are better off not speaking them. Do you understand?"

She nodded. "Are you advising me to—"

"I'm advising you to seek the truth about your heart. If you are in love with a man who makes you question—"

"Father, I have two days to decide."

He smiled at her with understanding. "I was once given moments to decide if I should side with the Scot's king, who had been thrown into prison, or England's king, who ruled more territories day after day."

"How did you decide?" she asked.

"I let God lead me. My path came in the form of a soft breeze from the north."

"A soft breeze?"

He nodded. "Aye, child. Sometimes, we just need to listen."

He left her to pray, which she did for the entire day. She didn't leave her chambers save to visit the garderobe, or open the door for her food, of which she ate little.

She didn't hear the captain outside her door, poised to knock three separate times, or hear his footsteps when he walked away. Nor did she receive the answers she was looking for.

She was almost fully certain of her decision, which she'd made on her own when the morning of the second day came. She dressed in her habit, with her wimple and veil. She was ready when Louise came to get her. She saw Matilda so happy for her that Silene had to keep her thoughts away from her uncle and his wife. They were part of the group to have her say her vows now. They had to secure her place so that John's place in the church could be solidified. It had nothing to do with God.

She didn't see Galeren in the great hall for breakfast. Now that she hadn't seen him for a full day, she missed him. Neither Will nor Morgann had seen him. She tried to sit with them, but they were called away.

It was better this way, she told herself while she ate alone.

As long as she obeyed, she was sure John wouldn't force his dear friend to marry Cecilia Birchet.

Everything would be well. She would go on with her life as planned, but where would she go? If her feeling was correct, not to St. Patrice's.

Would she stay here? Forced to be with the captain every day? Would she somehow die? She made the sign of the cross and didn't realize she had until Father Nate and Bishop Graham slipped into the bench beside her and asked if she was well.

She smiled but she felt anything but well, or in the mood to confess why. Rather than lie and tell them she was fine, she rose from her place. "If you would both excuse me, I would like to go pray."

They excused her with bows. She wanted to run, but it would be unseemly. Still, she lifted her skirts above her ankles and hurried out of the hall.

She was suffocating and pulled off her veil to get to her wimple and pulled that off next.

Quickening her pace, she turned one corner on the way to her chambers and crashed into a wall.

A living, breathing wall, with strong arms that came around her to hold her steady.

"Captain!" she breathed on his chin, tilting her face to see him.

She didn't want him to let go. She didn't think about where they were or who might see. She forgot it all in his embrace, gazing into his warm, green eyes.

"I have missed yer face, lass."

She smiled. He always made her feel beautiful just by the way he looked at her. "And I have missed yours, Captain."

She felt the muscles in his arms tremble before he reluctantly released her.

"Come, please speak with me, Silene."

She agreed and hurried with him down two more halls, until they came to an outside balcony and stepped onto it.

He looked out over Dundonald's lands instead of at her. "When I found oot aboot the church and yer vows, I tried to see ye. Why did ye hide from me? Were ye goin' to speak yer vows withoot even a word to me?"

He still hadn't looked at her. She wanted him to. She tugged on his shirt. He finally turned.

"I'm not certain, Captain, but I think I'm in love with you."

He turned the rest of his body until he faced her fully and took her hands in his. "Then come! Let us leave now!"

Could she? Could they get away? For how long? "If ye were killed, I would—"

"Lass—" He drew his forehead close to hers. "Better is a moment with ye than a thousand years withoot ye."

"I want more than a moment, Galeren. But I...I cannot..."

She watched tears pool above his lids.

"Silene, if ye dinna come, I fear ye may be killed here. My grandsire told me to get ye away from these men. I intend to do that. Please, lass, if I am killed, ye can speak yer vows. Fer death would have parted us."

"Nay!" She tried to step away, but he held her by the arms and wouldn't let her go.

"I want to fight fer ye, Silene. But I canna fight against God. Tell me ye do this fer Him and not oot of fear of yer uncle and I will walk away."

They heard a sound inside. Silene looked around the balcony and saw Morgann. He appeared to be searching the halls.

She called to him and the captain approached and waited at her side.

"Ah, Captain. I was sent to look fer ye."

"By whom?"

"The steward," Morgann let him know. "He said to tell ye he awaits ye in the great hall."

"Thank ye, Morgann. Ye may go."

Morgann's blue eyes met Silene's. He smiled briefly and then looked away. She called out to him before he left the balcony.

"'Tis good to see you, Morgann. Are you well?"

"Aye, Sister," he replied, and then was gone.

She hadn't expected his cool response. Aye, he was the stoic, serious one, but they had become friends. He had warmed to her on their journey. Now, it was all gone. She suddenly felt like weeping.

She felt the captain's gaze on her and turned to him.

"What is it?" he was quick to ask.

Everything was about to change. It had already begun. None of the men would treat her the same way when she became a nun. "I am sad."

His jaw tightened as he bit down on words he could not utter, save one. "Why?"

There were too many reasons, so she chose one. "What is going to become of us?"

The weight of his brow brought shadows to his eyes. "There is no us if ye say yer vows."

"Cap—Galeren, my uncle has vowed to destroy my life if I betray him."

"Then," he said quietly, "ye are speakin yer vows fer the wrong reason."

She was quiet. He was correct, but it didn't matter. "One of us must leave."

His gaze deepened on her. "Silene, is that what ye want? To be apart from me?"

"I need you not to be where I am, and all will be well."

He shook his head and looked into her eyes. "I canna agree to that."

"We must part," she cried on a hushed voice. "There is no other way."

She ran from him, crying all the way to her chambers. The more she told herself that living without the captain was not impossible, the less she believed it.

She wanted to go to the church and wait for the leaders there, but she needed her white cloak.

She met Louise in the hall.

"Why are ye crying, Sister?"

Because I'm about to lose a man who walks around with a kitten cuddled in the crook of his shoulder. "I am overwhelmed by everything going on."

"Aye, I heard ye were sayin' yer vows today."

"Aye."

"And that makes ye weep?"

"Nay," Silene told her honestly. She understood that Louise was jealous of the captain and would likely turn on her, but she wanted a friend and, right now, Louise was here.

"I weep because I would be sacrificed for anything. I thought I had time, but now I do not have any time at all."

Louise nodded, looking, for an instant, sympathetic to Silene's plight. But then she stopped at the door to the chambers without going inside. "Sister," she said, moving in closer, "I would advise ye to forget Captain MacPherson. I hear it could kill ye…or him."

Silene's blood ran cold. Not Louise, too! "Are you threatening me?" she demanded, having had enough of this.

Louise shook her head. "Not me."

"Then who? I wish to know! Is it my uncle?"

"Sister, I canna tell ye."

Silene opened her mouth to say more but heard voices around the corridor.

"I must go," Louise said, taking the opportunity to hurry away without answering her question. She was gone without a sound.

Silene quickly opened the door to her chambers and slipped inside. She felt too shaken up to talk to anyone.

She heard men's voices pass her door, and then it grew quiet again. She went to the hearth and stared into the flames.

Forget the captain or die.

She could not get warm. Her head was spinning, making her feel ill. Too much was happening at once. Her vows were upon her. She could not make the wrong decision because of lack of time. What did her heart want her to do? If she said her vows to God, she could not, *would not* break them. If she did not say them, she could take a husband of flesh and blood—and possibly anger someone enough to see her dead.

John surely knew that Galeren came from Invergarry. If he wanted her dead, he had men enough to do it. Her uncle had reason to hate her. She would have destroyed his connection to the powerful church.

Perhaps it wasn't someone as dangerous as her uncle who threatened her. Perhaps it came from one of Galeren's many admirers. It didn't matter—someone had threatened her to Louise. She should tell the captain.

Oh, how would she ever forget him? He would always remain in her heart, her thoughts, there to haunt her. There to tempt her to regret her choice.

"Cleanse my heart of him, Lord, I pray. Let it be that when I see him, I feel nothing. Nay. Let him repulse me."

Someone knocked softly on her door. Her heart thrashed against her ribs.

"Sister Silene," a child's voice came through the door.

Margaret!

Silene hurried to the door and opened it. "Margaret," she said, bending to level her gaze with the girl's. "What are you doing here?"

"Captain MacPherson asks that ye follow me."

Silene stepped out of the chambers without thinking about what she was doing. Could she ever resist him?

"Where are we going?'

"Ye will see when we get there."

Silene smiled for the first time so far that day. Perhaps she would fall down a hole on the way and never be seen again.

She followed Margaret around the western wall of the castle to the small barn. She remembered being here once before, long ago. There were stalls, smaller than the ones in the stable, but none of the barn animals stayed in them. There were three ducks that clapped their wings and honked angrily at her intrusion. Three hens and a rooster sent feathers flying. There was a pig, and a goat—and a man with a kitten on his shoulder and a little boy at his side. It was Alex. He was crying. What was going on?

"Captain?" she asked, looking up at him in the lantern's light. She didn't feel repulsed. She felt like she'd happened upon a mythical creature, golden and green and ready to offer his life to her.

"I brought the children here to bid them farewell."

"Farewell?" she echoed, feeling the emptiness of it. "You are leaving, Captain?"

He nodded. "'Tis time."

Well, that was it then. He was leaving. He wouldn't be here to tempt her with the shape of his succulent lips when he spoke, the sultry green of his eyes when he smiled at her. She'd wanted him to leave. She also wanted to be unaffected by him—but she wasn't. In fact, she felt so affected just by looking at him that she was unsteady on her feet, foggy in her head.

He hurried forward when she swayed, overwhelmed with everything that was happening.

"Are ye ill, Silene?"

She shook her head. She didn't believe it. She never felt so bad in her life.

"Good," he said with his arm beneath her, "because I want ye to come with me. The time fer waitin' is over."

It was all too much, too fast. She tried to remember the reasons she couldn't go with him. "Captain, do not ask this of me."

"Why not, Silene? Do ye not love me?" he whispered so only she could hear.

Oh, aye, she did. She loved him enough to give up her vows. "Louise told me that I should forget you or it could get one of us killed. She said the threat was not from her, but she would not tell me anything else."

His brows dipped over his eyes, creating shadows like phantoms in a verdant forest. "All the more reason to go now. I have everythin' worked oot with the men. They wish to come. 'Twill help to have them with us should the army come."

What was he saying? It was as if his words were jumbling around in her head.

She touched her hand to her head and fainted in his arms.

CHAPTER FIFTEEN

GALEREN WANTED TO run. He looked down at Silene and seriously considered running away with her. He could toss her over his saddle and flee to Invergarry. Let anyone come. No one would be able to breach the MacPherson stronghold. If they did, they would find themselves facing the most savage warriors that ever lived.

But he wouldn't take her away when she didn't want to go. Whether because of fear for their lives, or because of her desire to belong only to God, she was staying. That meant he was staying, too.

He'd thought when she saw how serious he was about leaving that she would go with him—not faint in his arms.

"All is well, children," he told them. "Sister Silene has fainted. She will awaken soon. Let me put her down. Alex, get my plaid and set it down here."

He waited, smiling down at Margaret. He shifted Silene's weight and held her in one arm and plucked Daffodil off his shoulder. "Hold her fer now," he told her while Daffodil meowed in protest.

His gaze shifted to Silene's face. He closed his eyes and swallowed.

"Captain?"

He opened his eyes to Alex spreading out his plaid.

Galeren couldn't lay her in the grass outside and risk someone seeing him carrying her. He'd already put her in enough jeopardy.

"Why did she faint, Captain?" Alex asked him, finishing up.

"She has many things to think aboot. Mayhap meetin' the men of the church has been too overwhelmin'."

They looked at her and nodded as if they understood.

"People will speak ill of her if they hear aboot this."

Margaret and Alex listened and nodded as he set her down on the plaid and remained on his haunches. He tapped her cheek, "Silene? Wake up, lass."

"Wake up, Sister Silene," Margaret echoed.

After another moment, her eyes fluttered open.

Galeren's heart quickened as his blood rushed through his veins. "Silene?"

"What happened to me?" she asked, looking up at him with her wide, worried, blue-green gaze.

"Ye fell faint," he told her.

"Ye are heavily burdened with decisions," Alex added.

Galeren and Silene turned to gape at him.

"Alex," Galeren said, resting back on his thighs. "How d'ye understand things meant fer adults?"

The child blinked his stunning eyes, one green and one blue and shrugged his scrawny shoulders. "I feel it."

Silene sat up slowly, her gaze steady on the boy. "What do you mean? How do you feel it?"

"I just think of everythin' I know aboot somethin'. After a bit of deductions, I come to a conclusion. If 'tis correct, I feel it. 'Tis as if I found a piece to a puzzle."

So, his *feeling* wasn't based entirely on emotion, but on the science of deduction. She still felt a kinship with him stronger than the blood they shared.

"Come," Galeren offered her his hand. "I will escort ye ootside fer some fresh air."

"Oh, Captain, your plaid," she lamented when she saw his plaid on the barn floor.

"'Tis nothin'. Can ye make it?" His smile vanished. "We shouldna stay in here any longer withoot a chaperone. I will take ye back to the castle."

She had less than an hour before she was to say her vows.

"Will ye be able to get to the church when the time comes?"

She nodded and smiled, and Galeren's heart broke and fell in pieces at his feet.

She was going through with it then. He saw her considering what she was doing and nod again. She'd chosen a different life. He wanted to change her mind, but he wouldn't fight to take her from God. Very well then, he would let her go, but he wouldn't leave her here alone. They would remain friends. The threat of him would be gone. If there was someone besides the steward who would hurt her, he would find out who it was and deal with him. He would stay here with the army until she left to wherever she would live. He would stay for John's bairns, but he would keep his distance with John and Matilda Stewart.

How was he going to see Silene? Speak with her and not desire her every day, in every way? How would he love her and never be with her? He almost groaned out loud.

They left the barn and started back for the castle. Margaret held Daffodil but the kitten wanted to ride with Galeren and finally leaped from Margaret's arms into his. He petted the kitten's head while she snuggled into to crook of his neck. Since Matilda refused to let them keep Daffodil, he had decided to leave the kitten in the barn where other kittens her age grew up. The children promised to care for her and play with her every day.

He wondered now, with tiny Daffodil purring near his ear, if she would have followed him all the way to Invergarry. She seemed quite attached to him, as he was to her.

"When will you be leaving?" Silene asked him.

He laughed a little. "I'm not leavin' ye here with someone who would threaten ye, lass. When 'tis time to take ye back to St. Patrice's, I will escort ye—and then I will go home."

"Captain," she said as she turned to him. "I do not want to sever whatever is between us, but God has made it clear by our mountainous obstacles that our way is not together."

"Aye, we have obstacles, but why should such a treasure come withoot a fight? We can overcome the obstacles if we dinna give up."

"Not if we are dead," she argued.

"I will protect ye, Silene. D'ye not trust me?"

"I do, but I also fear my uncle. You are the most adored man. These people do not follow John. They follow you, and *still* someone would threaten your life! They are not afraid. It has to be Uncle John." She whispered so the children could not hear these things about their father.

"Aye. I will keep my eyes on him. I have not fergotten that he has already betrayed me."

"You see? He is not to be trusted, Captain."

He knew what she was saying was important. But he didn't want to waste any more time with her thinking about her uncle. He didn't care about the steward. He only cared about her. He should have fought this sooner. The first time he saw her on the cliffs. He should have let her ride with Mac, but why put his friend through it? He should not have ridden with her until she could ride on her own. He'd allowed her to crawl under his skin while he watched her pray and when he fought others for her life and left ten dead. He should have pushed her away when his heart stirred for her, awakening when she refused to leave three hungry children in a village.

He never should have kissed her.

But he wasn't sorry for any of it.

"Captain?"

He smiled at her and then blinked out of it. "Aye?"

"You have not heard a word I have said."

It was true. He couldn't deny it. "I was rememberin'…"

"Remembering what?" she pressed.

"When I first laid eyes on ye, and all the days after that. They were too pleasant to leave fer thoughts of John."

She tossed him a wistful smile. "Aye, I think of those things often."

He frowned and looked away at the castle looming closer.

"Speak plainly please," she said.

Before he could stop himself, the words left his mouth, rolled off his tongue. "Fergive me, but if ye are goin' to be a nun, I dinna think there should be any doubt—or any need of time to think aboot it."

"There were no doubts before you!" she insisted.

He cast her a regretful side glance and opened the castle doors. "Bring Daffodil to my chambers," he called to the children and then watched them race up the stairs.

He didn't care who saw him with Silene. She'd soon be a nun and that would be the end of everything.

"I will be ootside yer door, ready to escort ye to the church."

"Nay. I do not think 'tis a good idea. You know you are a temptation to me, yet you always insist on being at my side."

"My desires…and yers dinna come before yer safety."

"I will be safe going to church, Captain."

Aha. He was back to being *Captain*.

"I do not want to see you."

"Verra well," he said, sounding like a hammer coming down on an anvil. "Ye willna see me."

SILENE STARED AT the purple gown folded neatly on her bed. She wanted to try it on. Just one more time before she gave it away. Perhaps it would fit Louise.

She only had a few moments left before she was expected at the church. She left the gown where it was and dressed in her habit. She looked at the door. Was he out there waiting to escort her? She wiped her eyes for the hundredth time. She wasn't doing this for her uncle anymore. She was doing it to keep her and Galeren alive. And though that was a serious reason indeed, it wasn't the right one.

She opened her chamber door. He wasn't there or down any of the halls. She walked, alone, out of the castle and into the late afternoon sun. She looked around at the village and the surrounding structures and trees, all cast in a soft, summer glow. It calmed her racing heart.

When she stepped through the inner gate, someone took her wrist. She turned, expecting to see Galeren.

"Uncle," she muttered and then pulled her wrist free. "Have you come to make certain I reach the church safely?"

"Of course," he said with a grin. "I need ye."

"Aye, ye do," she agreed with a knot twisting in her belly. She meant nothing to him.

"Now that we have a moment, I would like to ask you if you have seen my parents."

He regarded her with a wry gleam in his eyes. "I was with them last month. I have taken good care of them in yer name, gel. Ye are a blessin' to them."

She smiled. "How is Sherman, our Spaniel? He was just a pup when I left."

Her uncle nodded. "The dog is well, accordin' to yer sister. He still hunts and was oot when I arrived."

Silene closed her eyes to keep from screaming at him. He was lying. Her family didn't own a dog named Sherman. Her uncle was her enemy. She doubted that he had visited her parents at all.

"I wish you and I could have had more time to visit and get to know each other, my lord."

She wanted to find something redeeming about him.

"Well, ye canna live yer life with regrets now," he warned.

She couldn't find anything.

"Uncle, I would like some time alone with God right now." She knew he could not deny her and claim to be pious.

He nodded hesitantly. "Verra well." He sounded insulted that she had just dismissed him. He walked away and entered the church, leaving her alone in the coming twilight.

It was time. She looked around. Was Galeren somewhere behind a tree or cottage, watching her?

She prayed for strength but when she tried to move her feet, she found she could not budge them. She knew that if she went inside the church, she would never see the captain again. The feeling washed over her like a wave, a certainty she could not deny. It made her feel ill. She clutched her belly and cried out softly.

"Silene!"

The captain's voice in the indigo shadows made her blood rush through her veins and her breath pause.

"Are ye ill, lass?" He came to her as if from a dream, his eyes wide with concern.

She took a step to meet him and went straight into his arms. "Can we still get away?"

Without a word, he released her and slipped his hand to hers. He tugged and began to run.

She went with him. Holding his hand with one of her own and hoisting her robes over her ankles with the other. He led her to his horse and helped her mount. She would have to ride on her side, so she pulled her skits over her knees and waited for him.

He mounted and sat behind her, tucking her into his lap.

With a flick of his wrist, he snapped the reins and set the horse to flying through the outer gate. There was no time to go back to the castle and get her things. She was leaving Dundonald, her uncle, her vows, with nothing but the clothes on her back. Not that she had much in the first place. She didn't care about the castle or her uncle. But leaving her vows frightened her.

They rode until the world went black and his horse needed to rest. He would get her a horse tomorrow, he promised. She didn't mind riding with him.

They'd gone far, perhaps twenty miles. But was it far enough to rest? Was her uncle close?

They made a small fire and ate little. Galeren sat against a tree and held her in his arms when she snuggled close to him. He covered them with a fur hide he had tied to his horse when he thought they were leaving earlier and forgot about it.

She smiled and pressed her cheek to his chest. "'Tis good," she nearly purred.

She didn't know why she felt so peaceful. It was because all the weight of having to make such life-changing decisions was lifted. Even for a little while.

"I feel like a devil fer takin' ye from what ye have wanted fer so long now."

"I wanted to leave," she promised him.

"I tempted ye," he answered.

She shook her head. "I do not feel temptations, Galeren. I feel love."

He lifted her cheek on a deep breath. She could hear his heart pounding. He kissed the top of her head. "I didna know havin' these feelin's could be like this. 'Tis both thrillin' and terrifyin'."

She nodded in agreement. "I am afraid John will find us. Will Invergarry not be the first place he goes?"

"Aye. That is why I must go there. I must let my kin know what is comin'."

She felt the sting behind her lids and did everything she could to stop her tears. He would feel them on his chest. In the end, she failed.

"I do not want to be the reason your family goes into battle."

"Lass?" The deep, purring resonance of his voice fell around her like a favored blanket, coaxing her to let him stay under the blanket with her. "My kin dinna mind fightin'. 'Tis in our blood. We are put to the field at a tender age. Taught to fight and stay alive by our fathers and our mothers."

Their mothers? "Aye," she remembered out loud. "May and Rowley Hetherington are your mother's parents. Your mother was a border reiver."

"Aye."

"She fought men."

"Aye," he agreed "She is small in stature, but her speed is still spoken aboot at the table. No man I know has ever beaten her to the final blow. She doesna waste a moment of time tryin' to fight. She flies at her opponent in the first instant—or even before. Somehow attachin' herself on his back and cuts his throat. If 'tis the practice field where he finds himself, she holds the dull edge of her knife to his neck and wins."

Silene listened in both horror and awe. What kind of woman learned how to fight that way?

A woman who either conquered or was conquered. A warrior created in war, ready to fight to live or die trying.

"Tell me more about your family—the women in particular." She wanted to hear about these courageous women, and she wanted to keep listening to his voice.

"My Aunt Aleysia taught us how to sweep a man clean off his feet and onto his arse. She was and remains the only warrior who ever took down the merciless Cainnech MacPherson, High Commander to Robert the Bruce, and lived. She also taught us to run through trees."

Silene looked up at him. "What do you mean? How can you run

through the trees?"

"The trees around the stronghold are all connected by boughs or planks. We run along those. There are traps everywhere, as well. Her idea." He smiled. "An army will have a difficult time if they go through the forest."

He told her about his Aunt Julianna, who taught them all about different poisons that could either kill their enemy, paralyze them, or put them to sleep. "She taught us how to remove the tiny stingers of wasps, hornets, or the fangs of spiders, and more. 'Tis fer close contact, should ye find yerself at the enemy's mercy. Ye only need to touch yer enemy to kill him."

"Oh, my!" she whispered, astounded and rested her cheek on his chest again.

"Her husband is the youngest of the three brothers," he continued. "Uncle Nicholas was raised as a servant and became an earl. He is more of a diplomatic warrior. He can serve or slay with his tongue. He has lived in the huts along the Marañon River, verra far south of here."

"They sound fascinating!" she breathed. "And what of your father?"

His tone grew warmer when he spoke. "My father singlehandedly took down Berwick Castle, Till Castle, and dozens of others. In between, he learned to read because he wanted to find a story his mother used to tell him aboot a king called Arthur and his isle called Avalon."

"You love him very much."

"Aye," he agreed. "He and my uncles have built a stronghold that can withstand much. If John's men go through the forest, they will die. If they make it to the shepherds, many will die before they reach the battlements. There are over one hundred warriors within the stronghold. They are always ready fer battle."

She shivered in his arms. "I am a bit anxious about meeting them."

"No," he told her, "dinna be. They will love ye as I do."

She lifted her head to look at him and smile, but she should have known better. He smiled and she was lost.

When he dipped his head to her, she closed her eyes and tried to prepare for the feel of his…

…lips. They were warm—like the rest of him, firm but yielding, molding to her, tasting her in swift, breathless kisses. She loved kissing him. His lips were so soft. She wanted him to take her deeper and reached her hands around his nape. His dark, golden hair fell over her fingers. His mouth covered hers. His tongue licked and danced over hers, flicked across her teeth while his lips caressed hers.

She'd chosen this man over speaking her vows, but she had in no way given up the first place in her heart to anyone but God and she still might say her vows in the spring if being with Galeren proved too difficult.

Her uncle wouldn't care. His secured place on the council was gone. Not only gone but stained because of her.

"What about Mac and the others?"

He raised a brow. The corners of his teasing mouth rose. "D'ye think of my men while ye kiss me?"

"Not always," she teased back.

His smile grew into a wide grin and then they both laughed.

"They know where I wanted to take ye. I had hoped ye would change yer mind and gave them orders to collect anythin' we left behind and meet us at the stronghold."

Aye. She thought of her purple gown and nodded.

"They will also have a bit more information as to what actions John is takin'."

"You are clever, Galeren," she told him, staring into his eyes. "I love being held in your arms. I love your face and the things you talk about. I love how you feel in my hands." She ran her palms over his chest.

His smile warmed on her. She inhaled a deep breath and prepared to be kissed by him again.

"Ye are mine," he whispered, breaking their kiss for just an instant. "I will never let ye go."

Chapter Sixteen

GALEREN HELD HER in his arms while she slept. He kept his horse close by and his knife in his hand, ready to run and cut anyone down. He hoped no one came. He wanted to keep holding her. They had kissed and spoke until she could no longer keep sleep from overtaking her.

He tried to work out in his mind, while he counted the stars, how quickly things had gone bad in Dundonald. He had always known that John was ambitious, but he never knew what lengths the high steward would go to be king.

Silene was the steward's kin, a novice of the Almighty, and an innocent, genuine soul unsullied by the deeds of men.

How could John or any other man even think of hurting her? He wouldn't let them near her.

He rubbed his thumb over her back while his hand relaxed on her. She'd let him hold her. He was certain he was the only man who ever had.

What would he do if she chose to wed herself to God when she was finally safe? He prayed again that she would be released from her vows. That she would give herself to him.

And I will give what Ye ask of me, he prayed and closed his eyes.

He woke just before dawn to the sound of Silene's soft voice. She was deep in prayer, whispering things about him.

He didn't feel right about listening to something so private.

"Lass?"

She stopped and opened her eyes and inclined her ear to his lips to hear him.

An arrow whooshed above her. It would have gone straight through her if she hadn't bent to him.

Galeren moved in a blur of speed, pulling her down and covering her body with his. There was no time to think. Only to react. Galeren had decades of practice. He rolled over her and grabbed his bow and quiver in the leaves. He took a half a breath's time to pause and look down into her big, beautiful eyes. He didn't smile or speak. He just looked and then he looked away. He rose up from behind her with his arrow nocked and ready to fly. He saw a man kneeling behind the stump of a tree. He released the arrow. Without taking the time to aim, he'd sent his arrow into the man's head.

His eyes caught another movement. His second arrow flew and met its mark into the guts of another.

"Stay behind me, love," he commanded and moved slowly to the right.

His arrow was ready when he saw a third man behind a small cottage. Galeren made his way toward it.

"Do not shoot me, Captain!" the man called out and left the shadows with his hands up.

What? It couldn't be.

It was Silene who spoke his name softly into the dawn. "Morgann."

Galeren held the shaft of his arrow against his cheek. His fingers pulled back the bowstring.

"Captain, please."

"Ye dare plead mercy from me after ye betray me? Who? Who told ye to do this?"

"John," Morgann answered.

"Morgann, why?" Silene asked behind him.

"I dinna care why," Galeren said through his clenched teeth. "I'm goin' to kill ye."

Morgann closed his eyes waiting for death. But Galeren didn't want to kill him in front of Silene. Letting him live was punishment enough. His name would be known to every senior officer as a traitor.

"On yer knees," Galeren ordered.

Morgann quickly did as he was told.

"How many of ye are there, Morgann?"

"Three in the nearest vicinity. Ye killed two of them. There are three more headin' northeast. There will be more comin'."

Galeren scanned the surroundings carefully. Nothing moved. He deemed it safe to do so. He took Silene's arm and then took off for cover, grabbing hold of Morgann as he went.

Morgann, he thought, letting the truth pound into his head. Young Morgann had betrayed him.

"Which one of ye shot the arrow at her while she prayed?" Galeren asked him as they rounded up their horses and left the small clearing.

"'Twas Jack MacKinny," Morgann told him somberly.

Jack MacKinny, Galeren thought as he rode away. Bastard. He was glad he killed him. He wanted to ask Morgann if Mac and the others betrayed him as well. But he didn't want to know. Right now, Morgann's betrayal was enough.

He didn't allow his former friend near Silene. The only words Morgann could utter without losing his head were, "I'm sorry."

"Will ye ever fergive me, Captain?"

"Since when d'ye seek my absolution?" Galeren put to him.

"I have always looked up to ye, Sir."

Galeren laughed but the sound was void of any mirth. "And what did John offer ye to make ye look the other way?"

"Land in Ayr," Morgann answered with shame in his eyes.

"Well, lad," Galeren said to him. "Now ye know ye have a price."

He turned away from Morgann and rode closer to Silene.

"What aboot ye, Captain?" the traitor boldly called out. "Ye are runnin' off with the woman yer steward and friend charged ye to protect. A novice who was goin' to become a nun before God and the church today. D'ye think ye are so different from me?"

Galeren met Silene's gaze. He wanted to smile, but he couldn't. Morgann was correct. Galeren was guilty of those things.

But when he looked into her eyes at his reflection, he didn't see a shameful man. "Mayhap, 'tis not aboot what we did but why we did it. My heart has found my love," he said, keeping his gaze on her. "What I did was not fer greed or pride, but aboot love." He tore his gaze from hers and set it on Morgann. "And aboot wantin' to keep her safe from men who wanted to kill her. That now includes ye, Morgann Bell. The only reason ye are not dead is because I didna want her to see me do such a thing to a man she considered a friend." He waited while the young man closed his eyes that were staring at the ground. "Ye can try to run away," he continued, "but ye know I will catch ye. Ye know what I will do to ye."

Morgann knew of Galeren's deeds. All the soldiers knew how savage he was in battle. He feared nothing and no one and won every fight. He'd beaten every man who came against him. He was the valiant captain in gold who was always the one sent on a mission when trusted men were needed. He'd also been sent out often to hunt and kill the king's enemies, which he did proficiently. Each had been found. All of them killed.

Morgann didn't need to be bound or secured. He wouldn't leave.

They rode all day, stopping only to eat and to pray. They traveled northward. They didn't rest in the large burgh of Kilmarnock but made camp outside the town of Stewarton.

As their second night together since leaving all behind drew near, Galeren found the most out-of-the-way clearing to make camp.

He tied Morgann's wrists and ankles together. A precaution more necessary as they slept. He held Silene in his arms as he had the night before, and it was she who crawled into his lap, pressed her windburned cheek to his chest and closed her eyes.

He didn't care if Morgann saw and she, apparently, didn't care either.

"We will reach Paisley Abbey, ootside of Glasgow, tomorrow," he told her. "I have some friends there who will hide us while we rest. 'Tis the last place John will think to look fer us."

Silene appeared alarmed. "Do you trust the men there?"

"Aye," he told her. "Mac and I helped them rebuild some parts of the abbey when we first arrived there with King David. John hates the abbey because his mother died there while givin' birth to his brother, Robert."

"My uncle is a devious man," she said with her head tilted and her lips near his ear. "And if I speak my vows and put a man like him in a higher position, am I not guilty of his crimes right along with him? And would I be using God to do it?"

He didn't know what else to say but, "Aye. I suppose so."

She trembled in his arms. He comforted her with warm whispers of how beautiful she was to him. He told her about being captivated by her the first day on the cliffs.

"I have never thought of myself as beautiful," she told him with a smile he could hear in her voice.

"I dinna know how ye could see anythin' different. But yer genuine humility is quite lovely in and of itself."

"I have no hair," she reminded him.

"I canna imagine how much bonnier ye will be when it falls around yer face."

He was sorry he could barely see her face. He wanted to kiss her, but he worried it might lead to more. He wanted it to, but he knew he couldn't. He had made a vow and he intended to keep it. But when the vow was over, he would marry her if she would have him. Until then, he would help her trust him, give her time for her to think about a life with him. He wouldn't push too hard. He would offer her patience and try to get her home to Father Timothy as soon as he could. They both needed his advice.

"You have quite a silver tongue, Captain," she laughed softly, stirring the hair along his neck.

"I speak only the truth." He smiled and instinctually closed his arms around her more tightly, breathing against her, letting his hands rove over her back. He longed to take hold of her and pull her between his legs. But he stopped.

"Let us get some sleep now, lass."

"Aye," she agreed quietly and closed her eyes.

Seven more days of this, not including the time spent at the abbey. He couldn't do it. He certainly couldn't sleep with her like this after tonight and think he was strong enough to resist her.

But tonight, at least until her next prayer time, he wasn't letting her go.

The next sennight was not always torturous for Galeren. There were days when he looked toward her cleaning something from the campsite. Most times, she caught him looking and blushed all the way to her scalp.

They kissed—often, but when he asked her what she thought of one of the priests from the abbey marrying them, she told him she couldn't marry him yet.

He would wait until she could.

There was no sign of Mac or the others, but Galeren wasn't worried. If anyone could be trusted, it was Mac. They kept Morgann with them, mostly because Galeren didn't know what to do with him.

The soldier did his best to strike up conversation, but Galeren had nothing to say to him. He was part of the plot to kill Silene if she showed signs of not speaking her vows. Galeren would never trust him again.

"We are close, aboot half a day away," he told her from the top of a cluster of hills. "Beyond the hills."

They traveled along the wild river Garry where small waterfalls gushed over the braes. They trotted their horses through trees and over rocks. Birds flew overhead, shouting at the intrusion.

Home. The sounds echoed in his head. "I return home as often as I can, but not nearly as often as I should," he told her when she drew near. "Before, I wanted to fight. Now, I want to have a home and hearth of my own with a bonny wife and bairns."

Morgann called out from behind them. "Captain, are ye bringin' me to yer home to kill me there? Will yer kin kill me?"

Galeren didn't turn to face him. "If one of them wants ye dead badly enough, he will do it."

"But why would they?" Morgann pushed.

Now, Galeren pivoted on his heel and glared at his prisoner. "Mayhap because ye turned on yer captain."

He considered releasing Morgann in the forest around the stronghold. The lad would meet his end at the tips of a spiked ball flying from the branches. The traps were set up for intruders and enemies, which Morgann now was. Galeren wouldn't bring him into the stronghold, but would leave him outside the walls in the home of one of the shepherds.

He wanted Mac and the others to see him and know what he'd done. So he kept the man. Let them decide and agree what to do with him.

"I admit I am still anxious about meeting your family. What will they think of a novice who flung her vows to the four winds and ran off with the captain of the king's army? That is not a good first impression."

He promised all would be well. They would understand and even if they didn't, they would still love her because he did.

They came to the pastures, miles of it frosted with early autumn dew. Hundreds of wooly sheep and coos dotted the land. On the other side were more pastures and the deadly forests.

Just ahead, the walls of the stronghold rose high from the ground. Men dressed in plaids and weapons patrolled the land from the sky. They didn't point their arrows at him as he headed toward one of the good-sized cottages near the forest. No one was home so he tied Morgann to a tree.

"There is nowhere fer ye to escape to, Morgann, so dinna try. Either the forest will kill ye, or I will. Stay here and take refuge when the shepherd returns. 'Tis gettin' colder oot. Dinna be a fool."

Morgann's eyes glimmered with…what was that? Tears? Galeren turned away.

"What is the other option, Captain?" Morgann called out to him. "What if I dinna try to run. What will ye do to me?"

"I dinna know that yet. But right now, this is all the mercy ye will get from me." He turned away and went to his horse a few feet away, where Silene waited. Safe and alive, no thanks to Morgann. Galeren did not want to show the young soldier mercy. His betrayal cut too deep. Galeren had thought of him as one of his elite, one of his friends.

"Come, love," he said to Silene. He was ready to leave.

"I will pray that all goes well for you, Morgann," she promised before following Galeren.

"Ye have my thanks, Sister."

"He is with the men who tried to kill ye, Silene," Galeren reminded her.

"I know who he is," she told him softly, ending that conversation.

She slowed coming under the shadow of the walls. "This place is so large! Is there an entire town inside?"

He smiled. "Ye will see, lass."

"'Tis Galeren, son of Torin!" one of the guards shouted from above. "Open the gates. Wait! Who is that with ye?"

Galeren knew how difficult it was to bring anyone inside. The three brothers, including his father, who built the stronghold meant to keep it safe. It had taken over two hours to get Mac inside when they were here in the summer.

"'Tis…" He glanced at the habit she wore beneath her cloak and smiled. "'Tis Sister Silene Sparrow, niece of the High Steward of Scotland, with me," he called back.

She followed him when the gates opened, then slowed again when her horse brought her inside. Her eyes widened at the stalls and vendors mingled with tents and theatrical performers. There was an enormous church and even a mill. Children ran to and from the smith and the carpenters' tents, laughing and playing beneath the early autumn sun.

Spreading outward behind the marketplace were cottages both big and small scattered around the farming land and the wall beyond.

He watched her as she lifted her hand to her open mouth and her gaze rose to the web of walkways branching out from three main manor houses. Each walkway led to a smaller house and other houses.

They rode to the enormous middle house and dismounted.

A stable hand was there immediately to take his horse. He grinned and welcomed Galeren home.

"Is there anything I should know or do when I meet your parents or your brothers?" She wrung her hands together and bit her lip.

He took her hands in his and covered them. "They are not royalty. Just be yerself."

"Galeren?" a woman called out as she approached with a babe on her hip.

He turned to her and his smile grew when he saw his cousin, Elysande.

"What brings ye back to us so soon, Cousin?" she asked with her gaze slipping to Silene in her robes.

"El," he said after an embrace and a kiss to her cheek and to the head of the babe in her arms. "This must be the babe ye were carryin' last time I was here." The babe was beautiful like her mother, with raven hair and large, blue eyes.

"Aye. Raphaella," his cousin told him.

He kissed the babe's head again, swearing to himself that this one would know him. "I would like ye to meet Silene Sparrow, the high steward's niece."

His cousin smiled at her, eyes glinting like sapphires in well water. "Fergive me, but what is a nun doin' travelin' with ye?"

"Hidin'," Galeren answered. "She is hidin' from a powerful enemy. This is the safest place I know. And she isna a nun."

"Well, this is the perfect time to be here," she told them, not too alarmed by the news. "Everyone is gathered in my father's solar to welcome home my brother, Tristan, and his new wife."

"Oh." His gaze slipped to Silene. Everyone would be there. It would be intimidating for her. Why, he almost felt intimidated.

He blinked away from her to his cousin and took in a deep breath. "'Twill be good to see Tristan again." What was he going to tell his kin about her and who was possibly after her? Where was Father Timothy?

"How are ye, El?" he asked to fill the silence. "How is Raph and yer brood?"

His cousin turned a shade of pale green and closed her eyes.

"Elysande," Silene pushed forward. "Are you…"

His cousin nodded and then heaved.

Was she what? Galeren wanted to know.

"I will be fine in a moment," Elysande said between doubling over and more dry heaves.

"Nonsense, we will not leave you."

Galeren liked Silene's willingness to help. She had done it for everyone. Even Morgann.

"D'ye want us to get Raphael or one of the nurses?" he offered.

"No," she insisted. "I am well. 'Tis just that…"

"What?"

"I am with child."

His gaze fell to her flat belly and then he smiled and embraced her again.

"I will tell my husband tonight when we are alone and in our bed. I just need a wee bit of fresh air and rest."

"Of course," Silene reassured her calmly. "Is this yer first babe?"

El laughed. "'Tis our sixth."

Silene looked surprised and then she smiled when El insisted they go inside.

"How d'ye feel?" Galeren asked Silene when they were alone.

"She was very nice," she told him. "I'm sure the rest will be the same way."

He shrugged his shoulders and walked away. "Eh, I dinna know aboot that."

She pinched his sleeve and pulled him back to her. "Will you protect me from the mean ones?" she whispered, tilting her lips to his ear.

"With my life," he promised and turned his lips to hers.

The front doors opened and a handsome giant stood on the other side.

CHAPTER SEVENTEEN

THE SAVAGE HIGHLAND warrior was bigger even than Padrig. He wore his pale blonde hair cut close at his temples with a dangling tail in the back. His eyes were as blue as the sea, his shoulders as wide as oceans.

Thankfully, he looked quite happy to see Galeren.

Beside him was a much smaller woman patting her hair. When she looked up, her cheeks were bright pink.

"Little brother!" The Highlander pulled Galeren into a tight embrace. "We were worried aboot ye when we heard aboot the Black Death."

"I am well, Bors," he promised and then introduced Silene to him.

Bors cleared his throat and introduced her to Constance, from the village. Come," he told them. "Everyone will be pleased to have ye home. Tristan has also returned. 'Tis a blessed night."

"When you say everyone," Silene asked him. "How many do you mean exactly?"

Galeren's brother laughed. "Not many really. Ye missed supper—though I'm sure somethin' will be brought in fer ye. We are goin' to our uncle Cain's solar. 'Tis just the immediate kin by now."

Silene swallowed. She knew from Galeren's stories that number was high.

She wouldn't be afraid. God was giving her back a family. The bigger the better it would be.

She stayed behind when Galeren stepped into the solar. She needed a moment more to prepare. His parents were inside, and not only them, but his uncles and aunts, his cousins.

She felt ill, but strangely…calm.

They were happy to see him. She could hear his mother ask him what had happened, as if some kind of motherly instinct came alive in her and she knew things no one else knew. A few more words with his mother and then a man's voice.

Galeren was there, appearing through the doorway to take her hand and pull her in.

She stepped into a large room decorated with tapestries depicting three stags, and running deer, gardens, all embroidered in warm, rich tones. The fiery hearth was built against the north wall. Polished wooden chairs were set by windows or by the fire. Some were positioned together, while others were alone with a small table of books nearby.

There were men and women sitting and standing, with children running around them.

Every eye fell to her but all their faces blurred as Galeren urged her forward. She would not faint. She would not faint. She heard someone's shocked whisper. "They are holdin' hands!" And another's saying, "Aye. A captain and novice!"

Galeren held up his hand to quiet them. "She needs to stay here fer a wee bit. Fer protection."

"Who would hurt a nun?" a dangerous Highlander said in a low, bear-like voice.

An old priest stepped around one of them and offered her a consoling smile. He was bald, with weathered skin, large, clear, sable eyes and a kind smile. Father Timothy.

"She is not a nun yet," Galeren was quick to point out—and not for the first time. "I intend to offer her a different life." He smiled and shrugged. "We shall see what she chooses." Everyone cheered and it made her want to be a part of this family, cheering for love.

"In the meantime," Galeren went on. "She has an enemy and he might show up here. She needs our protection."

Three older men stood out from the crowd and nodded. His uncles, no doubt. She knew immediately which one was Galeren's father.

More cheering went up.

"Are ye a woman of God?" the priest asked her quietly.

"Aye, Father. I spend time with Him every day."

"We will protect the woman of God to the death!" a deadly Highlander called out.

"At the threat of war?" Galeren put to them. They were his kin. He needed their help.

"At the threat of death!" the men shouted.

After another toast, she was introduced to everyone. For the most part, she remembered them.

She was offered a chair by the hearth and given a small cup of wine.

Galeren had left her alone for a moment when his uncle pulled him away for a word, which was likely about her.

She caught sight of Galeren's mother. One could truly not miss her in the large room. Her long locks were plaited down her back, but torchlight found a way to dance over the top of her pale blonde head like a halo in a painting Silene had seen. She drew the eye like a moth to a flame. Her radiance was made even more glorious by her thoughtful smile when she set her cornflower blue eyes on Silene.

She was coming over!

She was petite, like a veil that a strong wind could sweep away. All the women here were beautiful. How could Galeren think her pretty?

"Greetings," his mother said brightly. "Do I call ye Sister or Silene?"

"Silene." Galeren called her Silene. She felt a slight smile tilt her lips. She couldn't help it, she loved when he spoke her name, but it was destroyed by her next thought. What must this woman think of her? Braya Hetherington MacPherson had fought battles over borders while Silene couldn't even resist a man.

"Silene," his mother repeated with a warming smile. "My son appears quite enamored with you."

Silene nodded. Her eyes moved to find him as if they had a will of their own. He stood with some of the most handsome men she'd ever seen, but Galeren stood out with his mother's face and his father's piercing green eyes. There seemed to be more of a smolder in Galeren's gaze, though, he *was* looking at her.

"He is very kind and patient," Silene told her. There was so much more to say about him, but she was sure his mother knew. And besides, Aleysia d'Argentan MacPherson was approaching.

"Tell me," Braya leaned in and looked intently at her. "Would you say he is knightly?"

Her eyes flicked for just an instant, but Silene saw it.

"Oh, aye!" She tried to stop herself from sighing and grew a little lightheaded. "He saved me from men who had vile intentions toward me."

"Very knightly, indeed. Aye, Aly?"

"I would expect nothing less from one of Torin's sons," Aleysia replied.

She was every bit as striking as Braya, but darker. Elysande looked almost exactly like her save for the gray in Aleysia's hair.

"And God used him to save me from an arrow," Silene added.

Both mothers looked equally stunned and impressed. "God used him," Aleysia repeated with a smile. "There is no higher honor."

Braya nodded and the two women giggled as if they were young maidens.

Silene knew she would like these two. And there were more. Julianna Feathers MacPherson, Nicholas MacPherson's wife had red hair like Silene's. It was plaited into a thick braid that hung over her shoulder. It made Silene want to grow her hair again.

"There will be many broken hearts when the lasses learn that Galeren the Bonny has lost his heart to a maiden," Julianna told her. "That is when you will really have to watch your back as well as your front."

The others laughed good-naturedly. Silene wasn't sure if she should actually pray about such a matter as jealousy. She knew she would be miserable if he loved another.

"'Twill not matter if she is to become a nun," Aleysia pointed out. Her voice was so soft and serene, Silene wanted to rest in it. "Or has our dear Galeren stolen your heart?" There was no malice in her tone, only curiosity.

"He has not stolen it, my lady," Silene said softly. "He has asked for it."

"And your reply?" his mother asked.

The small crowd of women suddenly parted and Father Timothy came forward.

"'Tis my turn to speak with her. If ye will excuse us. I willna keep her overly long."

They all agreed and watched quietly as he invited her to the private chapel.

She turned to look over her shoulder at Galeren.

He was surrounded by men, but his face was turned toward hers, his eyes, watching. His mouth, smiling.

"It can get a wee bit overwhelmin' when they are all together," the priest told her while they left the manor house and walked toward a beautiful stone church. Its face and left side were covered in bare vines. All around the church were pale green bushes and a few evergreens.

Silene imagined what it looked like in the beauty of spring.

"Come." Father Timothy opened the heavy, wooden door and ushered her inside.

When she stepped into the foyer, the smell of candlewax wafted through her nostrils. She followed him into the inner sanctuary where hundreds of tiny lights lit the altar. They both knelt at the cross before slipping into one of the stone benches.

"'Tis beautiful here," she told him when he sat next to her.

"Ye are welcome here whenever ye want to be here. The doors are never locked. Ye can also go to the main church in the village square," he paused to chuckle, "but ye willna be alone."

She smiled. He made her feel at ease.

"Galeren has told me much about you, Father."

"All good, I dare hope." He didn't look worried.

She nodded. "All good. He loves you very much."

"Aye. He is a good lad. And he is in love with ye, lass."

Silene shifted on the bench. He certainly didn't waste time. Nor had his mother. "But ye know this already."

Her mouth fell open. What should she say? The truth, of course. This was the man she had wanted to speak to since she began to question her life.

"Aye. I know he loves me."

"How do ye feel aboot it?" His eyes were large and filled with compassion.

"I...I love him, as well," she answered quietly, afraid that her admission would be heard.

"Is he the reason ye didna say yer vows before the church?"

She wanted to tell him about all of it—about not wanting to further aid her uncle and more. But at the center of it all was Galeren.

"Aye. He is the reason. Every time I think I have made my decision, I doubt it is the right one. As I was heading for the church where they waited for me, I could not—my feet did not want to take me inside. They wanted me to run to Galeren."

He smiled. His skin wrinkled and he winked his eye. "Ye know what to do, lass."

She shook her head and began to cry.

"Silene," his soft voice covered her. "God doesna think as we do. If ye love Galeren, marry him and have his babes. Ye can bring them here to pray with ye."

She stopped crying and looked at him. She hadn't considered that. Oh! She would like to do that!

"So, you do not think He is angry with me or with Galeren?"

"No, child. He isna angry with ye. Remember, He is good."

She smiled, feeling the weight lift off her. Galeren trusted this priest's opinions on God, and since it did match with what the priests at Paisley Abbey had told her, she wasn't beyond forgiveness, she chose to believe Father Timothy, too.

They spoke of spiritual things until Galeren came looking for her. "'Tis gettin' late," he told her. "My mother is eager to show ye to yer room and bid ye good eve."

"She will be angry with me fer keepin' ye," Father Timothy told them with a forced worried look.

"I enjoyed our time together, Father. Perhaps another day."

He grinned. "How aboot tomorrow?"

She laughed softly and agreed to breaking fast with him after her morning prayers.

"Did ye speak to him aboot us?" Galeren asked her while they walked back in the moonlight.

"He brought *us* up to me."

Galeren smiled but said nothing.

"He told me you were in love with me."

Now he laughed, but it was more to himself than out loud. "I told him but I didna think he would tell ye."

Aye, she knew it, but to have him admit it…well, it made her swallow back hot tears. It snatched her breath just enough to make her want to cough. Her heart pounded so rapidly it made her want to fall into his arms, the only place she was safe.

"He reminded me that God is good." She smiled at him when he turned to her.

She took his hand, weaving her slender fingers through his bigger, callused ones. "I am free to marry."

She felt his fingers tighten around hers the slightest bit.

"Are ye now?" he asked with mirth dancing across the lilt of his voice and addling her brains.

They played a little, but they both knew how sober the matter of God was.

She nodded and rested her head on his arm. She loved being close to him.

"I wonder how many suitors will call fer yer hand."

She laughed and then lifted her other hand to his arm. "I'm going to miss sleeping with you, Captain."

"Lass," he said, stopping before they reached the torchlight of the manor house. "I would love to bring ye right back to the priest and marry ye tonight, but my vow *was* said. I canna break it now. I fear if I hold ye next to me another night…in a bed, I willna have the strength to resist ye."

"Of course," she agreed immediately. She looked up at him. "When is your vow over?

"In four or five more days. I must check with Father Timothy, and then we will wed, if ye will have me."

She laughed feeling butterflies in her belly. "Of course, I will. But…"

"Aye, love?"

"I know nothing of intimacy," she confessed.

"No?" he asked in a low, doubtful voice. "I feel intimate with ye every time our gazes meet."

Her heart felt about to burst. "I love you, Captain." She wanted to shout it from the walkways for all to hear, but she whispered so only he could.

He took her in his arms and pressed her close. "And I love ye, Silene Sparrow."

He bent his head to hers. She closed her eyes and trembled in his arms as his mouth covered her. He tasted of eagerness and wavering control. His tongue swept like a curious flame over the deepest caverns of her moth His hands moved across her back, drawing her closer as his lips molded with hers.

She groaned in his mouth and they both broke away from the other at the same time. It took every ounce of strength she possessed not to leap back into his arms. He looked as if he were going through the same battle.

She smiled at him and he smiled back. Neither of them saw the pair of eyes watching them from the treetops.

The doors to the first house opened.

"Ah, there you are!" Braya Hetherington MacPherson threw up her hands. "Wait until I get my hands on that priest!"

"Forgive me for keeping Father Timothy," Silene said quickly and softly. "I had many questions. He was quite patient. 'Tis my fault. If you are angry, please let it be with me."

"Oh, I'm not angry with him," his mother promised. "Now come, Silene, my dear. Let me show you to your room."

His mother took her arm and led her forward, walking together. She was a full head shorter that Silene, though she strode as if she were royalty.

Silene told her about her conversation with Father Timothy and her decision not to speak her vows.

"Well then," his mother said. "Are we going to have a marriage celebration here soon?"

Behind them, Galeren walked with his father, the legendary "Shadow" of King Robert the Bruce's army, Torin MacPherson.

"Braya, my sweet," he said to his wife, "our son is required to woo her."

"Woo me?" Silene asked turning to him.

"Aye," his father said. "Woo ye. Court ye. Pay lovin' attention to ye. He must do these things fer ye. Pen ye a sonnet or read to ye."

Silene believed she would like this wooing. "What do I do for him?"

They all stared at her. "Wooin' is fer ye," Galeren's father told her. 'Tis somethin' a suitor does for the lady, to win her heart."

She covered her smile with her hand. She liked Torin MacPherson but she decided that if Galeren was going to woo her, she was going to woo him back.

They brought her to the middle house, which was Torin and Braya's house.

"We break fast in the dining hall at an hour after sunup," Braya told her.

"Oh, dear!" Silene said bringing her hand to her chest. "I promised to break fast with Father Timothy. Forgive me for—"

"We are happy ye and the good Father Timothy are gettin' along so well," Galeren told her. His parents agreed.

"Make no plans for supper though," his mother said, trying to look stern—which made her husband smile as he stared at her. "You will sup with us."

"I would love to. Thank you."

Galeren's father beamed at her. "Ye are courteous. 'Tis a good trait, that."

Now Galeren was smiling at her. "Aye," he agreed.

"Do you know any of the tales of Arthur Pendragon and his knights?" Braya asked her, leading them inside.

"Nay," Silene told her, looking around at the carved wooden

archways, and the well-lit halls. The house was deceptively huge, with a stone stairway and cut flowers everywhere.

"If you stay with him," his mother said, passing her, "you will learn them. Galeren knows every story as well as my husband knows them."

"Then your husband taught him well."

Braya's smile warmed on her. She didn't need to turn around and see the men. She could feel their gladness coming off them.

"Your home is very warm and comforting," she complimented, winning them over.

"You will like your room then," her hostess told her, walking her toward a softly lit hall with three doors. One on the left and two on the right. She brought Silene to the lone door on the left and opened it to a dimly lit room. The only light was from a candle in the window.

"This is our son Lucan's room. He is in England presently."

"Have ye received any word from him?" Galeren asked softly as his mother went inside and lit more candles.

"Not for two years now," his mother told him.

"And where is Lionell?" Galeren asked his parents. "I didna see him in the solar."

"He is oot somewhere." His mother waved her arms and laughed to herself, but there was no mirth in it.

"Let us not speak of this before bed. 'Twill make fer troubled sleep," his father said, stepping forward.

"Aye," his wife agreed with a smile. "We will speak of it tomorrow at supper and both of you shall tell me about my parents."

Silene nodded and looked around as more light fell on the room. She let her gaze rove over the polished wooden walls. The large bed with four wooden posts. Blankets of fur and wool were piled high on the bed. Three heavy, wooden chairs, laden with more furs, a table, and more filled the room.

"I'm moved that you offer this room to me."

Braya looked at Galeren and smiled. "Oh, I almost did not remember. My son has given me your prayer schedule. I have let the guards know that they may see you."

Silene didn't know how to thank them enough for all they had done. She would make herself useful around the house. She knew how to cook. She could clean, launder, sew, all of it. It was all required learning at the priory.

"Well, love, I will let ye sleep," Galeren bid her good eve but neither of them wanted to part.

If Silene's chest could have opened, she was sure her heart would have burst forth and into his arms, perhaps kiss him once more.

Now that she believed she was free to marry Galeren, it was all she could think about.

She bid him good eve with a heavy heart and missed him before he shut the door to the room. They would wait until his vows were fulfilled. But it would be difficult.

CHAPTER EIGHTEEN

MORGANN HEARD RUSTLING above him—in the trees. *They walked in the trees here.* He looked up but he saw nothing in the moonlit branches. Was he losing his mind to the constant cold? It wasn't freezing, but he hadn't moved in hours. The slight chill in the air and his shivering were becoming unbearable.

He was thirsty. Thirst always came first.

He deserved this. Silene had almost died. He was so glad she was alive. He didn't owe this kind of allegiance to anyone, even after what the steward had done for him.

John had found him on the road to Edinburgh. His feet were burned and blistered from the heat below and having no shoes. He hadn't eaten in…in truth, he had no idea, save that it had been a long time. He wasn't used to it. One never grew used to starvation. But he'd gone without eating before. He knew what to expect. He was weary. Bone weary of living.

He was twelve.

John had taken him in and given him back his life. He never went hungry again. He learned how to fight with a sword and shoot an arrow. He grew strong and fit and John put him in his army at fifteen.

He'd known of Captain MacPherson since he'd come to Dundonald. Everyone knew of him and his closest group of men. Morgann used to watch them ride through the inner gates, home from doing the king's duty, champions of Scotland. He'd aspired to be friends with them, men like them. He looked up to the captain and worked hard honing his skills in the hopes of fighting next to him someday.

But it wasn't fighting that brought them together.

It happened one cold winter's day when John and some of his men, including Morgann, rode home from Kilmarnock. They stopped to rest their horses by the river Irvine. John was restless and went to the water's edge. He lost his footing and fell into the freezing water. The current was pulling him farther away from shore. Some of the men jumped in to save him but they, too, were swept away. With no time to think, Morgann jumped in. He swam with the current, directly to the steward and managed to grab hold of him. He swam back with John in his arm, but his limbs were too numb to go back for the other two.

When the captain, who had just returned from hunting their lunch, saw what was happening, he dove into the water and saved the other two men.

John threw Morgann a celebration that night and asked the captain to personally train him.

At first, Morgann had been happy to train with the captain, until John came to him and demanded that he find out if the captain was truly loyal to him. How about his men? Morgann couldn't refuse. So, while he was training under the captain's tutelage, he was also keeping his eyes on the captain and his men.

He didn't report everything to John. Mac and the others questioned many things the steward did, but Morgann never spoke of any of it.

When John ordered Sister Silene's death, Morgann didn't want them to do it. He went with MacKinny and D'Ato to stop them. But the captain would never believe him. He was a traitor. That was all that mattered.

No one came home to the cottage. It was empty, abandoned. He thought he saw a couple going toward a house on the hill. He thought of calling out to them but he'd have all the MacPhersons on him in ten breaths.

Something moved above him. He looked up again, afraid to see one of them aiming an arrow at his heart.

He saw nothing.

Wait!

Those were not branches. They were planks nailed into the boughs. It took ballocks for someone to run around so high up. One wrong move…

The captain had told them that he and the other children at the stronghold were taught to climb and run in the trees. The captain had taught some of his men. Morgann and Padrig had never done it.

He caught a movement in the canopy. "Who are ye?" he called up.

Silence. And then… a kitten's meow? What the—? Someone or something stepped over a few more of the planks and branches drooping closer.

Finally, Mac fell from the low branches and strode to Morgann. His dark eyes flashed like fire while he looked Morgann over. "What are ye doin' here?" he asked. "Bound to a tree?"

Morgann was too afraid to tell him.

No. What's the worst Mac could do? Kill him? He'd prefer it to what his life would be like now.

"I betrayed the captain."

Mac stepped closer. Close enough for Morgann to see the captain's wee kitten tucked in Mac's cloak. "How did ye betray him?"

"What are *ye* doin' here?" Morgann demanded, trying to avoid what was to come.

"Whatever 'tis," Mac said with a smirk. "I'm not the one tied up."

"I'm cold and hungry, Mac."

The scarred, scruffy Highlander pulled out a knife. He hooked the blade under the rope and, with two strokes, cut Morgann free.

Morgann fell to his knees because his legs were numb. He could not rise.

Mac pulled a blanket from his saddlebag and tossed it around Morgann's shoulders.

"We canna build a fire, but we can take shelter in the house."

Morgann looked up at him. "Why are ye helpin' me?"

"It canna be all that bad if the captain didna kill ye."

He reached down by the side of the door and pushed a black rock over to reveal a metal key. He winked at Morgann and inserted the key into the door. "The captain told us aboot the keys a few years ago."

The door opened. Morgann's heart was racing so hard he thought it might fall from his mouth. If any of the patrolling guards saw them, they would be shot.

They entered the cottage and without lighting any candles, found the bed. Mac fell onto it, holding up his palm when Morgann would have protested. "Ye were tied to a tree a few moments ago. Be thankful ye have walls around ye and a roof over yer head."

Morgann said nothing. He had no defense.

"Now, tell me of yer betrayal," Mac insisted while he let Daffodil out of her shelter.

"Can we sleep and—"

"No," the scar-faced Highlander cut him off. "Tell me what I wish to know."

Morgann sat up on the floor and told him about his original loyalty to John Stewart and how it had moved to the captain. "I wanted to tell the men not to shoot her, Mac. I did tell them. But they wouldna listen to me. They didna care that she was a novice."

Mac bolted up. "Silene was shot? Does she live?"

"Aye." Morgann let him know. "Followin' the steward's orders, Jack MacKinny shot an arrow at her but missed."

"MacKinny!" Mac's gaze went dark. "That bastard!"

"Why did the steward order her death so quickly?" he asked Morgann. "How does he not know she wasna taken against her wishes and that is why she didna speak her vows?"

Morgann shrugged his shoulders. His duty was not to ask questions of his lord, but he would ask them of the captain's close friend.

"What are ye doin' here lookin' over the stronghold wall. Who were ye watchin'?"

"The captain," Mac told him truthfully. "The others and I traveled separately. I didna know whether or not he had arrived. I wouldna try to get into the stronghold at night."

"Where are the others?" Morgann asked, afraid and ashamed to see them.

"They will be here. Enough questions. I'll do the askin'. Tell me everythin'."

Morgann told him about how MacKinny almost succeeded. "The captain killed him."

"But he let ye live."

"Aye."

"Ye are fortunate. I would have killed ye."

Morgann nodded. "She told me she was goin' to pray that all goes well fer me."

"Aye. She is thoughtful."

"All the more reason I hate myself fer my part in this."

"We will discuss it in the mornin'," Mac said. "Get some sleep.

Morgann closed his eyes to the dark, cold house but at least he was warmer.

He fell asleep and dreamed of running.

The next morning, he opened his eyes to the tip of a blade at his throat and two pairs of green eyes staring down at him.

"Mornin', Captain," he said nervously. He looked at the kitten tucked into the captain's neck to calm himself.

"Wake up. Ye willna sleep all day."

"Cap," said Mac with a plate of food in his lap. "He says he betrayed ye."

"And her," the captain added. Mac agreed.

"Captain, I wanted to stop them from killin' her," Morgann finally told him, but it was too late.

"I think he should die fer his crime."

Mac shrugged. "Mayhap, but he is a soldier in the House of Stewart. We will have to give account before a dozen councils if we kill him."

The captain looked at Morgann as if he wanted to kill him with his bare hands.

Morgann rose from the floor.

"Where is the food? I will prepare ye somethin', Captain."

"And mayhap poison me?"

Morgann shook his head. He wanted to get away from the captain before he drove the man to run him through. He could see it in his eyes. Murder, violence, unforgiveness.

"Where are the others?" Morgann heard him ask Mac.

Morgann lowered his head. He felt like the lowest worm. What would Will and Padrig say when they heard what he had done? Who would believe that Morgann cared for them all, even more than he cared for John? They had taken him in like a brother. He had fought by their sides more than once. There had been times when, before bed, he thought he would give his life for theirs.

His secret had weighed on him heavily, making him somber and serious.

He was sorry. He was sorry and he wanted to tell her.

He heard the captain and Mac moving behind him. When he turned, he saw them cloaked and hooded and leaving the cottage.

Morgann followed them. When he stepped outside, he saw Will and Padrig riding up the hill. His heart sank. He wasn't always sure about Will, but Padrig was loyal to the captain.

The hulking Highlander was going to kill him. Morgann began to panic. He didn't want to be here to hear his sentence, deserved or not. He wanted to run. He could run for a horse, get the—

The captain turned his head and looked directly at him as if he could hear his thoughts. The warning glint in his eyes convinced Morgann not to make the captain chase him.

He remained still and waited for his punishment.

They brought the horses to the small shelter behind the cottage. When they returned, Will greeted Morgann with a playful slap and tossed a travel bag to him. "Take that to Sister Silene later, will ye? 'Tis her clothes."

Padrig came to stand beside his brother. "How did ye get here so fast?"

"I traveled close to the captain," Morgann answered.

The captain chuckled with malice. "Is that what ye call it?"

"Call what?" Padrig queried.

"I..." The captain was truly going to make him confess to them. He swallowed and waited a moment more, hoping the captain would intercede. But he didn't.

"I...I was traveling with Jack MacKinny—" They smiled. "And Richard D'Ato." Their smiles faded. They didn't like D'Ato. They often spoke of him gathering information for the English king, though he was a Scot.

"What were ye two doin' with him?" Will asked, then looked around as he walked away toward the cottage. "Where is MacKinny anyway?"

"He is dead," Morgann told them quietly.

Padrig stared at him. Will stopped in his tracks. "Who killed him?"

Morgann ran his hand down his face. With each question he answered, he was getting closer to the pit from which there was no escape.

"The captain shot him after he tried to kill Sister Silene."

Padrig's eyes opened wide like twin chasms of darkness and the promise of pain. "Is she hurt?"

The captain shook his head.

"MacKinny had orders to kill her," Will said.

"Aye."

"Ye rode with him and that other traitor, D'Ato."

"Aye," Morgann heard himself confirm while he watched the captain enter the cottage. Morgann looked up to him. He was sorry he was weak.

They all entered the cottage and stood near the hearth fire the captain had prepared.

"Who were the orders from?" Will asked him, then answered his own question. "John."

His gaze met the captain's. "He wants her dead, though he doesna tell us this himself. That he told Morgann says much."

Padrig nodded and stared into Morgann's eyes, unsettling his bones. "What did ye do to stop them?"

"I pleaded with them."

"MacKinny shot his arrow," the captain told them, rubbing his chin on the kitten. "By God's goodness, he missed."

Will fell into a chair. "So, ye are the steward's man? What else did ye do fer him?"

"I...ehm...he wanted me to report to him all that the captain and any of ye said against him."

"Ye spied fer him. On us." Mac, who was quiet up until now, spoke up.

"In the beginnin' 'twas so," Morgann confessed. "But things changed. Ye became my brothers. My reports to him were always the same. That ye are all loyal to him and havena wavered." He looked at the captain. "Especially ye, Sir. He mostly wants to know of ye but I have never told him anythin'."

The captain stared at him.

"What d'ye think we should do with ye?" Mac asked.

"Whatever ye will," Morgann told him. "But I would appreciate it if after ye kill me, one of ye would tell Sister Silene that I am sorry."

"I will tell her," the captain said, "after I kill ye."

GALEREN PULLED HIS sword from its sheath and pointed it at Morgann's throat. Mac moved an inch forward. He raised his palm to stay Galeren's hand.

"Cap, have mercy. He is but a pup."

Aye, a pup. Galeren withdrew his blade. He wasn't about to kill a pup. He wanted to make the lad shyte in his breeches. To let him know he would never be taken back into the fold.

"Ye may go," he said. "Ye are free. I willna pursue ye."

"Where am I to go?"

"To him," Galeren answered with a streak of menace in his voice. "Tell him I let ye live because ye were followin' his orders. *Him*, I will kill if he comes here."

"But Cap—" Morgann persisted.

"Come on, lad," Mac warned and pulled him out of the cottage.

Will laughed and closed his eyes. "Who would have ever believed 'twould be Mac who cared fer the traitor?"

Galeren swung his gaze to Will. "Ye think I should have killed him?"

"I think ye did what ye had to do, Cap."

The door opened and Mac appeared. "He doesna want to leave."

Galeren held up his hand and turned to Padrig. "Tell me, what did ye learn?"

"The steward is puttin' together a regiment of men. We dinna know the purpose, fer he cast us all oot. But almost all the men refuse to fight against ye, Cap. So, he is hirin' mercenaries. He is comin' at this harder than we thought."

Galeren shook his head. "He is predictable. Did ye hear anythin' aboot the church?"

"Aye," Will grinned. "The church denounced him, accusin' him of trickery and lyin', sayin' his niece was a nun when she was a novice."

"I see," Galeren said, not knowing whether to be happy the steward lost his place on the council or not. "We will be prepared fer whatever John brings."

"If he hires mercs," Mac told him, "then we kill him. When the mercs find oot they are not gettin' paid, they will disperse."

"Killin' the high steward and runnin' will make us outlaws."

"Mac," Galeren said, looking at his friend through the corners of his eyes. "Ye seem bent of remindin' me of the laws."

"I dinna want ye swingin' at the end of a noose, Cap. We will have to return to save ye, and 'tis likely that one of us will get caught."

Galeren didn't argue. He didn't want that either.

He wanted a life, a future with Silene. He knew now how love changes a warrior. It makes him care about living and not dying on the battlefield. He hadn't slept last night. He'd tried not to think about her in bed alone just across the hall. His body ached for her. The muscles in his arms trembled for her. They did, even now.

"Captain?"

"Aye, Padrig?"

"We also saw Lord Birchet. He was packin' up everythin' he had in Dundonald, includin' his daughter, and takin' them home."

"Good," Galeren said, happy to hear it. "I'm sure she will find a man who deserves her."

He laughed briefly and the others joined him.

"Silene is a much better choice fer ye, Captain," Will said.

"Thank ye," Galeren answered. It meant much to him that his men thought he was deserving of her.

He wanted to see her but when he'd knocked on her door this morning, she was already gone.

He was happy she liked Father Timothy and even more grateful that Father Timothy convinced her that she'd made an acceptable decision.

He would make her his wife in four days. It was getting harder to wait.

"I am returnin' to the stronghold," he told the men. "Come with me and eat at my kin's table. 'Tis big enough. The three of ye can come back here tonight and sleep. I have been told that Jamie the shepherd who lives here is off on a visit to his brother in Perth. He willna be back until next month."

They left the cottage with him and headed down the hill, and back to level ground and the stronghold gates.

Galeren looked around for Morgann but he didn't see him anywhere. Had he gone through the forest? Galeren hated to admit it, but he hoped not. Morgann wouldn't make it a quarter of a mile before he set something off in the trees.

Where was Silene? He checked the church when they finally opened the gate. No one was inside. Where would Father Timothy have taken her?

"Are ye goin' to marry Sister Silene?" Will asked him.

"Aye, I am. And dinna call her Sister. She is just Silene."

"But," Will challenged, "ye can have yer pick of so many lasses. A different beauty every night."

"I only want her."

Will finally accepted that the captain was in love with one lass and walked on ahead with Mac.

"Is yer father still the friendliest of the three brothers?" Padrig put to him as they drew near the manor houses.

"He isna the friendliest," Galeren told him with a sly smile. "He only makes ye believe he is. That is how he brought down the most English strongholds in the kingdoms. From the inside."

"Like our young Mr. Bell," Mac pointed out.

"Not quite," Galeren disagreed as they entered his father's house.

He spread his gaze over his parents in the dining hall. Father Timothy and Silene sat with them. When he saw her, he smiled and went to her, as if pulled by unseen tethers.

She looked especially lovely today in a forest green tabard, belted at the waist, and reaching to her knees with hose underneath and boots. Her habit was put away.

"Good mornin', lass." He knew he looked pitifully happy to see her. He didn't care. "How were yer prayers?"

"Calming," she told him, smiling, "and thankful."

"Ye are a blessed man to be takin' Silene as yer wife, Galeren," Father Timothy told him happily.

"I know, Father."

"She has to be special to have won our son's heart," his mother said as she beamed at Silene. Silene made a good impression then. He hoped his kin had done the same.

He pulled out a chair and sat beside Silene at the table. His men sat at the table after Galeren reintroduced them to his kin. He watched her notice his men were sitting with her. Her premonition had been incorrect.

"Thank you for retrieving my bag from Dundonald, Will," she said with a wide smile after Galeren gave it to her. "I have a special dress in here that I did not want to lose."

He winked when her eyes caught his.

"How is Morgann?" she asked on a low voice in case he didn't want his parents to know about the lad.

"Free. I sent him off."

"Oh."

She looked off to the side and bit her fingernail.

"What is it, love?" he asked.

"I had hoped to bid him farewell."

He blinked. Here she was, betrayed by him, and still wanting to bid him farewell.

"Silene," his mother interrupted his thoughts. "What do you think of wee Daffodil? Is she not the most precious baby kitten you have ever seen?"

"Aye," Silene laughed softly reaching up to stroke the kitten on Galeren's shoulder. "I have come to love—oh!" She turned to him. "The children!"

"There were tears," Mac told her. "But they canna care fer Daffodil now, and they know that. They unselfishly gave her up fer her own good."

Silene stared up at Galeren. "You trained them well, Captain."

"I worry if they will be well," he whispered.

She made a note to say extra prayers for Alex and Margaret. "I think you will see them again," she told him.

He smiled. "That is good news to hear, my love."

She moved a little closer to him. "I like when you call me your love."

He wanted to kiss her, but he thought it would make her uncomfortable in the sight of everyone. He dipped his mouth and kissed her shoulder instead. "Have I told ye how beautiful ye are to me, *my love*," he whispered near her ear instead.

She blushed and kept her head down. But she was smiling.

Galeren looked around, happier than he'd been in many years. He was home with the woman he loved, his kin, and his friends around him.

Where was his youngest brother, Lionell?

Galeren hadn't seen him last night. He remembered when he was here last, Lionell stayed out late and slept in even later.

"Where is Lionell?" he asked his parents.

"My guess is he is asleep," his mother told him, sipping her warm milk, a drink she relished from her reiver days. She didn't look up from it when Galeren rose from his seat, handed Daffodil to Silene, and strode for the stairs. They hadn't seen Lionell last eve and if Galeren didn't do something, they wouldn't see him today either.

He arrived at Lionell's door at the same time a serving girl was bringing a jug of water and a basin. Galeren took the water from her and, with a grin, dumped it on his sleeping brother's face.

Lionell bolted upright, roused so alarmingly from his dreams. He swung his arm before him, as if he were wielding a sword. His other sleeve was empty, hanging limply at his side. He opened his heavy lids, revealing vibrant, green, bloodshot eyes.

"Galeren? What the hell are ye doin' back here so soon and what d'ye want?"

Galeren grinned at him. "Greetin's Lionell. That is a good question. What I want is ye at the mornin' table every day and on the practice field after that. I want ye to come to the table now and meet the lass I love and plan to wed in just a few days. Mostly, I want ye to not give up on yer life."

"I canna fight, Brother, or d'ye not know?" He turned his empty sleeve toward Galeren.

"I know, but there is still much ye can do.

"Aye," Lionell laughed and cupped his groin. "'Tis good I can still f—"

"Get oot of bed," Galeren commanded. "Get cleaned up and come to the table. When ye are there, ye will watch yer tongue or I will take ye outdoors and knock yer teeth oot."

Lionell glared at him. "I am not one of yer soldiers, Captain. Get oot of my room."

"If ye are not at the table shortly, I will throw ye oot of the house, Lionell. Dinna push me to see how far I will go. I will go far. I'm goin' to help ye whether ye want me to or not. Best give in to me now."

His brother lifted an auburn brow and snarled. "Never."

Chapter Nineteen

"Lionell lost his arm in battle last year," Braya told Silene and waited for more warm milk. "He does not know how to live his life anymore. My poor husband has tried everything to help him. Bors has also tried."

Silene looked at Father Timothy. What did he think Lionell needed?

He gave her an understanding smile. "Ye can add yer prayers to mine."

She nodded and smiled at him.

A loud clang resounded in the dining hall.

"What was that?" Silene began to rise.

"'Tis just them fightin'." Mac took her wrist until she sat again. "That is why he gave ye the kitty to hold."

They tried to carry on conversations between the thunderous noises coming from down the hall.

No one was doing anything about it.

Silene thought a one-armed man would not be a very good fighter. What was Galeren doing to him? "Perhaps we should—"

"No," Galeren's father shook his head. "Mayhap this is what Lionell needs."

After a few more startling bangs that nearly brought down the walls, it finally grew quiet.

"Highlanders fight, lass," Father Timothy advised her with a wink.

Highlanders fought. Aye, it seemed they did. Galeren's mother and his aunts and uncles had all fought to stay alive or keep what was theirs.

"I understand," she told the priest.

A few moments later, Galeren entered the hall. His luminescent, golden locks were more disheveled around his face. His léine was torn at the arm and the left side of his jaw was turning purple.

He returned to his place at the table and smiled at his father. "His right hook is still efficient." They laughed and Galeren turned back to her as if nothing had happened. "Lionell will be here shortly."

"Are you hurt?" Silene asked him as Daffodil jumped back into his arms.

"No, but I'm goin' to teach him to hurt me."

"Why?"

"Because he needs to be able to fight. From as young as we can remember, we are taught to protect our lives and the lives of those we love. 'Twas pushed into our heads over and over until we put away fear of dyin' in battle—because battle is a way of life fer a Scot. Lionell lost his ability to fight. He is losin' his ability to live because of such a loss. I'm goin' to help him."

She swallowed and held back the tears she would shed. "And I will pray for him with Father Timothy."

She wanted to kiss his beautiful lips, breathe his breath. She would kiss his dimpled cheek, his bruised jaw. But there were too many people watching.

She had no idea how much longer she could resist falling into his arms, his bed.

She thought of being naked and intimate with him and it didn't frighten or embarrass her as much as she thought it would.

It excited her and made her long for him in ways she was not familiar.

She didn't tell Father Timothy about her sexual desires. Perhaps she should tell Galeren. He was the levelheaded one. He would know what to do.

But in the meantime, his closeness at the table, whispering things in her ear—well, it was positively thrilling. Every time his thigh touched hers, she felt a lick of fire up her spine. If she gazed at his masculine profile, she found herself wanting to crawl into his lap and kiss him senseless.

Everyone grew quiet. Silene turned to see why and saw a man standing at the entrance to the dining hall.

He was starkly handsome with russet hair shot through with broad strokes of gold that fell past his shoulders. His mouth was full and sulky and cut in two places. One cut was beginning to swell.

He wore a beige léine with black trousers and bare feet. One sleeve of his léine was empty and tucked into his belt. He looked around the hall and nodded in greeting to Mac and the other men, after greeting his kin.

"I'm only stayin' long enough to greet ye, Mum, Father, Father."

His parents and Father Timothy smiled at him.

"And who is this short-haired beauty?" He set his eyes on her, his smile charming. Silene's belly flipped. She smiled while Galeren introduced her.

"Are you certain you cannot stay?" she asked him.

"Mayhap I can be persuaded."

Oh, dear, but Lionell was astonishingly pleasing to look at. Like Galeren, he resembled both his parents, but Lionell favored his mother. He also had a silver tongue and boldness that exceeded Galeren.

"Well then," she told him playfully. She knew what his mother wanted. "Let me make a plea on behalf of your kin. Do not be in a rush to go."

He tossed her an incredulous grin and then moved toward the door to leave.

She wouldn't ask again, but she didn't think he wanted to leave.

"Lionell," Father Timothy called to him. "Stay to please an old man."

For a moment, Lionell seemed to have decided and took another step toward the exit. Then he stopped and returned to the table. He took a seat near Bors. Everyone was quiet but relieved, especially Galeren. He felt the tension in his body leave and he relaxed close to her.

"Lionell," Silene said, drawing his attention. "Do you know that your name means little lion?"

"I didna know," he quipped. "But Galeren knows now, after tryin' to drag me from my bed."

"But here ye are," Galeren said with a smirk.

Somewhere to the right, Will laughed, and then everyone else did, including Lionell.

Soon, he accepted a cup of mead and shared a quiet word with Mac. His eyes found her. He smiled and then glanced at his brother. "Where did ye find him, Miss Sparrow?"

"Silene, please," she corrected. "And on the cliffs in Bamburgh. I had been there praying. He had come to take me to my uncle, the high steward."

"Go on," Lionell urged.

"Aye, please do," his mother agreed.

Silene smiled and glanced at Galeren. His apologetic expression changed into a smile even more radiant that his brother's. "He was quite patient with me having to stop several times a day for my prayers."

"Several times a day fer…prayers?" Lionell looked on the verge of bursting into laughter.

"They are verra important to her," Galeren told him on a warning growl for Lionell not to laugh.

"Verra well," Lionell defended in a friendly tone. "But who prays several times a day and canna do so in her head?"

Will chuckled while he chewed his bread. This time, Padrig kicked him hard under the table.

"A lass preparin' to be a sister in the church," his father answered Lionell's question.

Lionell's already large eyes opened wider as they fell on her and then on Galeren. "Brother, ye took a lass from God?"

"Lionell," Father Timothy said gently, trying to ease the high tension in the dining hall. "Ye speak of what ye dinna ken."

Silene tried to remember to breathe. She was finding it difficult, but she closed her eyes for a moment and held on.

"Of course," Lionell said, unconvincingly.

"I am going to raise bairns to know Him even more than I do." She smiled at him and bit into a fig. She demanded her hand not to shake.

Father Timothy and Galeren were smiling at her. They all were.

"Lionell, I pray that you are in their lives, in good spirit and health."

"Alas," he pouted. "Ye ask fer too much, lass."

"You are a MacPherson, son of the clever warrior who infiltrated enemy armies and brought down more castles than anyone else. Remember the stock from which you come. No one ever gave up."

She caught Torin MacPherson's soulful gaze on her. He smiled. She felt a little lightheaded.

The feeling didn't change throughout the day when she was busy meeting the rest of Galeren's family. She strolled outside with Galeren and Daffodil beneath the wooden walkways high above the ground.

His uncles were the kind of handsome that makes a woman go warm. Especially Cain. He was still rugged and fit from, she guessed, practicing his swordplay every day—and playing with his grandchildren.

Galeren shared a brief, private word with them about her uncle and then took her to meet Cain's son, Tristan, and his new wife, Rose. They had arrived last eve just before Galeren had brought her home. She and Rose got along right away and promised to find each other later.

Galeren had Lionell sent for and she watched Galeren practice with him. Lionell swung his sword wildly, as if he were off balance. Galeren pointed it out and had him start with the very basic of swings. Galeren was patient, as he'd been with her. It made her heart swell with pride over him.

She spoke with him between meeting up with everyone.

"What d'ye think of everythin' so far?"

She looked up and around at the people coming from or going to the market.

"'Tis like nothing I have ever seen before. No one is begging for food. No one is hungry or alone." Her gaze settled on his and he nodded.

"As long as we are blessed with enough, we share what we have."

"I feel happy here," she told him. "Like this could be our home."

"D'ye know," he asked, coming closer while they walked, "sometimes when ye smile, yer nose bunches up just a wee bit and yer tongue parts yer lips. The sight of ye and yer fiery hair fallin' over yer brow drives me mad."

She pressed her side against him. She wanted to be even closer—inside him.

She coiled her fingers through his. "Sometimes when you look at me, I can see myself there, happy and adored in your eyes."

"Aye."

"You are everything I have ever wanted," she told him. "God heard my prayers and prepared us for this day."

He kissed the top of her head. "There is somethin' I wish to show ye," he said and pulled her away by the hand.

"Where are we going?" she asked on a melody of laughter.

"Ye shall see." He hurried with her back to the middle manor house and pulled her to the stairs.

She let him lead her forward. Her feet felt as if they weren't touching the ground. If she had wings, she would have taken off.

They ran up the stairs and through a small hall to a door. Galeren opened it, letting sunlight spill into the hall in golden rays. Some of them fell over him.

The bright doorway led outside to the wooden walkways high above the ground.

"Come." He held out his hand and Silene thought he looked like an angel, ethereal and beautiful, illuminated in the shafts of light.

She took his hand and stepped out into the full sunlight.

They were about twenty feet up, above the world. She looked to her left and saw the forest colored in greens and golds and oranges.

"This way." He pulled her along in a quarter of a circle. Then entered the tower of the next house and came out over the forest and the village. They met some of his kin on the way around, including Elysande.

When Silene looked out at the view, she gasped at its beauty. "Oh, Galeren, 'tis breathtaking."

"As ye are, my love," he told her, stirring her blood with the huskiness of his voice. He took her hand and drew her closer.

Her heart soared. She could not wait to be his wife. She put her arms around his neck and laughed, feeling Daffodil there. He kissed her laughter from her mouth and closed his arms around her.

He swept her away on waves of pleasure and desire. Her body longed for more of him, and thoughts of his sleek, hard body made her want to touch him.

He broke their kiss to kiss his way to her ear. His strained breath fell hot and scintillating against her lobe. "Ye make me feel feral," he told her thickly.

"Are you trying to frighten me? Because you are not." She smiled when he closed his teeth around the pulse at her throat. He didn't hurt her. He held her close and she gasped at the hardness between his legs. He felt as if he were made of iron. "How will it…"

"It gets even harder," he told her against her ear. "Like a rod and I put it inside ye. Here." He pressed himself between her legs.

She realized she knew nothing about living a fleshly life. She swallowed.

"Dinna be afraid. I will be considerate of ye."

She smiled at him, not caring if her face was aflame. "Thank you, and I am not afraid. I will be with you, so I have nothing to fear."

She watched him smile from the moment it began in his deep green eyes. She could feel his happiness, almost like a tangible thing. Her words pleased him.

"Three more days. Will ye wait?"

"Aye," she told him. "I will wait."

She looked out over the hills and clung to him, and he to her.

"Why did you vow six years?" she asked. "How old were you?"

"Ten and eight."

"Oh. Was it difficult?"

"Some days were more difficult than others," he admitted.

She appreciated his honesty. "But six years?"

"I had to break its hold on me. I had become consumed with it. I didna want any master but one. I knew that if I vowed somethin' to Him, I would keep it. So, I made my promise fer six years."

She remembered to breathe. "I'm thankful the time is almost over."

His dimple reappeared while his gaze hardened. "As am I."

"We can do this."

He raised an eyebrow. "We? D'ye find it difficult as well?"

"Difficult not to be your wife, to lay in your bed and share myself with you, to wake up every day knowing I get to spend it with you? Aye. I find it difficult, indeed."

He began to pull her back, but she pushed away—out of his reach. He took a step forward.

In this moment, he did indeed appear feral, like a bird of prey swooping down on her.

She held her neck where he bit her and something below her belly flipped and spread pleasure throughout her body.

"We must part," she told him. "Or we will—"

He nodded, his brows dipping lower and casting shadows on his eyes.

She slipped through the door and then fell against it and bit her lip until it bled.

She didn't understand these feelings plaguing her. She felt warm and raw. Even the wind outside pained her. She couldn't think straight. Her belly constantly flipped. She wanted to feel his mouth on her. All of her, devouring her. She wanted his hands and other parts of his body on her. She wanted to take him to his bed and bind him to her. One flesh cleaved together.

She was afraid that iron shaft would hurt her. She had no idea why she still desired it in some primal way. Intercourse was the one thing about which she was never taught.

She needed to know.

She couldn't ask his mother. She would not feel right speaking about intimate things with a man's mother. She didn't see anything wrong with asking his cousin, Elysande, though. Aye! She would know best.

She didn't want to do it. How would she even bring it up? She wiped her brow and continued down the stairs. When she reached the first landing, she wasn't sure whose house she was in.

She entered the great hall and spotted Will and Padrig sharing a drink. She went to them, intending to get directions.

"What is a lovely lass doin' wanderin' aboot the halls unescorted?" Will asked.

"I am lost. One wrong turn and you could end up in another house." She laughed softly. She missed traveling with them, getting to know them.

"How have you brothers been?"

"We are well," Padrig said in a gentle tone and a smile to match. "Yerself?"

She lifted a dark red brow at them. Hmm. "May I ask you something?"

"Of course." They nodded.

"I have been feeling…ehm." She shifted in the tunic she'd changed into after her bag was returned to her thanks to these two. She tried again. "I have been…feeling…" she blew out a deep breath. She just couldn't do it. She couldn't ask them about such private things.

"Have ye seen Elysande?"

Padrig blinked. "What aboot what ye are feelin', lass?"

"Oh, never mind that." She laughed nervously and waved her hand.

Will pointed to the main exit directly ahead. She thanked them and hurried toward the exit to seek out Elysande.

She found her in the huge garden behind the houses, busy picking apples and some small pumpkins.

"Should you be doing all that bending?" Silene asked her and bent to help.

Elysande smiled. "I dinna hurt the babe by doin' a wee bit of work. I keep myself strong."

They talked about Elysande's husband and how he'd taken the news that he was going to be a father again. "He is quite proud of himself."

"For what?" Silene asked.

"Fer what, indeed." Elysande laughed. "My swollen belly is a sign of his virility."

Aye. She was the one to ask. "Ehm, Elysande? May I ask you a question?"

"Aye," Elysande allowed and bent to another two fallen apples.

"Lately, being…being around Galeren is sparking…feelings in me which I do not understand."

"Oh?" Elysande straightened and smiled at her. "What are ye feelin'? Can ye describe it?"

Silene could feel her face burning. "I was never taught…I am feeling like my senses are heightened. I…I see things with more clarity. I feel like I can hear better and I find myself listening for his voice. The sound of him—the sight of him makes my heart quicken. When he kisses me, I want more, but I do not know what it is I want."

Elysande invited her to her home, a large manor house connected by the walkway to the first house.

"What ye are feelin' is natural attraction and love fer him."

"What should I do about it?"

Elysande gave her a furtive smile that made her look even more beautiful. "Marry him. And do it soon."

"HE BETRAYED ME," John the Steward said while he thrust his arms into his coat. "I want his head and I want to be the one who takes it." He'd given his men two days to find Galeren and Sister Silene. When they found nothing, John knew he had to do it himself.

If John's captain was smart, and John knew he was, he'd be on his way to Invergarry by now to hide out in his family's stronghold. John was going to have to find a way to get into the fortress. Fortunately, he had Morgann Bell at Galeren's side and another means of information he hoped could be trusted. He would soon find out.

"What about the girl?" Alphonsus asked, already in his extra robes for the cool day.

John slanted his smile at the man. He didn't have to say, for his lust showed in his eyes. "She ruined my chance to sit on the council, because she wants a man inside her. I'm goin' to show her what an error her decision was."

"They say the MacPherson stronghold is impenetrable," the priest said. "How are we going to get in if they are inside?"

"I have some surprises under my belt. A hellcat, fer whom the captain isna prepared. She guarantees she can capture him fer me. We just have to get her to Invergarry."

"And her name?" the priest asked.

"Ah, that is my concern. Ye will find oot soon enough. I trust no one."

"Not even me?" Alphonsus asked him, looking insulted.

"Especially not ye," John told him, not giving a damn what the priest thought of him.

Chapter Twenty

She would be Galeren's wife in two days. Time could not pass quickly enough, though Galeren's kin kept Silene busy between her prayers, which Father Timothy told her could be shortened, now that she was no longer to be a nun, to however many times a day she wanted to say them. She found herself saying the ritualistic, structured prayers less and just speaking to God the way she would Father Timothy, more. She was happier at the stronghold than she could ever remember being.

With so many relatives, she didn't see Galeren as much as she would have liked.

She wooed him by baking hot apple and pumpkin pies. She darned all of the clothes his cousins, Adela and Geva, found for her in his room that needed repair. She hadn't minded sewing up holes in his hose, fixing tattered hems on his léines or coats. It really was nothing, but he smiled when he saw everything piled neatly on his bed and listened while she and Elysande told him how much she had done.

"Ye have my sincerest thanks, my love," he had said and then asked Elysande to leave. Of course, his cousin refused his request.

Pity. Silene wanted time alone with him. She sighed now thinking about it. They sat in the dining hall for the last meal of the day. She stared at him while he ate and laughed with his family and his friends.

She was thankful to be dining with the men. Thankful her feeling that she would never dine with them again had been wrong. Were they all wrong? Did she rely too much on them? What did it matter? She was here, in his stronghold, protected as he'd promised.

"How is Daffodil?" she asked when his gaze slipped to hers as if he could feel her watching. His smile deepened.

"Loud." He laughed softly. "At night. Until I put her with me in my bed."

Silene wished he was putting *her* into his bed. She didn't blame the cat.

"I couldna bring her," he continued, "so she could walk my kin's supper table and try to eat from everyone's plates."

Silene nodded and laughed, "Although I do not believe your mother would mind." She sobered a moment later. "I miss the children."

"Aye, as do I," he agreed, quieting.

"Galeren," she said, taking on a somber tone, "I am happy you brought me here, but if not for me, *you* would not be here. You would be at Dundonald with my uncle's children, teaching them to be good, honorable adults."

"They are not mine, lass, though I wish they were."

"I will give you children," she promised.

"Aye." His smile returned. "As many of our own that we can stand makin'."

She felt her face go flush. She smiled and looked away. Many children—here with him. Her heart flipped at the thought.

"Captain," she said softly. "Perhaps after supper you would not mind taking a walk with me."

His smile warmed her heart and other hidden parts of her. His gaze softened and glimmered with affection. "I wouldna mind."

She nodded. She'd been embarrassed at first to seek out time with him, but she saw Braya smile at her from her seat beyond Lionell. The women here were strong and bold and feminine. They admired strength in each other. They would not think her odd for being bold.

Galeren had tried to see her a number of times, but their meetings never lasted overly long before someone found them and pulled her away.

He'd been patient, understanding that his "kin" wanted to get to know her. But she could see the longing in his gaze for her. Tonight, she wanted to give him that time back. If he wanted to kiss her, she would allow it. She might even kiss him first. She smiled thinking of it.

His dimple deepened across the table.

"Can ye both stop tryin' to make me ill?" Lionell drawled and swept his mane of hair off his face. Having only one hand made it impossible for him to tie it back or braid it. So, he left it hanging around his face.

"Are ye sure 'tis not the way ye fought today that sickens ye, little lion?"

"I told ye I was no good at it," Lionell argued.

"No one is good when they first begin a thing," Galeren said, showing who was the wiser brother. "That is what practice is fer."

When they all retired to the solar for a drink, Galeren took her hand and led her outside.

The weather was surprisingly warm but Galeren still put his arm around her while they walked.

"I have missed ye, my love," he told her. "I dinna know why I thought 'twould be less hectic here."

She smiled against his chest. "'Twill settle down soon. Your kin are happy for you. You have been chaste since you were ten and eight. Your mother thought you might be fulfilling your calling to be a priest."

"A priest!" He laughed. "No. My callin' was to be a soldier. I wanted to be the best and havin' a lass in my life and couplin' on my mind would have likely gotten me killed. I know by lovin' ye that if I ever go into battle again, I will fear dyin' and leavin' ye."

"I do not want you to fight anymore battles, Galeren!" she cried out. "Please!"

He didn't answer. He was still a captain in King David's army. He couldn't just walk away from his duty.

"Galeren, will you always be a captain?"

"No, love, but I am still young. No doubt there will be more battles ahead fer our weary countrymen."

"They will need you," she guessed out loud.

"Aye, they might."

"I will pray that they never need you again."

She heard his heart accelerate, and his breath shorten. He kissed the top of her head.

She stopped walking and saw that they were in the stronghold's gardens. They were alone.

She felt his fingers under her chin to tip her face to his.

"I canna wait to be yer husband," he ground out huskily over her lips.

"I cannot wait to be your wife." She pulled him in and parted her lips to welcome him.

She trembled against him as his arms came around her and encircled her in his strength.

His lips molded to hers with heat. His tongue plunged softly inside and moved over hers in a dance as ancient as time.

She never wanted to leave his arms again. His kiss sparked this flame inside her that burned all day and night.

"Has anyone seen Morgann?" she asked, knowing this would make them forget their desires.

"No. He may have gone through the woods."

"Oh, Galeren," she brought her hands to his chest. "He knew they were dangerous, did he not? Do you think he would be so foolish? I hope not."

"He knew I could be deadly and that didna stop him from betrayin' us."

"But did he?" she put to him. "You and Mac have told me everything he said. He never told my uncle anything you or the others may or may not have said. And he claims he tried to talk the others out of killing me."

"He was there when they shot at ye," he brooded now. "He should have fought them."

"Why? I have not been his friend for years. He has no allegiance to me. I barely know him."

"Ye were in my care," he said in a low voice.

She smiled softly at him. "So, 'tis *you* he betrayed."

He looked heavenward and let out a long breath.

"I am not telling you to forget what he did, but I know there is room in your good heart for forgiveness."

"Good heart?" He laughed and shook his head. "My heart isna always good, lass. As a matter of fact, when I fight and kill, I would say my heart goes black."

She smiled as they walked back to the manor house. "We will work on that."

"Anythin'" he promised her. "I will do anythin' fer ye."

She wanted to leap into his arms and let him carry her to her rooms. She would not invite him into the rooms and tempt him further.

"Until I see ye tomorrow?"

Perhaps it was best if they didn't see each other. How could she tell him it was for his own good? How could she tell him anything when he brought her hand to his lips for a kiss?

"Until tomorrow, my love," she whispered.

Was he going to kiss her? She'd prayed about it. She'd asked the

Lord to let him kiss her again. It was so wonderful and thrilling.

He looked into her eyes. "I love ye, Silene. Pray fer the time that is left to go by quickly."

She giggled. The next thing she knew, she was crushed in his embrace. His hand was under her nape and the other held her up.

When he kissed her, everything seemed to lose its light. None of it was important. All she needed was him.

He ran his tongue over her and pulled at her lower lip with his teeth.

She wanted to know where he learned such things and what else he knew about what to do with his tongue.

He kissed her softly and with rigid control. She had to call on all her defenses to break away from him. She did and turned for her door.

Inside, she shut the door and had a fleeting thought to go find Father Timothy and confess these wanton thoughts to him. Elysande's advice was to wed Galeren. She would if she could! Perhaps confessing to the priest was what she needed. These feelings certainly did feel sinful. Elysande said it felt sinful because it felt so good. Why did Silene think she had five babes and one on the way if it wasn't pleasant? Elysande had asked. Silene could now understand why. And this, just from kissing!

She looked at the large, masculine chair and her purple gown draped over it. She would wear it when she wed Galeren. She closed her eyes and prayed for the days to be quick.

When she opened them again, she looked around Lucan's room. She didn't know what Galeren's room looked like, but Lucan's room was very warm and comfortable. She should stay here for the two days—away from the temptation of him.

She had a duty to God to help Galeren fulfill his vow—and make a new one to her.

She would stay here until the morning of her marriage. His aunts and female cousins would all help her if they knew why she was staying locked up in her room.

Father Timothy would be here early to escort her to church for prayers. They enjoyed their mornings together when everyone else was asleep. But if he was opposed to coming into her room, she wouldn't be praying with him.

She would stay here and pray and rest.

She undressed and, after a time on her knees, she climbed into bed. Her thoughts were filled with the captain. His laughter, his scent of woodsmoke, the sound of his deep, lilting voice across her ears, the sight of him surrounded by children and a kitten on his shoulder, playing with his hair. She thought of every moment with him until she fell asleep.

And there, she dreamed of him.

She awoke to a knock at her door. Her room was dark but a quick glance to the half-open window revealed the blue-gray haze of dawn.

She'd slept late.

She opened the door partway as she wore only her chemise. Smiling on the other side was Lionell.

"Good morn, Miss Sparrow. I was goin' fer a walk in the gardens and thought ye might like to join me."

"Good morn to you, Lionell. My apologies but I cannot. I am staying in my room until tomorrow when 'tis time to become wife to your brother."

"Are ye hidin' from Galeren?" he asked. "D'ye not want to wed him?"

"Oh, aye. I do want to wed him. Very much."

His autumn-colored brow fell for a moment but then he sighed and offered her a sheepish look. "Fergive me."

"Oh, but what for?" she asked.

He held up his palm to stop her from saying anything else and let his gaze rove over her face. "Though I do find ye lovely, mayhap one of the bonniest lasses I know, I was only tryin' to make my brother angry. I dinna know why. He would likely kill me."

She shook her head. "Nay, Lionell. He would not kill you."

"Lady, ye dinna know how he beats my arse—and that is when he isna angry!"

Silene fought the urge to giggle. Perhaps it was Lionell's brash but charming demeanor. The prioress would have fainted had she heard how often he used the word arse.

"He wants you to learn how to defend yourself. Who better to teach you than such a skilled warrior as your brother? My guess is you will grow weary of having your backside beaten and will learn how to fight back, and when you can fight *him*, you can fight anyone."

"Mayhap, I dinna want to fight," he told her.

"Do you want to live within these walls for the rest of your life, never to venture out again? Because, I can tell you that in just a few short days of traveling, we were attacked more than once."

He stared at her, looking like he might say something more. But he thought better of it and nodded.

Silene felt sad for him and she felt sadness from him. But he'd had enough pity.

"I'm just about to begin my morning prayers. Would you care to join me?"

"In yer room?"

"I will keep the door open."

He shook his head but then whispered, "Aye."

Smiling, Silene led him inside, left the door open and kneeled beside the hearth fire.

After a moment of him probably fighting himself on whether to stay or go, he knelt beside her.

FATHER TIMOTHY SHUFFLED down the long hall to the three doors at the end. He might be a wee bit late, but he was going as fast as he could. He liked staying active by walking though. It kept him young for his age of almost eighty years. He didn't mind coming to the manor house to escort Silene back to church. He enjoyed their prayers together in the morn—so much that he neglected Cain's son, Tristan, and his ten-year return to pray with her instead.

She was a delight, thankful and joyous in prayer. The old priest felt revived and invigorated after his prayers with her. She was devoted to God and Galeren, and soon she would be devoted to the clan.

He was happy she would be a part of the MacPherson family.

When he came to the third door, he saw that hers was open. He peeked his head inside, about to call her.

He saw her and Lionell by the hearth in prayer. Lionell. How had she managed that?

He looked up. "Ye are good."

Chapter Twenty-One

GALEREN SCOWLED AT Lionell when his brother ducked and then leaped back avoiding Galeren's strikes, then came back to punch his brother in the jaw.

Mac and the others playfully jeered their captain.

"What distracts ye, Brother?" Lionell asked and returned to his fighting stance.

"My thoughts drift to Silene. I want to see her, and she will not allow it."

"Aye."

"What d'ye mean, *aye*?" Galeren's stare turned to a dark glare.

"She told me," Lionell told him and thrust his sword at Galeren's belly.

Galeren smacked the blade from Lionell's hand and stepped closer to him. "When did she tell ye? *What* did she tell ye?"

"This morn. A wee bit before dawn, in truth. Are we still practicin'?"

Galeren shook his head. "I might kill ye."

Lionell nodded. "That is what I told her."

Galeren ran his palm down his face and clenched his painful jaw.

"Brother, ye had better explain. Start at the beginnin'."

So, Lionell told him. "We prayed together."

Galeren couldn't be angry that she had gotten this lad to pray. "Why is she stayin' in her room and not seein' me? Is she angry with me? Afraid? What did she say?"

"She doesna want to end up in yer bed a day before yer vow is over."

Galeren gave him a doubtful stare. "She told ye that?"

He knew Silene better. She wouldn't bring up such things with his brother.

"She told Adela," Lionell told him. "Adela told me."

So, she was staying away for his sake. He should have known. "'Tis considerate of her," Galeren decided out loud. "But I still feel like breakin' down her door."

"One more day, Brute. Ye can do it," Lionell said and made way for Galeren's next opponent.

"'Tis refreshin' to know ye dinna have complete control over yerself, Cap," Mac said, stepping forward. "Ye are mortal like the rest of us."

Galeren swung his heavy claymore and cracked it against Mac's. They practiced for another two hours and then headed for something to eat.

"Where should we start?" Mac asked Lionell, rubbing his sore thigh.

"Start what?" asked Galeren.

"'Tis the last day of my vow," Mac told him. "Lionell is goin' to take me and the lads to the village."

"Ah, aye, the end of yer vows," Galeren said. "Where is Will? He didna practice today."

"Last I saw him," Padrig advised him, "he was sharin' words with yer cousin, Geva."

Geva! Uncle Nicky's daughter!

He rose from his seat in the dining hall and pushed his chair out behind him. Beautiful, sweet Geva with Will? No. What was his friend doing? Why would he go after Geva? Aye, his cousin was captivating, with large, sable eyes and glossy, chestnut locks that fell to her waist. She also possessed just enough sauciness to hook Will, but his uncle would skin his arse if he touched her.

Galeren was on his way to Nicholas' manor house when the front door opened and Will stepped inside.

A swirl of dried leaves blew into the house.

"Where is Geva?" he asked.

Will blinked his eyes and shrugged. "I havena seen her since this morn."

Relief flooded through Galeren. He let himself smile but Will narrowed his eyes on him.

"Ye thought I was with her. Ye were comin' to save her from me. Aye? I know that look in yer eyes, Cap."

"She is my cousin. One of the youngest."

He did his best not to insult Will. "Ye are not known fer stayin' by the side of one lass, old friend."

"Of course," Will said and smiled but did not look at him. "I must go."

Galeren watched him leave and cursed under his breath. He would think of what to say later. He wasn't used to being cautious with his men's sensibilities especially Will's.

He hadn't left the house and was drawn as if on an unseen tether to the door of his brother Lucan's room. He stared at the wood for a moment, as if it were the biggest obstacle in his life.

He breathed, and then he knocked. After an eternal moment, he heard her approach the door. It opened.

He couldn't wait to see her face.

Elysande appeared on the other side. "Oh, Galeren, Silene canna see ye now. She is deep in prayer."

He wanted just a glance. It was all right. He could wait until tomorrow to see her.

He spied a glimpse of purple and heard his aunts and other female voices. "She must be verra deep in them not to be distracted by all of ye." He smiled and went back to the practice field.

His friends were all gone, eager to share the beds of village maidens. He unsheathed his sword and swung it in the air. The long metal blade danced in the sunlight, cutting through shafts of light. He balanced himself with his other arm—something Lionell had to learn in an entirely new way.

Galeren braced his legs and brought his blade down again. This time, metal struck metal.

Someone was there.

His father's blade parried then struck Galeren's edge hard enough to rattle his bones a little. He tilted up one corner of his mouth and brought his sword down in a chopping blow. He knew how his father fought, like a breeze suddenly changing direction. Galeren had to be quick or—his father swept the flat end of his blade across the backs of his knees and threw him off balance. By the time he rose off his arse, his uncle, Cain, was upon him. He came in like a force beyond whatever one can think or imagine. His sword struck Galeren's three times before Galeren could even parry. His father circled the two of them like a feline predator and came closer to the fighting. Soon, Torin would strike and his uncle would take an instant to rest his arm.

They had done it before all throughout Galeren's training, preparing him for the world outside the gates.

He parried his father's strike to his legs and struck his uncle's back with the flat of his blade.

They retreated but only to circle him, joined by his uncle, Nicholas, the youngest of the three brothers and least barbaric among them.

"Let us see if you were paying attention, Nephew," Uncle Nicholas challenged softly and struck from the right. Cain came from the left, his father, behind him.

He had been paying attention all those years. It was what kept him alive on the battlefield. He watched and listened and swung. A parry to the left, a jab to the right, swing around back and remove a head.

Of course, this was practice. He wouldn't actually take a head—but he could come close if they weren't careful.

He fought them for an hour with his cousin, Tristan, and his other cousins joining his side.

In the end, the younger men saw victory. Galeren was glad. For if his father and uncles had won, they would feel as if they had failed the lads and would begin the strict training again.

No one wanted that.

He looked toward the manor house…her window. She was there, watching him. She lifted her palm and smiled at him. His heart accelerated. He lifted his palm in response.

His father and uncles all came around him and ushered him away with advice about his wedding night.

"Bein' chaste fer six years has its disadvantages," his father supplied while they walked to the manor house. "Ye will be done before ye begin."

"Aye," his uncles agreed. "Ye need to go spend some time alone—"

Galeren held up his hand to silence anymore advice. "All will be well. Dinna fret aboot my weddin' night."

"But ye are both like virgins!" Cain protested. "Ye need some help from men who—"

"Uncle," Galeren cut him off, not wanting to hear of their prowess with his aunts and mother! "Both of us bein' like virgins is all right with me. I like the idea of us teachin' each other what is pleasin'."

His father patted him on the back and smiled at him. "Let us go drink to yer upcomin' nuptials and yer excellent skills."

They walked to the solar in Torin's manor house and drank their kin's fine whisky. Among many other things, they discussed what to do when the high steward arrived.

"He doesna seem like the type to let this go," Cain said. "We should kill him."

"What aboot King David?" Tristan asked. "Will no help come from him?"

"No. None," Galeren told them. "He can do little from where he is. Still, he willna kill us fer doin' what must be done if John attacks."

"The king will take your side?" Nicholas asked him.

"Aye."

"How do you know for certain?"

"Because I'm friends with John on the king's orders."

All the men straightened in their chairs and stared at him.

"I mean, the king doesna trust his cousin, John. He never has. He is sure John had his hand in his capture and arrest at Neville's Cross. He sent me to befriend his rash cousin and wait fer him to plot against his rival, David. That is what I have done."

"Ye have been a spy fer nine years, learnin' the high steward's secrets?" his father asked, looking prouder than ever before.

"Three years, actually," Galeren answered. "Before that, David was free. Once David was imprisoned, my role changed. I have learned much. The king calls his cousin a thief and a heartless, disloyal scoundrel. He is correct. John has his hand in the royal coffers. He robs the coin to pay killers to silence any Scots noblemen who comes against him. David knows aboot all of it because of me."

"Why has David done nothin' aboot it?" Cain asked. "Even if 'twas to order ye to kill him?"

"He wants John only after his cousin plots against him. John havin' Silene killed willna cause the king to move. 'Tis murder, not treason. John could always come back somehow and become king."

"Perhaps he won't plot anything against the king at all. They are cousins, after all," Nicholas offered.

Galeren shook his head. "Once he had the seat secured, he likely would have made his move against the king. I dinna care if we lost our chance, Silene wouldna make a promise to God to prove John wanted the throne, and I would never ask it of her."

They all agreed, knowing the king might not share their sentiments. Silene might have the king against her as well as the high steward.

Would he put his kin in danger to protect her?

"We will leave," he said.

"No, ye willna leave," his father told him. His uncles agreed. "King David isna only yer friend. Most of yer cousins fought with or fer him. And we," he motioned to himself and his brothers, "fought with his father, Robert the Bruce."

"Aye," Cain agreed. "But even if he still comes here—we will stand with ye, lad."

"Ye have my gratitude," Galeren said softly. He loved them. He didn't want them to stand against the king. If David went against him, Galeren would take his wife and leave.

He prayed it didn't happen.

"Son," his father said, "tell us how ye stayed true to the king's orders these years withoot some kind of friendship growin' between ye and the steward."

"Friendship did grow, but I can separate it from duty, save when it comes to my men. Fer them, our friendship comes before all else."

"Rumor traveled as far as Invergarry," said his uncle, Nicky, "that the high steward put you in charge of everything. He practically gave you his position."

"'Tis true, he handed everythin' to me, his army, even his children. That is why he canna muster his army against me and must hire a new one. My men willna fight me. Well, most of them. John didna completely trust me. He had one of his men implanted into my ranks. Morgann Bell. I found oot and tied him to a tree near Jamie Treskil's cottage."

"Jamie is in Perth visitin' his brother."

"Aye, as I later discovered. I saw Morgann alive after that and let him go free. Perhaps he went into the woods."

"Fittin' punishment fer a traitor," one of them said. The others agreed.

Galeren remained quiet. Now that a little bit more time had passed, he could think more clearly. He'd liked Morgann and to think of his head smashed to bits by a swinging boulder was unpleasant. Not so though for any mercenaries. He was glad he never told John about the forest.

He wondered if any of his kin worried about mercenaries getting in. He knew they had the upper hand in the walled town. They had positions along all the walls. But no defense was impenetrable. They were not in a castle but in a house with different ways inside. Galeren wondered if the stronghold was built the way it was for a reason. His father and uncles were clever. There was much defense here. They were safe here. Even the shepherds outside the gate were safe. Every house was within sight of someone patrolling the walls. "I was thinkin' of usin' Jamie's cottage tomorrow night fer our weddin' night. I want to be completely alone with her. Withoot any of ye tryin' to give us more advice or any of the women or Father Timothy—or Lionell at our door."

"Verra well," his father said. "I will make certain the cottage is heavily protected."

"There ye are, Galeren," Father Timothy said as he appeared and went to Galeren's side. "A word, please."

"Of course, Father." Galeren passed his kin a concerned looked and then followed the priest into the church.

MIDNIGHT SETTLED ON the manor house, but Silene couldn't sleep. She sat in her chemise in a chair by the open window and looked down at the moonlit practice field. He'd been there today, looking so fit, so graceful and yet savage as he fought. His father and uncles pushed him until Silene was sure he would fall, but he didn't. She knew they wouldn't kill him but, still, each moment struck her nerves until she thought she would cry out to him to look out!

She didn't have to. He saw every blow about to strike him.

And when the fighting was finally over, he looked up as if feeling her there, watching as she was. She missed him.

Just one more night and they would be wed. What would it be like to be his wife? What would it be like to have a family, a motherly woman who dotted on her? Braya spent a lot of her time with Aleysia and Julianna, who were often accompanied by their daughters, Elysande, and Adela or Geva. Braya had no daughter. Until now.

Silene didn't mind the adoption. She hadn't seen her own mother in years. She—

A soft rapping at her door drew her from her thoughts. Who could be knocking at this hour? She left the chair and padded to it.

"Aye? Who is there?"

"Arise, my love, my beautiful one,

and come away.

O my dove, in the clefts of the rock,

in the crannies of the cliff,

let me see yer face,

let me hear yer voice,

fer yer voice is sweet,

and yer face is lovely."

Silene lifted her hand to her mouth. *Song of Solomon* was one of her favorite scriptures.

"Open the door, my love."

She did as he bid her and opened the door a crack. When she saw his beautiful green eyes, she opened it a little more.

"What are you doing here at such a late hour?"

"I have come to wed ye, lass."

Daffodil meowed from beneath his hair falling loose to his nape. Her heart flipped and she couldn't help but smile at him. "The morning approaches."

"'Tis after midnight. 'Tis tomorrow and the end of my vow. Father Timothy awaits us in the church."

"Father Timothy?"

"Aye, he is the one who reminded me that I took my vow at midnight. Now, come quickly," he whispered, and his eyes glittered in the torchlit hall. "I want to be yer husband."

"Now?" What was he saying? Marry now? "Let me get my cloak."

He smiled as if England just broke off and floated into the North Sea.

"Will everyone be there?" she asked, leaving the door open and reaching for her purple gown.

"Just us tonight, my love. We will have Father Timothy do it all over again tomorrow with our kin and yer gown. Aye?"

She smiled, nodded, and grabbed her cloak.

"Come," he beckoned, "tonight, I am chaste no more."

His words along with his low, whispered voice dripped down her spine like a flame igniting her blood. She was going to be his wife. Now. Her belly tightened. Her heart thumped hard in her chest. He hadn't been with a woman for six years. He was hungry for her now.

She wasn't afraid. She remembered his hardness when he kissed her. Perhaps she was a bit afraid. Suddenly, she wanted to do what she could to postpone it. No. She wasn't going to say her vows because she loved this man. She was happy to be his wife.

They reached the church and held hands as they entered.

Silene smiled when she saw Father Timothy. He was fast becoming her dearest friend.

"Did Galeren explain how this is possible?" he asked after their warm greeting. "He made his vow at midnight exactly six years ago. It ended tonight."

Eager to get on with it, Galeren took her hand again and led her before the altar.

Father Timothy smiled and went with them, with a Bible in his hand. He began with loving looks at them from under his fuzzy gray brow and reading from the Holy Scriptures.

"Silene Sparrow, d'ye consent to becomin' Galeren's wife? To love and honor and obey him till death d'ye part?"

She smiled. "Aye. I do."

He smiled lovingly at her then turned to Galeren. "Galeren MacPherson, d'ye consent to becomin' Silene's husband? To love, honor, and protect her till death d'ye part?"

He consented with a wide, dimpled grin.

A few more words were said, that Silene didn't remember later, and then Father Timothy told them to kiss.

"In the sight of the Almighty, I pronounce ye husband and wife."

That was it. She was Galeren's wife. She thought the ceremony was a bit short and smiled at her husband's eagerness. She wondered if she would still be smiling in the morning.

They thanked the good priest and Galeren handed him Daffodil for the night.

"We are not going to the manor house?"

He shook his head and led her up the hill toward Jamie's cottage.

CHAPTER TWENTY-TWO

THE COTTAGE WAS simple in design. There was a small table and chair near the hearth that was built within the wall. Dried, garden herbs hung from the low ceiling. A curtained wall separated the kitchen area from the sleeping quarter, which consisted of a separate room with a bed and some trunks. There was a shepherd's crook hanging on the wall. A larger hand-carved chair was set opposite the bed.

There were fur coverings on the bed, and it looked able to accommodate two people.

"The night is finally here," he said, coming up behind her and kissing her earlobe. "I thought I would go mad yesterday when I couldna see ye."

She trembled a little when his arms slipped around her waist and he buried his face in her nape.

She lifted her arm and ran it through his dark golden locks. She expected to feel Daffodil there. She smiled and drew in a quick, deep breath to calm her nerves. She loved him. She just promised her life to him. Truly, there was nothing to be frightened of.

"Silene, I love ye, love. I will be gentle."

How? She wanted to ask him. How would he be gentle when he was so eager for her? When he'd been chaste for so long? What if she disappointed him?

"Galeren," she turned in his arms to say, "I do not know what to do to please you."

His eyes roved over her face, her red waves falling to her brow. "Love, lookin' at ye pleases me." The catch of his breath proved his words.

Somehow, she, with her plain, freckled face and shorn, bright red hair had won the heart of Galeren the Bonny. She didn't have to do anything to please him. She already did please him. It made her want to please him more.

She took his hand and led him to the bed, her heart banging so loud in her chest she was sure he could hear it.

He followed, a willing subject.

She released his hand when they reached the bed and turned to face him. She untied her cloak and let it fall around her ankles, her gaze fixed on his while she stood before him in her thin chemise.

He took her in as if he had waited his whole life for her.

She was emboldened by the power he was giving her by not throwing her onto the bed and taking her like a savage. Though she was not always opposed to savages, this was her first time.

He was patient, as always, in tight control of himself, letting her move at her own pace. She had never touched a man before him. She wanted to take her time and explore him. She began with his léine, pulling it free from his belt. She could feel his eyes on her, looking down at what she was doing, patient, waiting…

She pulled the léine up, exposing his flat, muscled belly and bit her lip. He lifted his arms so she could continue undressing him. She loved being the only woman in six years whom he allowed to touch him so intimately.

He had to finish undressing when she couldn't reach his head.

She wanted to step back to revel in what she'd uncovered but she wanted to touch him even more.

Lightheaded with power, she moved her fingertips lightly over his belly, dancing over the hills and valleys that fashioned him.

He groaned at her silken touch as she rubbed her palms over his chest that was dusted in swirls of dark gold. His shoulders were wide and carved from stone. She leaned in and kissed one of his arms, thick with sinew, able to protect and comfort. She wasn't afraid of him. Elysande and Adela had told her what happens on a lass' wedding night. Her new cousins were correct to tell her that after a few passionate kisses, she would not care about any pain. She wanted him to know she wasn't afraid.

She leaned up on her tiptoes and hooked her hands on his shoulders. "Kiss me, Husband."

His broad hands circled her waist as he bent his mouth to hers.

Contact with his lush, hungry mouth made her nerve endings feel raw. The sensual path of his hands—one up her spine, and one below, and moving even lower made her blood boil. He pulled her body against every inch of his. He was hard and tight everywhere.

He slipped his hand between them and unhooked his belt, for which Silene was thankful since his many weapons were digging into her.

With that out of way, Silene could feel his passion without any interference. She almost broke their kiss at the fear of the beast between his thighs, but she would not succumb to fear.

He didn't let her go. Instead, he bent over her when she arched her back and kissed her until she broke away to pant with need of him.

She blushed, but she didn't care about being shy when he dipped his face to the breasts her arching back offered. He cupped one in his hand and lowered his mouth to the other, sucking through her thin chemise.

Her nipples were so hard and tight, they almost pained her. His scintillating tongue and teeth eased the pain but also made her ache below her belly, between her legs.

He moaned and fell on his back on the bed with his legs hanging over the side. He laughed, taking her with him to land atop him.

He took her mouth again, molding his lips to hers, playing with her tongue, firing her blood.

He used one foot to release the other from its boot, then did the same with the other foot. His movement beneath her caused him to rub against her crux and shook her world on its axis.

She'd never felt anything like it…there. He was steel against her, about to break through his hose and impale her.

Instinctively, she wanted to straddle him, and he wanted it, too.

Freeing her breasts, he pulled her chemise up over her bare thighs, the alluring curve of her bottom, up over her breasts. He pulled the chemise close over her head and released it at her nape, locking her arms behind her.

He was now the one in control.

For an instant, she was overly aware of her body and the fact that she was naked before him. But when he tangled her wrists behind her neck and arched her backward, she had no time to consider if her breasts were too small before they were in his mouth.

She cried out at the thrill of it and was glad they weren't in the house. She trusted him not to hurt her, but he never promised not to make her go mad with need. She threw one leg over his hip and then the other. Her hot flesh caressed him and made him groan like a bear in pain.

With her arms behind her back, she had no way to hold herself up. He did it for her with his free hand laid gently at the valley between her breasts. He kept her steady while he worshipped each breast in turn. She felt herself growing wetter and more ready to receive him.

When he yanked his hose free, she gasped at the feel of his heavy erection beneath her. He was long and thick, for she tested his length with a quick upward rub.

Her legs tried to close.

"I willna hurt ye, my love," he whispered and set her hands free.

She rested her palms on his chest and sat up on him.

His smile of complete seduction singed her nerves.

With his cock firmly between her thighs, he stroked her with himself until both their muscles trembled. He curled his arm around her and pulled her down for a kiss. His mouth ravished her, her chin, her throat while his hand pressed her lower back closer against him.

She felt his heartbeat hard and fast against her, growing even faster. He closed his eyes and wet his lips with his tongue.

He guided Silene over him in a sensual dance.

She closed her eyes, but her fears were drowned in his seed, shooting into her, onto her.

He fit his hand between them and took hold of himself while he stared into her eyes. He pushed the head of his erection against her wet entrance.

She wanted him. All of him. She wanted this intimacy with him. She kept her breath slow and steady while he pushed deeper and deeper, opening her. He retreated slowly, leaving her gasping. He was big and forceful without forcing her. He pained her—but just a little. Instead of simply ramming his way inside her, he withdrew, letting her feel the length of half of him.

He returned and thrust softly, slower, breaking her barrier and filling her again.

While he spilled more of himself into her, he remained deadly still, not letting himself fully enjoy her yet.

Well, Silene thought, she wouldn't have that.

She already knew what felt good to her and what was still painful.

She kissed him and took him deeper until she felt his hilt. She let him move her the way he liked. In. Out. In. Out. Both, sleek and swollen.

Something began in her like a force she could not fight. She didn't want to. It was as if a hundred waves were rushing over her. Her body tightened and quaked. The waves built to a towering tidal wave with her on top.

She rode it faster, her muscles, taut and shaking. She cried out in painful ecstasy and looked at him for assurance that this was normal.

He was in the same ecstasy as she, filling her over and over, until he threw up his arms as if in surrender.

She trailed her palms down his arms before she withdrew and rolled off him.

"Ye play with fire, lass," he said huskily. "I will roll ye over on yer belly and take ye from behind."

She laughed, believing him to be boasting about what his spent body could do—and then she was on her belly and he was on top of her.

HE HAD TO keep in mind that her body was untried until tonight. He wanted to have her from every angle. His body was well honed. He didn't need much rest, and besides, he never wanted the night to end.

He spread her knees with his and leaned down to whisper in her ear how she made him feel. He loved her and he told her so as he found her entrance and pushed.

She closed her eyes and cried out into the blankets as she grew wet for him again.

He moved slowly, surging against her, lifting her, pressing her down, retreating, his heavy breath falling on her ear, her neck.

He never wanted to leave her body. He'd been with other lasses before his vow. He'd had no idea what love was.

Coming together in the past was nothing like this. No lass he'd ever met or spoken to was like Silene. His heart was hers and it would be hers until the end of his days.

Wanting to look at her, he rose up to turn her beneath him. He lifted one of her legs and put it around him. He almost slipped out and thrust himself back in.

Her eyes opened wide and she crossed her arms over her chest.

He'd already seen her lithe body and she was being overly aware of it now? He smiled and instead of telling her how lovely and perfect she was to him, he wanted to show her.

He heaved himself into her once, twice, three times, until her arms uncrossed and curled around his neck.

He gazed into her eyes. Somehow, he, a soldier who had killed many on the battlefield, had won the heart of Silene Sparrow.

He didn't care how. He was glad he had.

"Am I hurtin' ye, lass?" he asked on a tender whisper as he moved inside her.

She shook her head. "I am so happy to please you."

He slowed, his gaze not leaving hers. "Ye please me too much."

"And you, me." She clutched his shoulders and opened her legs wider, taking him deeper.

Short, little sounds came from her lips and felt like whips across his back. He kissed the sounds from her. He kissed her chin, her neck.

He felt her tight sheath swelling around him, making it impossible to stop. He thrust deeper and shuddered on retreat. She clung to him, moving in perfect rhythm with him. Her long legs wrapped around his waist, her arms around his neck and her hips wedged against him.

He knew she was about to climax. The thought sucked the blood from every part of him but the part that was inside her. At least, that was how it felt when he erupted inside her. He moved faster, wanting to pin her to the bed.

When she tossed her head back and cried out his name, another rush followed and then the gentle subsiding.

They finished together and laughed for no other reason than that they were happy to be together and they made each other feel good.

She was bolder than he thought she would be. He loved it. He knew she was brave. He also knew that he was exhausted.

"Where are ye goin'?" he asked her when she left the bed.

"To put on my chemise," she answered. "I am cold."

He waved her over with his hand. "I will warm ye, love. That is why God gave men fur."

She giggled and hurried into her chemise and then back into bed.

He engulfed her, holding her close.

Soon, they were asleep and didn't hear the front door opening.

CHAPTER TWENTY-THREE

SILENE WAS DREAMING of running on the cliffs, laughing with the children and a fat, yellow cat following them. The skies darkened suddenly, and a man called to her—or was it the waves crashing against the rocks below? She turned and saw Galeren lying dead beneath someone's bloody sword. She began to scream.

Wake up, Silene. Wake up.

She opened her eyes and looked around the dimly lit room. Someone was there with them. Someone was watching in the shadows. She moved to rouse Galeren, but her uncle stepped into the soft glow of a dying candle. He shook his head while two more men stepped out of the shadows on Galeren's side of the bed with their swords at his heart and his throat. They would kill him if she made a sound.

Her uncle motioned for her to get out of the bed.

How had he known they were here in the cottage and not inside the gates?

She obeyed his silent command and left the bed quietly.

The instant she was out of it, her uncle grabbed her. He closed his hand over her mouth and pulled her to the door.

She took an instant to see her glorious husband awaken and one of the men lift his blade. She struggled in her uncle's arms and tried to scream. She would never stop.

He dragged her toward the outside door. As they passed the light from the glowing hearth fire, she saw a woman cloaked in a hooded mantle run into the room. Whoever she was, Silene prayed the woman could save Galeren.

She tried to scream but a fist to her jaw silenced her.

GALEREN OPENED HIS eyes. He was still in the cottage, still in bed. He tried to get out of it, but his wrists were tied to the bedpost behind his head.

His head. It pounded like thunder between his ears. He'd been struck, likely with the hilt of someone's sword. Where was Silene? Now his heart throbbed as loud as his head. Where was she? Who took—her uncle. He remembered. He'd heard something in his sleep. His eyes opened and he had a moment to see John pulling her away before he was struck.

He had to get free and find her!

Who tied him to the bed? "Who are ye?" he called into the shadows. It was still night. Where were the stronghold guards?

They didn't know he and his new wife were here. They were ordered to heavily protect the cottage *tomorrow night*. "Come oot so I can see ye," he beckoned, clenching his teeth. "Where is my wife?"

"Until death parts you, correct?" a woman sneered stepping forward. She looked like a wealthy lady out for a ride in her fur-lined mantle and hood.

Cecilia.

She hadn't come alone. Four more men appeared, all drawing

swords.

"If she is harmed in any way, I will wring yer neck with my own hands."

She turned up one end of her lips. "How will you do that with your wrists tied to the bed?"

Galeren's blood boiled. "Tell me where she is or ye will find oot."

"What does it matter? You speak as if you are confident of breaking free. Let me assure you, you will never be free again."

He gave her quick, doubtful grin.

For a moment, she looked worried.

"How did ye get past the guards?"

She shrugged. "A small forest fire in the opposite direction drew them away from their posts." Her mocking smile deepened into a snarl. "Not so well protected is it?"

She was correct. If he lived through this, the guards would be reprimanded for leaving their posts.

"Where has he taken Silene?" he demanded again. "I saw the steward take her."

She looked as if she had things to say…or scream. "She is homely with her short, orange hair and dotted face. Truly, Captain," she implored. "What is the point you are trying to prove? That you are not a simple-minded man who thinks with his—" she pointed to the fur covering him from his waist down. "Anyone who knows you, knows you are not such a fool."

Galeren was at a loss for words. She wouldn't see any point that wasn't in her favor. He didn't feel like coddling her.

"You have power and wealth," she reminded him. "The people adore you. You will not give up everything for her."

"Aye. I already have. She is beautiful, Cecilia, while ye are quite ugly. Where is she?"

She screamed again and stomped to one of her men. She snatched the soldier's knife from his belt and rushed toward Galeren.

He stared into her eyes, hating that he was going to die this way and not in battle.

Oddly, his heart slowed, as if preparing him for a blade to the chest.

"Cecilia!" a man cried out.

Galeren knew the voice. He opened his eyes to see Will standing in the doorway.

"Ye said ye were only helpin' the steward get the gel. Ye told me ye had nothin' in yer heart fer him."

"I lied," she told him with a sly smile.

"Will!" Galeren shouted. "What the hell are ye doin'?" No. No. It couldn't be. Not Will. He pulled on his bindings. He wanted to hit him or worse.

"I love her, Cap. I have fer some time."

Galeren closed his eyes. He wanted to scream or kill. This was one of his closest friends! The one who…he remembered the children's confession. The one whom they saw Cecilia kissing. She was the reason he was late in joining them.

"He told me you and your bride were here in the cottage and not in the stronghold," Cecilia told her. "He wants you dead, Captain."

"No!" Will shouted. "Ye swore he wouldna be hurt!"

"But ye didna care aboot Silene, did ye, Will. Ye didna care aboot what happened to her."

"I—"

"And if I married Cecilia?" Galeren asked. "What would ye have done then, Will?"

"Once we were married, he would have done nothing," Cecilia assured them. "I do not love you, William. You are pretty, but he is pretty *and* powerful."

"Get away from him, Cecilia," Will warned her.

Galeren had never seen him so serious. What had come over his friend? This was Cecilia! The one Will used to complain about. He saw one of her men inching up behind Will.

"Behind ye!" Galeren instinctively shouted.

Will turned, unsheathing his blade. But he was too late.

Galeren pulled and tried to free himself until his wrists bled. He watched her soldier run Will through and his friend sink to the floor. "Will!" he shouted again. "Will!" But Will didn't answer.

Galeren set his deadly gaze on Will's killer. "I'm goin' to kill ye."

The man laughed.

"Get out!" she shouted at her men. "All of you! Out!"

When they were gone, she didn't spare Will a glance but rushed to the bed.

"Captain, I do not want to kill you. I love you."

He shook his head. "Ye dinna love me, and I dinna love ye."

She smiled, looking as serene as a windless loch. She was mad and spoiled to the point of no return.

"Captain," she purred, pulling back his fur covering with her finger. "If I cannot have your love, let me at least have your body."

He pulled and tugged on his bindings as she exposed him.

He was flaccid, sickened by her and the death of his friend, concerned only for Silene.

She lifted her skirts, ready to mount him.

"Cecilia!" he said in a commanding voice. "Ye will get nothin' from me this way." He knew what she wanted to hear. "Untie me and I will show ye what bein' chaste fer six years has done to me." He'd already showed his wife, but Cecilia didn't know that.

He saw her shiver. She attempted to climb atop him but he bent his legs. If he had to kick her into the hearth fire, he would.

"Untie me, Cecilia."

She blinked and smiled. "You are like a sorcerer, Captain." She patted her flush face.

"Cut me loose. If havin' my body is what ye want, I will let ye do to me as ye will."

She pressed her index finger to the dip in his hip.

He clenched his teeth, not wanting her to touch him. "Cecilia—"

"Shh. I'm cutting," she whispered, leaning up over him and cutting his binds.

The instant his hands were free, he cupped them around her nape and smashed his forehead into hers, making her reel. "Next time, I will crack open yer skull. Now, tell me where my wife is."

"Men!" she croaked out. They came running. The first reached him in an instant, before he had any time to plan an attack. It didn't stop Galeren from snatching Cecilia's knife and jamming it into his opponent. The one who killed Will. He looked into the man eyes and twisted the blade.

Galeren let the man go and took an instant to ready himself for more, then flung the bloody blade into the neck of the second man.

A third and fourth rushed toward them. Galeren fought them, ducking and stepping out of the way of their blades. He punched one and knocked him out, grabbed his sword and cut the last man down in two brutal swings.

Without pause, he rushed to his hose and boots and put them on.

Cecilia screamed in horror. Blood spurted from a deep gash in her throat, "Galeren!" she cried out. She'd been cut in the fighting.

He lifted her in his arms. She would be dead soon. There was nothing he could do. "Where did he take her, Cecilia. Where is she?"

"She is all...you...care about." Cecilia managed, growing weaker.

"Aye. She is all. Tell me what I wish to know."

Tears filled her eyes and they closed. "The steward...told me to meet him at Laggan."

Galeren looked down at her and shook his head. "Ye shouldna have come here, Cecilia."

She did not answer.

He took his plaid and Will's sword and left.

He knew where Laggan was, but he didn't believe John was on his way there. Especially at night. There were too many small rivers he would have to ride around. Like Morgann, John knew that Galeren could track him.

John wouldn't take the chance of telling Cecilia where he was truly going. Any fool knew that she would tell Galeren if he persisted.

He took a lantern and tied it around his horse's neck and then followed the tracks down the hill. Most went south, back toward Ayr. One set led north.

He would kill John if he had to. If John hurt her, Galeren would kill him.

SILENE WOKE UP in a strange forest, tied by her ankles to a tree by a small fire. Her jaw felt sore. He uncle had struck her.

She was supposed to pray for her enemies. She could not pray for her uncle yet.

"Ah, ye are awake."

Her uncle's voice. She closed her eyes again, not wanting to speak to him. Ever again. But she could not do that.

"This was foolish of you, Uncle. The captain was your loyal friend, and yet you allowed him to be killed."

"Ye both betrayed me, Silene. I am the one who will never fergive. But Captain MacPherson isna dead," he corrected. "I handed him over to his betrothed."

"I am his wife!" she argued.

He slapped her hard in the face. "William of Lorn told Miss Birchet and I aboot yer blasphemous vows to my captain. They willna hold up fer long. I am bringin' ye to Father Alphonsus. He will annul yer marriage and ye will speak yer vows. I have given ye another chance,

Niece. Though ye dinna deserve it. Ye care more fer a cock than—"

"You disgust me."

His gaze grew dark and Silene was afraid she'd gone too far. She was helpless tied to the tree.

"And ye think ye dinna disgust me?" he asked incredulously. "My dear, ye are nothin' but a whore."

She heard something in the forest, just beyond the tree line. Her uncle heard it, too.

He rose with his sword as dawn broke. He went to the tree line and peered inside, and then entered.

Silene smiled, but she was worried. Was it Galeren? It had to be! He was alive! But what lengths would her uncle go to in order to keep her with him and get her to Father Alphonsus?

Should she call out a warning? "He is coming!"

A loud, crashing noise sounded from the trees, and then everything went still.

Silene waited what seemed an eternity and then heard someone returning.

Thrilled to see her husband come from out of the trees, she tried to free herself, to no avail. The rope her uncle had tied her with was thick and scratchy around her ankles.

She saw a figure. It wasn't Galeren. Her heart thumped madly in her chest. She grew terrified and mournful. How could her uncle have beaten him? But no. It wasn't her uncle either.

Morgann ran toward her. "Sister! Sister, we must make haste!" He looked over his shoulder at the trees. "He will be comin' any moment now. I dinna know how hard I struck him."

Morgann? Morgann was saving her?

"Morgann! Oh, thank you, Morgann! I knew you had a pure heart!" she cried while he cut her loose. "Where have you been these last few days?"

"No time now." The rope was thick, and his knife was dull, and her uncle was coming, walking a bit crooked. But coming.

"Where is the captain?" he asked fretfully, sawing at the rope and looking over his shoulder.

She shook her head. "Alive, I pray."

"Bell!" the steward called out. "Ye, too? Ye betray me fer her, as well?"

"I canna let ye kill her, my lord," Morgann stood up and faced him. "She is my friend and…so was the captain before I betrayed him."

"After all I have done fer ye, ye ungrateful son of a whore!" her uncle accused. "I took ye in. I—"

"Ye asked me to kill a nun!"

"She isna a nun," her uncle told him. "She wed the captain today."

Morgann turned around to look down at her. A smile lit his face. She thought how handsome he was when he smiled like that.

"God chose well, Sis—Silene."

She smiled at him. She would speak to her husband on Morgann's behalf. She would—she heard a slight thump. Morgann's smile froze on his face.

"Morgann?" she whispered, already bringing her hands to her throat. "Morgann. Nay!"

The young man folded to his knees and then his face hit the ground. A knife protruded from his back.

Silene wept for him and prayed he wouldn't die. Though her vision was blurred with tears, she could make out her uncle walking closer.

"John!"

She turned at the wonderful sound of her husband's voice. He lived! Oh, thank You! Thank You!

She took hold of the knife Morgann had used to try to free her and continued at the task.

Galeren appeared unhurt and handsome, wrapped up in his plaid. When she finally freed herself, she wanted to run to him. But their reunion would have to wait. Her husband was here to fight, proving it by wielding a sword and standing ready to battle.

"Ah, Galeren, old friend. Have ye come to try to kill me with the blade ye already have in my back, or with that one in yer hands?"

Galeren shrugged off the accusation. "In yer back, yer heart, whatever it takes to kill ye if ye hurt her."

The steward's pained expression grew darker. "Ye and Silene took everythin' from me. I…I was goin' to let ye live because ye *have*, indeed, become my friend, one who is dear to my heart."

Her husband smiled and Silene remembered what he had said about his father. *He isna the friendliest. He only makes ye believe he is. That is how he brought down the most English strongholds in the kingdoms. From the inside.*

Galeren's smile radiated with beauty, as his mother's did. It was practiced and insincere like his father's.

"Then come away from her," Galeren said.

Her uncle shook his head. "I need her. This isna over."

"Tis," her husband corrected. "'Tis over now. We were wed earlier. She is now my wife.

"Annulled by Father Alphonsus."

"It cannot be annulled, Uncle," she told him. "'Twas consummated enough that I am likely carrying his babe."

"John!" Galeren thundered lifting his sword to fight. "Come away from her or ye will force me to cut ye down!"

"Ye willna kill me. The king would—"

"Believe what I tell him," Galeren shouted. "Fer I am *his* captain, not yers."

"Wh…what?" her uncle stammered.

Silene smiled. He was his father's son.

"What are ye sayin'?"

"Come away from her and I will tell ye my great secret."

Her uncle's eyes widened first in horror that he'd been tricked, and then with rage. "Ye report to King David?"

Instead of waiting for an answer, the steward spun around and lifted his blade. But he didn't run toward his captain. He ran screeching at *her*.

Silene lifted the hem of her chemise over her calves and ran for her life. Her uncle was going to kill her. She had no doubt. She prayed to escape.

She turned for an instant to look over her shoulder. The steward was upon her, reaching for her.

And then Galeren was there, in the air over him. He'd bounded off a tree stump and fell on the steward as her uncle's fingers curled around the neckline of her chemise.

The two men went down and took her with them.

They weren't fighting. Something was terribly wrong.

She screamed when she saw that Galeren had landed on her uncle's sword. The blade protruded from his back and flashed with blood in the morning sun.

He moved! He wasn't dead! When he rose up on the steward, she saw the hilt against his belly to the right. It hadn't seemed to cut through anything more than flesh and perhaps some bone.

She made the sign of the cross.

He swung around to hold his blade over the steward. But her uncle grasped the hilt sticking out of Galeren and began to twist it.

Silene knew the damage would be much worse in another moment. She was still holding Morgann's knife. Without thought or plan, she fell with it upon her uncle's chest, burying the blade deep.

She looked down at what she had done. She felt ill. She had just killed a man. But… her husband still lived. She felt his hand on her. He was alive.

It didn't take Galeren's men long to find them after a villager's daughter told Lionell that she'd seen the captain riding off into the night.

After a quick examination by Padrig, he deemed the sword could be safely removed from his friend and proceed to pull it out. Mac had whisky in a pouch at his belt. They poured it on Galeren's wound, then brought his horse back to him.

He couldn't ride alone without slipping from the saddle. Padrig offered to ride with him and hold him up.

Thankfully, Morgann lived and was taken back to the stronghold with Mac.

Her uncle was dead. She had killed him. She was responsible for making his children fatherless. How would God ever forgive her? How would she ever forgive herself?

"Where is Will?" Padrig asked.

Her husband grimaced. "Padrig, he…he is dead." He turned his head to look at Silene riding close by. She saw his eyes shimmer with unshed tears. Will. She lamented. Will was dead.

"How?" Padrig demanded. "Where is he?"

"At the cottage," her husband told him, grimacing in pain, then holding up his hand to stop her when she would have ridden closer. "He was tryin' to save me. I had been…knocked oot and tied to the bed. I couldna help him. I am sorry."

Padrig hung his head. Silene loved her husband for not telling Padrig that Will had betrayed them.

"My love?" he said, turning to look at her, as if knowing what she had done and what it had done to her. "We will get through it together, aye?"

She smiled and nodded. Her life would never be the same, but she would be able to face it with God and her warrior husband at her side.

One month later…

GALEREN LET LIONELL adjust his formal plaid. He was wedding Silene today for the second time in the sight of all his kin. His side only pained him a little. He'd developed an infection and had grown quite ill. But besides Silene, he had plenty of people looking after him who helped him grow better, stronger.

Silene also was growing better every day. With him and his kin, and, of course, Father Timothy constantly at her side, she smiled more and more. She'd spent much time with the priest, discussing her feelings and thoughts and praying with him. Father Timothy was a soothing balm.

Galeren didn't mind that she went to the Lord with her troubles before she brought them to him. She was almost fully recovered and finally laughed with him at Daffodil jumping off the walls.

"Ready?" Lionell asked.

It was what he wanted over and above everything else—to spend the rest of his days with her. He nodded and followed his brother outside and to the church.

His kin were there waiting, as well as his men, Mac, Padrig, and Morgann. He'd forgiven Morgann since he himself had done the same thing, and because Morgann risked his life for Silene, but mostly, because Silene had asked it of him.

Agnes had arrived a sennight after a letter had arrived from the prioress saying that the girl was leaving the priory. Galeren had penned an invitation to come to the stronghold. She had accepted.

Silene's father had died last month. No one had told her. Her mother had been brought to the stronghold by the men. Their reunion was tearful and somewhat strained. It would take time for them to come to know each other. They had time.

They buried Will and forgave him. Galeren knew that when a man loved a woman it made him do mad things.

He reached Father Timothy and waited for the bride to appear.

Tonight, they would sleep in his room, where they had been sleeping for the last month.

They had tried making love, but he had suffered three broken ribs and moving under or atop her was too painful to enjoy. There were other ways to please her—and she, him. But tonight, he felt well and fit. Tonight, they would begin their lives together.

He heard the crowd of witnesses whispering and looked toward the entrance. Geva entered the church, followed by Adela, and then Elysande at the rear.

After her, Daffodil came traipsing down the aisle, meowing. She knew where to go and padded straight for Father Timothy, her new dearest.

Galeren held his breath at the sight of Silene coming in last. How could she think she was anything but ravishing and beautiful? Especially so in her purple gown altered to perfection to fit, though her belly hadn't yet begun to swell with the growth of his babe.

Her hair had grown but was still short enough around her nape for him to kiss her neck every chance he got. What there was of her hair was pulled into an intricate knot at the back and loose locks around her temples.

She was bonnier to him than a thousand sunrises. Whatever life he'd had before, this was the one he wanted now. To be here—with her and everyone and everything he loved.

He would send men to Hethersgill and bring his grandparents, if his grandsire still lived, to Invergarry and mayhap one day, he would see Margaret and Alex again. He would ask their forgiveness for losing their father.

His smile grew into a wide grin when she reached him.

"My love, I'm happy I told ye to keep the dress."

She lifted her fingers and giggled behind them. "I'm glad it pleases you, my beloved."

Father Timothy cleared his throat to quiet them and opened the holy book. Daffodil clawed her way up the outside of his robes and fell into his pocket.

Galeren and Silene smiled at Daffodil and then at each other as if they were parents smiling over some sweet thing their child had just done.

Father Timothy began reading and Galeren watched her, noting how radiant she was and feeling weak at the sight of her.

He didn't remember too much of the ceremony until it came time to kiss his wife. She tasted of honey and pumpkin. It made him hungry for more of her.

The celebration took place in the great hall with everyone in attendance. They ate and drank and sang songs. They told stories until late into the night.

They had received word from Dundonald that Father Alphonsus and eleven others were excommunicated from the church at the request of Bishop Graham, which gave them more cause to celebrate.

Galeren and Silene were the first to leave the celebration and locked themselves away in his room. Within a year, they would have their own cottage built next to Bors' house.

For now, his room would have to do. It was huge but sparsely furnished, save for a few wooden bookcases, an ornate table and chair by the window. Other than a few small tables there wasn't much else. His bed was, of course, huge with four posts and wood carvings on the foot and headboards.

He took her wrist after he bolted the door and pulled her into his arms. "My kin love ye."

"I'm glad. I love them, too." She coiled her arms around his neck and let him kiss her until they laughed.

Soon, their mirth turned back into kisses, and as they pulled at each other's clothes, Galeren finally gave up all control, tore her chemise down the middle and carried her to bed.

The End

About the Author

Paula Quinn is a New York Times bestselling author and a sappy romantic moved by music, beautiful words, and the sight of a really nice pen. She lives in New York with her three beautiful children, six over-protective chihuahuas, and three adorable parrots. She loves to read romance and science fiction and has been writing since she was eleven. She's a faithful believer in God and thanks Him daily for all the blessings in her life. She loves all things medieval, but it is her love for Scotland that pulls at her heartstrings.

To date, four of her books have garnered Starred reviews from Publishers Weekly. She has been nominated as Historical Storyteller of the Year by RT Book Reviews, and all the books in her MacGregor and Children of the Mist series have received Top Picks from RT Book Reviews. Her work has also been honored as Amazons Best of the Year in Romance, and in 2008 she won the Gayle Wilson Award of Excellence for Historical Romance.

Website:
pa0854.wixsite.com/paulaquinn

Made in the USA
Columbia, SC
20 March 2021